RETURN
TO
BULL CREEK

ROGER MEADOWS

This is a work of fiction. The characters, incidents, and dialogue are products of the author's imagination and are not to be construed as real. Any resemblance to actual events or persons, living or dead, is coincidental. The geographical area of this story exists but has been modified by adding the village of Sycamore and other changes to geographical features and names.

Cover design by Philip Meadows at xenopixel.com
www.xenopixel.com

ISBN 13: 978 1 7036 6005 0

Acknowledgements:

Thanks, of course, to my wife, Wanda, and our family. A big thanks to our son, Philip, who has designed all my beautiful book covers. I am grateful for input from my manuscript readers: Wanda, Mary Ann, Jack, and Philip. Anything they might have missed is entirely my responsibility. Thanks for the encouragement of the Joyful Readers book club.

I am also fortunate to have spent a great deal of time with my late grandfather, Washington Irving Meadows, who was born on Bull Creek in 1875. My late father, Lester Irving, was also born there in 1915. *Devil's Lane* and this novel are not biographical in any way, but they are seasoned with the flavor of stories about their lives in those earlier times.

Progress was slow in some of the Missouri hills in the decades after the setting of these two books. Therefore, I personally experienced life without electricity, the use of work horses for farming, and all eight grades of primary education in a one-room country school.

RETURN TO BULL CREEK

RETURN TO BULL CREEK

A sequel to *Devil's Lane*

ALSO BY ROGER MEADOWS

HANGMAN, A Deadly Game

A CHANCE ENCOUNTER

DEVIL'S LANE

Available in print or Kindle versions

ROGER MEADOWS

-1-

THE FUGITIVE

Washington, D.C., 1883: Attorney General Benjamin H. Brewster sat at his desk and contemplated the arrival of his first appointment of the morning. It was a prematurely hot March morning and he had to choose between sweltering in his wool suit or opening a window. He chose the latter, to get a little air, but with it he got flies, the sounds of horse-drawn traffic, and the smell of horse dung.

The problem he was to solve was one of many, a carryover from the prior administration, indeed from the Civil War, now many years past. It was not major in its proportions, but a nagging nail in the shoe, a torn cuticle, an aching tooth—to be solved once and for all. A fugitive must be brought to justice, and his visitor this morning was just the man to advise how it could be done.

Virgil Earp was one of the nation's most famous lawmen. He led a posse including his brothers Wyatt and Morgan in a gunfight with outlaws at a place called The O.K. Corral, putting that band out of business. Two months later, he was ambushed, suffering three shotgun wounds, shattering his left arm. The perpetrators were not convicted.

Brewster's secretary, Winton Smith, tapped on the door and announced his visitor. "Marshal Earp to see you, Sir."

Brewster rose, "Send him in."

Smith moved aside to allow Marshal Earp to enter. Brewster stepped forward to meet him and shook hands. "Marshal, thank you for agreeing to meet with me. Your reputation precedes you, and I am honored, Sir."

"The pleasure is mine, Sir," Earp replied. He was an imposing figure, tall and weathered, with drooping mustache. He carried his withered arm close to his side.

"Smith, you may bring coffee," Brewster said over his shoulder, as he led the way to stuffed leather chairs arranged in a corner of the office. "Please be seated, Marshal."

After they were settled, Brewster began. "Before anything else, let me say how sorry I am about the murder of your brother, Morgan. It's a travesty they got off. Despite my office, may I say between us, I hope Wyatt is able to obtain justice in whatever way he can."

"Thank you General. We can't keep letting these people get away with it."

"I agree, and it's just such a case that I'd like to talk about. I heard you were coming to Washington and thought it would be a great opportunity to seek your advice."

"I'll be glad to help if I can."

The two men paused as Winton Smith brought in a silver coffee service and placed it on the low table between them. "Thank you, Smith. We'll serve ourselves," Brewster said.

Brewster crossed his legs, balancing cup and saucer on his knee. "If I may, allow me to outline the case briefly, then we can discuss any salient points in greater detail."

Earp nodded.

"It involves a man by the name of Perry Madison, 'Colonel' Madison as he liked to be called. We want him for the murder of a U.S. Marshal, name of Elbert Strong, among other charges. Madison was in the Quartermaster Corp here in Washington during the war, and was a key figure in procurement. Well, in the grindingly slow pace of things in this town, a few years back, a Congressional Committee examining wartime finances had him brought in for testimony. You may see where this is headed."

"Yes, Sir, I believe I do."

"To get to the point, the third time Marshal Strong went to Missouri to fetch him, Madison went missing and Strong was found dead a week or two later, out in the brush."

"Hmm. Whereabouts you say this happened? Missouri?"

"Yes. Down in the Southwest Missouri hills. Apparently Madison took his ill-gotten wealth and tried to set himself up as some kind of superior country gentleman. The Committee, in its best judgement, tried to pretend as though they were soliciting his assistance in the study of wartime finances. Apparently he smelled a rat."

"He have family? Anybody there close to him?"

"I understand a daughter still lives there. Daughter and a son back east, here. Wife lives with her sister in New York. We sent an agent to talk to her, but she's not well in her mind, if you know what I mean. As to the second question, I doubt it."

Earp shifted in his chair and refilled his cup. "So...not much to go on. How can I be of service?"

"I may be presumptuous, Marshal, but I had doubts you'd want to tackle it yourself, but might have a recommendation who would be good for it. Also, I'd be interested in your speculation on what such a criminal might have done to escape; where he might have gone."

"It's a vast country out there as was brought to my consciousness again as I traveled by train all the way from California these past weeks. Forgive me if I say anything that might channel a search in the wrong direction, but let's think about him a bit."

Brewster leaned forward. "By all means, feel free to speculate. Whoever gets the assignment can start from scratch, but I'd be most interested in what you think."

"Well, here's a man who wants to live high, be important, but decrease his chances of being discovered. I doubt he'd risk coming east, and I doubt he'd head to Canada. Too undeveloped up there. Leaves South or West. He prob'ly would want to go into some kind of business, considering his background. South of Missouri, you have the Gulf, Mexico, and the Islands. Good bit of commerce out there; less without the slave trade, but still rum, sugar, and cotton…" Earp leaned back, pinched his lower lip and stared at the ceiling. "Lots of stuff going on in California these days. I just came from Colton in the south, but San Francisco is gettin' pretty hot, what with the railroad and all, and shipping coming in from Chiner."

"How would he best get there?"

"Two ways…well, three, actually. There's the train, there's land, horseback or stage, and there's ship. Before the railroad, lots of folks went down the Gulf to Panama and took a ship up the west coast."

"Which would you suppose?"

"…Or maybe somewhere or some direction I haven't thought of. Who knows? Just the nature of this business." Marshal Earp stared at his coffee cup, then looked up. "Joshua Lambert."

Brewster raised his brows. "Sir?"

"My recommendation, General."

-2-

THE MARSHAL

Margaret Madison tucked a stray curl of brown hair over her left ear and bent to the task of wiping down the slate blackboard behind her desk. She'd sent Pearl Bowman to the steps outside the side door to beat chalk dust out of the erasers. She had also given a final task for the day to the roomful of students. They were to pick someone in their class and write what they liked most about that boy or girl. They could draw their portrait also. She'd done it before and always got a kick out of the responses, especially from the younger ones. One wag last year had written something he might have heard somewhere, "For a fat girl, she don't sweat much." The task gave her some insight into the morale of the eclectic mix of students. Some tended to carry forward disagreements among the families in the Bull Creek watershed. And there were those in the upper grades that tried to disguise romantic attraction with bland phrases.

She turned to her desk and sat down to grade papers from the day's earlier assignments. Her mind wandered to feelings of satisfaction over her first full year as the teacher. She'd been a part-time apprentice the year before, learning from retired professor Abe Phillips, who had started the school in the community of Sycamore. Now she felt she had achieved success for the most part.

Her reverie was interrupted by a knock at the entrance door at the back of the room. All of the students looked up at her, then swiveled their heads as she strode down the center aisle. "You keep your minds on your work," she said. "School won't let out until you finish." That always motivated them.

She opened the door to a stranger, a large man dressed all in black except for a shirt that had once been white. She was taken aback by his stern demeanor; his weathered face with a thin, pink scar down his left cheek from temple to the edge of his jaw. When he saw her, however, he whipped off his hat and smiled.

"How'd do, Ma'am," he said, "I'm lookin' to speak with a Miz Madison. Might you be her?"

"I am. And who might you be?"

He thumbed aside his jacket to expose a silver badge. "U.S. Marshal Lambert at your service, Ma'am."

"And what is it you want with me?"

Joshua Lambert saw all eyes of the classroom staring at him over her shoulder and shuffled his feet, spurs jingling. "Uh, Ma'am, is there someplace we can talk?"

Margaret saw where he was looking and turned around. Her students quickly looked back at their desks. "We have about fifteen minutes left of the school day. Let me finish, and we can speak. Please go to the blacksmith shop and ask for George Zinn. He has benches out front. I'll want him to join us when we talk."

"Ma'am, I can do that, but are you sure we shouldn't keep this matter private? It's about your father that I'm here."

"Yes, I'm sure. I trust his advice and he knows everything I do about my father."

Lambert nodded, clapped his hat back on and left. As he turned away, he thought to himself, That's one fine-lookin' woman. She was tall, with a slender waist, dressed in a ruffled white blouse and long black skirt. Had a good head of brown hair that flowed down her back. Surely a rare sight for one like me, spending most of my recent years in Indian Territory. Hopeless, too, since I've got to move on. Also I suspect there's a connection to that Zinn fellow she told me to find.

Margaret released her students and they went streaming outside, most looking toward the blacksmith shop where the large stranger was seated on one of the benches facing George Zinn. Many of the children had a considerable distance to walk home, but some had horses staked out in the shade of the trees, or had a wagon or buggy waiting to take them home.

Margaret locked the doors and made her way the short distance to where the two men sat. George looked a bit uncomfortable, she thought, considering that another man was anticipating a discussion with her. He needn't worry.

"I see you two have met." They both nodded and Margaret took a seat beside George.

"If I may," said Lambert, "I'll tell you what little I know. I was minding my business out in Indian Territory when I got a message to meet Marshal Virgil Earp in Springfield. It was something of a relief, I must say, considering all of the squabbles and fights going on out where I been. They say it might become an official U. S. territory...but that's another story.

"Anyway, Marshal Earp gave me a new assignment, to track down your pa, Miz Madison. I don't have much to go on. That's why I'm here. I have the basics: that Marshal Strong came to usher him back to Washington, and on a rainy night they both disappeared. Later they found Strong's body in the brush. Don't seem like they got on it right away, so it's a cold trail."

"That's about it," said Margaret. "They were on horseback, but no one knows where he was headed. I immediately stopped the farm bank account, so I assume he had escape money hidden somewhere. We've not heard a word since, as far as I know. My family has pretty much come apart since then. My mother is not well, seeming to put the past out of her mind, but I guess you could ask her."

"They already did, without any success."

"I see. My older brother never lived here, and my sister went back east near him."

"They interviewed them also. What I hope to do here is see if you can give me anything at all on his thinking or his character, and also see the beginning of the trail for myself."

"I'll do anything I can to help. My father is not a nice man. He deludes himself that he is better than others...more important. His plan here was to set up a serfdom and preside over the lower classes. It makes me think that wherever he is, he'll try the same thing. George, do you have anything to add?"

"No. You're doing fine," George said. "That's how we all saw him from the first. You might tell the Marshal that the government took the house and land."

"Oh, you're right. They had enough feeling for the family to leave the bank account, so I was able to relocate. No telling how much he swindled out of the government, though, or what he had hidden."

"Who else should I talk to?"

"Let me think," said Margaret. "He didn't have much contact with the community. There's Hank Green, his foreman, and Sheriff Horton, who can show you the place where they found the marshal's body. The maid and the groom are brother and sister and they live in a cabin on my place. There's Anna Archer, another maid, who could certainly speak to his personality. She moved out of Taney County, but I can tell you how to find her."

"Sounds like it could take a coupl'a days. Anything against me campin' out on the school ground?"

Margaret looked at George. "Do you think Oley Jensen might put him up?" Then to Lambert, "he's the miller here, and also the preacher."

"I'll check," said George.

"And to save some time," Margaret said, "Why don't you come to my place for supper this evening. You can talk to Etta, the maid, and her brother Ike. George, you come, too."

"I'd better not," said George. "I have two teams comin' in after plowing to be shod, so I'll be working late. I'll get him to set it up with Oley, and I'll see you tomorrow." Just what I need, thought George, as he walked away. I saw how he looked at her. For weeks I've been trying to work up courage to ask her to marry me, but it just don't seem right somehow. I'm still living with Pa and Ma and she has a place of her own. It just wouldn't look right.

I trust her, but I'm jealous of someone else havin' the pleasure of her company. At least she has a chaperone. Etta would lay him out with her rollin' pin if he even looked cross-eyed at her. He smiled to himself at the thought, and told himself, Let it go.

ROGER MEADOWS

-3-
SYCAMORE

Joshua unsaddled his dappled gray gelding, Rex, and hobbled him, leaving him to pasture in the large schoolyard. Miss Madison had given him directions to cross the swinging bridge across Bull Creek and go up the west bank about a quarter mile to her place in a cove. Oley Jensen had welcomed him to stay in a spare room in their house, since their children had grown and gone.

Now, unaccustomed as he was to walking, he found himself enjoying the experience. Trees were leafing out and dogwood was in bloom. It was right pleasant, 'specially with the sound of the creek beside the trail. He found the place with no problem. It was a new cabin, larger than most, and was all new-squared logs and new-split bright shingles. It had a smaller, older cabin close by and a barn behind that one. Looked like two or three acres of plowed field, rail-fenced and ready for spring planting.

When he climbed onto the porch and knocked on the plank door, it was opened by a slender black man with a lined face and white hair. The man smiled at him. "You must be the Marshal. I'm Ike. Missus say you is to come right in." He didn't offer to shake hands, a carryover from his past, when it wasn't the right thing.

Margaret, now wearing an apron, was in the corner kitchen area with a black woman, obviously the sister Margaret spoke of. "Come on in," Margaret said. "You can have a seat at the table if you wish. That was Ike who let you in, and this is Etta."

Etta did a semi-curtsey and spoke, "How d'you do, Mister Marshal?"

Although he fought for the Union, Joshua wasn't quite used to the mixing of races, but he went with it. Kinda a good thing. "Pleased to make your acquaintance," he replied.

Later, all four were seated around the table and enjoying a meal of ham, potatoes, and wild greens—curly dock, slick dock, lamb's quarter, poke, and dandelions. Margaret suggested they could begin to talk about the subject of the marshal's visit. "Ike, you might tell about that night he disappeared."

"Yes'm. Mister marshal, that other marshal, he come evenin'. Colonel tole me to have the surrey ready early next mornin'. Later he come, said not do that, they just use the horses. I put everything away, fed they horses. Next mornin' when I gets up, horses both gone, both men gone."

"Anything else? Anything unusual?"

"No, Suh. Nuthin' out of place. Colonel rode a reg-lar saddle, the little one still there."

"I see. What kind of horses?"

"Marshal, he have a stable horse from Ozark, I think. Big sorrel mare. Colonel had his reg'lar one, a big black Tennessee Walker. Mean horse, name Devil. Good name. Try to bite me all the time, but jest got me onct."

Joshua smiled inwardly, and asked, "Anything else you can think of?"

"Oh, forgot. Rainin' like the second flood, so no tracks no place."

Joshua looked down, deep in thought.

"Etta, this would be a good time to serve some pie," said Margaret. "I'll get the coffee."

After they had had their gooseberry pie, Joshua turned to Etta. "Miz Etta, can you tell me anything I ought to know about the Colonel?"

"I don't like to speak out'a turn about any of God's children, but Miss Margaret say it need to be done. So the colonel…he not a nice man. Gave me and Ike a place to be, but very distant, like we mostly there only to please. Didn't treat us like real people. I'm ain't smart enough to think of anything that would help. Worst thing of all was how he treated Anna, precious Anna."

"How was that?"

Etta looked at Margaret, who gave an almost imperceptible nod.

"Anna was a girl brought in to help me and I loved her like the child I never had. When a terrible thing happen to her, Colonel, 'stead of helpin' her, turned her out in the cold." She paused and swallowed, wiping a tear from her cheek with her index finger.

Joshua waited for her to continue. When she did not, Margaret spoke. "It's a long story, but the short of it is that Anna was attacked by a man when she was out in the woods. Wasn't her fault, but my father didn't see it that way. Anna is all right now, and you might go by and see her when you leave here to wherever you're going. I can tell you how to find her, and you can wish her and her husband, Benjamin, the best from us. They had to move out of this area. Ben was falsely charged with murder and neither acquitted nor convicted. Resentment remained. They're up north of Aurora, a town west of Springfield, if that's where you're going. Would add a couple of days to your ride, but it's up to you.

"That's really about all we know. You might learn more from the sheriff and Hank Green."

Joshua sensed that the meeting was over and realized there wasn't much they could say that would give clues to Madison's whereabouts. "Just one thing, Miss Margaret. I suppose you have had no contact from him in any fashion?"

"Absolutely not. I believe that's the only thing that kept him from trying to clean out the farm account. I don't envy you trying to track him down."

"I'll do the best I can, and I thank all of you for your help and the fine supper." He went in turn to each of them, shaking hands, surprising Ike and Etta. With Margaret, he said, "I'll make sure you hear from me before I leave. I doubt this Anna you spoke of will have much that will help, but I might drop by as you suggest. Good night to all of you."

Joshua Lambert spent the next day and a half talking to Hank Green and meeting with Sheriff Horton. He and the sheriff followed the assumed path Madison had taken from his farm to where Marshal Strong's body was found. It was a couple of miles south, but from that point he could have gone any direction. His interview with Hank Green added nothing that would indicate where Madison would have gone. Lambert got the same impression about Madison's character he had gotten from the others. Green emphasized his admiration for the daughter, Margaret, when she was temporarily in charge of the farm.

Now he brought Rex to a halt at the rail outside the schoolhouse and dismounted. Looked like the noon break because the kids were all outside chasing each other in some kind of game. Margaret was also outside standing under a shade tree. Lambert approached, and doffed his hat. Margaret turned to him and smiled.

"How'd do, Ma'am," he said.

"Fine, Marshal. Any luck?"

"Can't say. Never know what will help, but I feel like I know a little bit about the man. Keep forgettin' he's your father."

"I've had to come to terms with it myself. What's next, if you can say?"

"Just the usual. I have a wanted poster to show you, which I'll mail to all major cities. I'll telegraph a description to sheriffs in several places, try to get a lead on which way he went.

I'll lick a finger and hold it in the wind and try to guess which way to try to pick up a trail."

Margaret was surprised at the likeness of her father staring at her from the handbill. It had been made from his Civil War picture. She also gave directions to where Anna lived, and shook hands with Lambert. He mounted his horse and rode away, up the wagon road, headed north.

ROGER MEADOWS

-4-
ANNA

Anna Friedrich Archer dug a clean sheet out of the basket at her feet and began to clip it on the clothesline. Anna was young in years, but mature beyond those years, due to the adversities she had faced and overcome. She was full-figured but slender of waist. Her cloud of red hair was braided in a single queue down her back while she worked. It was a beautiful spring morning, light breezes just right to dry the wash. She glanced over her shoulder at Eva, now mobile and hard to keep track of. "Evie, get away from the cistern!" she shouted.

Eva Mae stopped and looked at her, deciding whether to obey. Should I do that, or should I wait until Mama starts after me? Finally, as Mama continued to stare, she relented and toddled a short way and sat down in the grass. She started to pluck sweet clover blossoms from their stems. She babbled to herself, trying to think of what Mama called these little fuzzy things.

Anna worried about that cistern. It collected rainwater for use in washing and bathing. They had a dug well for drinking water and it was deep enough to be pure. The cistern was large and deep, but she didn't know how deep the water was. It had a framework around it and a lid, but still, it was a scary thought when there was a meddlesome little girl wandering around.

She enjoyed washdays, in a way. Everything dried outside had a special fresh smell, like you could bring perfume designed by God right into the house. She still washed outside in a big cast iron pot when the weather was nice. She'd had Ben set stones for a fire under it. Mister Coleman had provided a new-fangled washing machine for washing indoors, but she liked the old way best. Maybe it would be good in the wintertime. It had a big wooden tub with a lid and a hand-crank to stir the wash inside. It also had a hand-cranked set of rollers to squeeze out the water. Maybe she'd get used to it. Eva was finally out of diapers, so that helped some.

She looked toward the east, where Ben was plowing with the team, preparing to plant corn. Most of the farm was in fields for hay and pastureland for grazing cattle. It was beautiful rolling land, far different from the hills in Taney County where they both were born. It was pretty here, but she missed the hills at times, mainly the people who had been kind to her in her past troubles. Margaret wrote to her and always included best wishes from Etta, who she thought of as a surrogate mother since her own mother had been killed by a horse.

Anna finished hanging the wash and turned to go inside. Eva was nowhere to be seen. "Evie! Where are you?" She shouted. She dropped the basket and ran around the house to the front yard. Starting to be concerned, she ran all the way around, at last seeing her hiding in the middle of a lilac bush. Anna plucked her up and hugged her to her breast. She kissed her on the neck and said, "You little rascal. Don't run away like that. Mama loves you, but you should stay close to me."

Eva giggled and squirmed to get down.

It was about time to go inside and start dinner for Ben. He was coming in at midday, even if the plowing wasn't done. Mister Coleman had asked him to meet at the general store about a mile away to update the count on new calves. They were tenants on one of Mister Coleman's farms. Ben had told her the calving was all done, and they had a good crop. She opened the screen door and helped Eva up the steps onto the screened back porch and into the house. She was proud of her house, even though they were only tenants. It was a frame house with clapboard siding and was painted white—far different from the log house where she was born and where she and Ben had met. The first painted house she'd seen was down by Bull Creek and belonged to that Colonel Madison, but it was much bigger than this one, of course.

This house had a kitchen separated from the small front parlor and the two bedrooms. The kitchen had a sink that drained outside to a french drain. It had a hand pump for cistern water, but they got their drinking water from a pump in the back yard from the dug well. As she stood at the sink and began to peel potatoes, Eva banging a pot lid on the floor at her feet, she looked out the window and saw a horseback rider coming up the lane in the distance. Strangers always made her nervous until she knew what they were about. I hope Ben's coming soon, she thought. She stopped what she was doing and picked Eva up. The front door was latched, so she went to the back and hooked the screen door shut. Most people would come up there first, anyway.

She covered the potatoes in cold water and went quickly to the hall mirror and adjusted her hair, tucking the red curls that had escaped back into the braid at the back of her head. She took off her apron and smoothed her skirt. Then she waited and watched out the window as the rider approached. She went to the back door to see him ride up out back where she'd been hanging out the wash earlier. He dismounted from his big gray horse and looked toward the back door where she was standing. He was tall, dressed in black, and armed with a holstered gun. He paused, then walked toward the house, climbed the steps, and knocked on the screen door. Anna stepped onto the porch and he tipped his hat and said, "How'd do, Ma'am. I'm Marshal Lambert. Lookin' for a Miz Anna Archer." He hooked the lapel of his coat aside to show his badge.

Anna felt a chill down her back. Is this something to do with the trial? She thought. Is he after Ben? Was there some evidence against him? As these thoughts flashed through her mind, she forced herself to speak. "What do you want?"

"Just want to talk, Ma'am. I assume you're Miz Anna?"

"What about?"

"Miz Margaret Madison told me how to find you. I'm after trackin' down Colonel Madison. May I come in?"

"Oh. Yes, I'm Anna. But I'd like to wait until my husband gets here. It won't be long. Why don't you water your horse at that trough in the lot."

Anna felt Eva grasp her skirt, so she picked her up. She saw Ben approaching down the lane from the field, leading the team of horses. The redbone hound, Bone, trotted by his side. She pointed. "Look, Evie, Papa is coming with the horses."

"Papa," Eva said and pointed her own chubby finger.

They watched Ben come into the lot and approach the stranger. She could see them speaking, then they shook hands. The marshal moved his horse away to make room for the team to drink. Ben tied the team of grays to a rail and went around to the backyard and started pumping water, which ran down a small trough into the watering trough. Anna could see the men continuing their conversation and after they finished with the horses, they tied them in the shade of two different trees in the barn lot and headed toward the house.

Ben ushered the marshal in and offered a seat at the kitchen table. Eva climbed on Ben's lap.

"Ma'am, I'm sorry to come in during your noon. I should a'planned better," Lambert said.

"That's all right," Anna said. "It works better with my husband here."

"I appreciate it."

"What would you like to know? We can talk while I put dinner on the stove. You can join us."

"That would be most kind. As I already told you, I'm after Colonel Madison. I know the basic outline, but I always feel like it helps to get a picture of the person in mind. It helps me guess what he might do."

Anna bustled about the kitchen as she talked. "He is a mean, self-centered man. My mama died and my papa put me to work for the Madisons and abandoned me. I think he sold me, but that's another story."

"We've since figured that out," Ben said.

Lambert shook his head.

"Anyway, it seemed to be all right, but I didn't like the way the Colonel—I hate to call him that—started looking at me. Margaret and the maid, Etta, were kind to me, but after a year or so, a very bad thing happened to me. I was attacked in the woods by a man. Later, as things developed...." She paused and glanced at Eva. "...he turned me out of the house with winter coming on."

Lambert was perceptive enough to understand her meaning as Anna stopped at the stove to turn the potatoes.

"I was lucky," Anna said. "I walked for miles and hid in the barn where I lived before. I'd hoped it was abandoned, but Ben was living at the place. His pa had bought it. Ben's dog discovered me, and in his kindness..." Her voice broke and tears started down her cheeks. She walked up behind Ben stroked his cheek. "In his kindness, he took me in and made a safe place for me."

Lambert was surprised to find his own voice shaky. "What a scoundrel!"

"That's him. He was mean to his own family, even his wife. Margaret says she's not well."

"That's what I understand. I know you probably have no idea where he might have gone, but I can see he needs to be brought in."

"That's for sure," Ben said. "I'd bet on West, but you know your business better than I would. California, I'd be guessin'."

"My thoughts, too. We'll see. I'll get posters on the way to several places."

"I hope you get him," Ben said. "I'd like to be there when you do. You may have heard I had problems of my own. I shot a man in self-defense, but the jury didn't reach a verdict. It scared me at first when I saw you, thinkin' they'd come up with a reason to haul me back."

"Not so. I knew nothing about it."

"Well, it's the reason we left the hills...to make a clean start."

"I understand. By the way, Margaret sends regards from herself and Etta."

"Thank you, and good luck," Anna said.

After a quick meal, Joshua made his departure. What a nice young couple, he thought. Both of them have had more trouble than they deserve. She's a beauty but she doesn't know it, and he's as clean-cut as they come. I hope the world treats them better in the future.

-5-
MARGARET

Margaret always arrived at the Sycamore schoolhouse early so she would be first to arrive in case any of the children were brought in before early morning farm chores. It gave her a chance to organize her thoughts, and in a morning like this, to open windows to let in the fresh spring air. In winter, of course, she would make sure the big potbelly stove was going well. In this past winter, George faithfully performed that task for her. Before her father stole away in the middle of the night and the family farm was confiscated, she drove a buggy more than two miles to the school. Now she could walk a short distance down the west bank of Bull Creek, cross the swinging bridge, and be right in the large school yard. The morning walk on a day like this was particularly enjoyable with all the dogwood and redbud in bloom and wild flowers peeping out along the path.

As she sat at her desk, getting ready to begin the day, she heard the sounds of children outside. They would stay out there until she went to the door and rang a hand bell to call them in. Her concentration was broken by the soft sounds of footsteps coming from the side door. Due to the stealthy approach, she started, looking up to see a man standing there.

"Sorry to scare you, Ma'am," he said. "You looked in a deep study, so I didn't know what to do."

"That's all right, Mister...uh—"

"Coggins, Ma'am. Lester Coggins."

"Oh, yes. Elspeth, Buddy, and Sadie."

"Yes'm. I just wanted to say, I'm beholden for what you do for them. They ain't got a ma, you know, so life is kinda rough…'specially for the girls." Coggins stood before her, shifting his feet and chasing the brim of his battered hat around through his rough hands. He was tall and lean with a drooping mustache whose wings reached well below his jawline. He looked freshly shaved, however, evidence of his plan to approach her.

"I'm sorry for your loss, Mister Coggins. I know it is hard for young children. I'll keep doing the best I can for them while they're here."

"I reckon I know that. I wish there was more I could do. They need a ma." He looked uncomfortable and reddened beneath his deeply weathered skin. When Margaret did not respond, he cleared his throat and continued, "I don't mean to…well, I reckon I'd best be goin'.'"

Margaret rose and picked up her hand bell. "Good day to you Mister Coggins. It's time for me to call the children in."

"Thank you, Ma'am. I'm much obliged."

As the children began to enter the building, laughing, pushing, and getting organized, she thought to herself, *I wonder what that was about? I feel sorry for the troubles of others, and do what I can for the children. It's obvious that the Coggins children do not have an easy life, based on their clothing and their backward demeanor. He seemed to want to say more. I'll just have to wait and see what happens.*

Every morning she made a point of greeting each student as she set them to their tasks and especially had words of encouragement for those who needed it most, like the Coggins children. The Archers were well adjusted and excellent performers with their lessons, thanks to a stable home life. Of course she knew them well, but tried not to show favoritism. Josie, Jimmy, and Oren were siblings of Benjamin, the husband of her dearest friend Anna. They had two new sisters from the marriage of their father, Tom, to the widow Rebecca Tate. Jennifer was in second grade, but little sister Essie was still too young.

Then there were the Bowman children, Pearl, Ruby, Garnet, and Sapphire. Their older sister, Opal, had graduated, although she was no older than Margaret's eighth graders, Josephine Archer, Warren Harvey, and Luke Johnson, who were about to graduate, but had missed enough schooling that they had to make up some time. Warren lived over on Swan Creek and hadn't been able to attend regularly. Even now, he rode a horse to school and tied it in the shade of a tree during the day. Josephine was a different case. Her mother had died giving birth to her little brother, Oren, now in first grade, so she had to fill that void and missed quite a bit over the years taking care of him and her other two brothers.

Josie was a prize; bright and willing to help Margaret tend to the younger classes, which now included her half-sister Jenny after her father married Rebecca. Margaret felt especially close to Josie because of Ben and Anna. Too bad Anna no longer lived close by. Margaret thought of her constantly, reliving the circumstance of their meeting.

After she had made the rounds of all the classes, and given assignments, she settled at her desk. She smiled to herself at the memory of how Anna, despite losing her mother, and being abandoned by her father, blossomed into a beautiful girl. And then to be attacked by a man and put out in the cold by Margaret's father. All of her hardships had forged her into a person of strong character, helped along of course by the love of her new husband. My, my! thought Margaret. What am I to do about my own love life? I know George feels the same about me as I do of him, but he has seemed subdued lately. I wonder if something is wrong. I wonder if I should ask him....

Thomas Archer stopped the team and wagon in front of his house and went inside. Rebecca was working in the kitchen getting ready to prepare the evening meal. "Hey, Becky, I'm on my way to get the kids. Would you and Essie like to ride along, maybe see if you need anything at Guthrie's?"

Rebecca untied her apron and draped it over a chair. "Yes, that would be fine. I have a list."

Essie jumped up off the floor where she'd been playing and came running. "Can I get some candy?"

Tom smiled. "We'll see about that."

After driving down their lane and fording Hansen Creek, they drove down the wagon road along the east bank of Bull Creek. Spring rains had been generous, so the creek was running strong, its waters crystal clear over the gravel beds and wide layers of limestone.

"Suckers and redhorse ought to be runnin' soon," said Tom. "Wish Ben could be here to grab them."

"You miss him, don't you?" said Rebecca. "Do you think they can ever come back?"

"Don't know. Haven't heard anything out of Ferd for quite a spell. Maybe he's given up his resentment against the family, but I doubt it."

"I wish it could be so," Rebecca said. She reached around Essie on the seat between them and squeezed her husband's hand.

Ferdinand Harvey had started a feud against the Archer family over a line fence, resulting in a so-called devil's lane. At one confrontation, shooting started, resulting in the wounding of Tom Archer and Ferd, and the death of Ferd's son, Clint. The resulting murder trial against Tom and Benjamin Archer had ended in a hung jury.

Essie, Jenny, and Oren stared through the glass of the display case and debated the choices of stick candy. It was a tough choice. Jimmy, at age eleven and determined not to be considered a kid, stood aloof. Josephine assisted her stepmother in gathering groceries and supplies from her list, and soon Tom Archer helped his blended family into the wagon and headed home. He managed to get Jimmy his stick of candy without public ceremony.

-6-

THE CISTERN

Marshal Lambert had been given space to work in the Greene County sheriff's office in Springfield, Missouri. Now, the waiting and inactivity was driving him crazy. He had sent out telegrams and had mailed wanted posters to police departments in all the major cities he could think of that might have some bearing on his search for Perry Madison. He was used to being outside, on his horse, investigating, chasing, and collaring fugitives. Oh, the sheriff allowed him to participate in their activity sometimes, but it wasn't the same. He had boarded Rex in a stable and he exercised him daily, but mostly he rode a desk chair, waiting, thinking.

The Attorney General had arranged for Madison's Army file to be sent to him. It was a thick file with copies of all orders he had received throughout his career, going back to his application and acceptance into West Point. It included the endorsement of his New York senator. It had periodic physical examinations, starting with the entrance at the Point. There were no battle wounds, Lambert noted, since Madison had never been near a war zone. Biggest risk, he thought to himself, would have been a paper cut, or falling out of his desk chair. Lambert read the file several times.

There was a large map of the United States and western territories on the wall in a conference room and he would go in there and sit and stare at it. It was a vast country, much of it unsettled. What would I do if I did what he did and I wanted to disappear, to start over? he thought. And what will *I* do if I don't get any feedback? Talk about needle in a haystack! He hoped his telegram would move somebody into action. It read:

> WANTED FOR MURDER OF U S MARSHAL ELBERT STRONG FUGITIVE PERRY MADISON AKA COLONEL MADISON WANTED POSTER IN MAIL STOP FUGITIVE LEFT SW MISSOURI DEC 1881 DIRECTION UNKNOWN STOP FIVE FEET TEN HUNDRED SEVENTY POUNDS AGE LATE FIFTIES SILVER HAIR STOP LAST SEEN RIDING BLACK TN WALKER STALLION LEADING LARGE SORREL MARE STOP DO NOT APPROACH STOP CONTACT SHERIFF GREENE COUNTY MISSOURI ATTN MARSHAL LAMBERT

In keeping with his assumptions about where Madison might go, he concentrated on cities south and west—Little Rock, Baton Rouge, Mobile, New Orleans, and Kansas City, Oklahoma City, Dodge City, Denver, San Francisco. In a second round, he sent the same to Dallas, Santa Fe, and Phoenix. Wait and see, wait and see.

Anna was working in the garden, planting seed while the soil was still soft from the rain of the day before. Ben had scratched out shallow furrows in the plowed garden that morning before he headed to the field. The garden was on the north side of the house with the rows running east and west. Eva was running about nearby, playing in the yard, and Anna frequently looked up to keep track of her. That girl could disappear in the blink of an eye sometimes! She was full of energy and loved to use her relatively new mobility to the fullest extent.

Anna worked west along a row, planting grains of sweet corn. All danger of frost was past and it was the right phase of the moon. This morning she was planting corn, peas, and beans. Radishes and lettuce were already up, as were tiny carrot tops.

Ben planned to dig deeper furrows tomorrow for sweet potatoes and Irish potatoes. Next would come pumpkins, cucumbers, and squash. They hadn't moved in time last year to have much of a garden and she dreamed of how it would be. She straightened and wiped the sweat from her forehead and looked back for Eva. She was nowhere to be seen. Anna went running toward the house shouting her name, and finally found her, after a moment of panic, around in the front yard.

As she carried Eva around to the back yard, she said, "Evie, you must not get out of my sight. Mama worries when she can't see you." She squatted down and looked Eva in the eye. "Do you understand?"

Eva looked at her a moment before replying. "Yesss."

"All right. Now you stay here or you will have to take a nap."

"Not sleepy."

"Then do as you're told."

She finished the end of the row, lightly covering the seeds as she went. As she turned around and glanced toward the yard, Eva was not in sight. At that moment she heard a loud cry. She went running toward the back of the house and to her horror, saw the lid to the cistern askew. She dashed toward it and flipped it off. In the swirl of black water below was the tiny, thrashing figure. Without hesitation, Anna jumped in, to one side, and as she plunged down in the cold water she was able to grasp hold of Eva's dress and pulled her to her bosom.

Anna's feet hit the bottom and she bounced up, finding that she could keep her face above the surface by tilting her head back while standing on the bottom. Eva was choking and gasping for breath. Anna held Eva up and draped her over her own tilted face and slapped her back.

Eva coughed and coughed and finally began to cry.

"It's all right, Baby. Mama has you," Anna crooned. She shifted her hold and lowered Eva in her arms, holding her head above the surface.

Anna looked up at the circle of light. The walls were made of stone and were covered in green slime. There was one small pipe down the side to feed the pump in the kitchen. It would be impossible to climb the pipe or the wall. The top was probably six feet above her head. And the water was cold, having been filled by the rain of the day before. Please, God, help us. Send Ben home early. Maybe a neighbor will drop by. Please, God!

Eva was still coughing and sobbing. "Mama, Mama, I'm cold!"

"I know, Baby. Papa will come and help us out. Try to be a brave girl." She tried her best to believe her own words.

Ben drove the team of mules over the plowed ground. They were pulling a spring-toothed harrow to break up the turned sod. A drag was attached behind that Ben rode on. It was a ten-acre field, much smoother with fewer rocks than he was used to, even in the bottoms along the creeks at home. Still, he missed his family and the community of friends along Bull Creek. Only dark spot was that Ferd Harvey and the accusation of murder that went unresolved. Ridiculous. Somebody on that jury was bought. Nuthin' I can do about it. Thank the Lord for Anna and Eva and for Conrad Coleman giving me a chance to work this farm.

Looks like I can finish before noon time. Wonder what Anna fixed? I'm gettin' hungry already. Must be her good cookin' I'm thinkin' about.

Anna clung to the pipe to steady herself. She clasped Eva to her and could feel a little warmth where their bodies touched, but they both shivered in the cold. In the dim light Anna could see Eva's lips turning blue. Eva still had spasms of coughing, but had ceased crying, reduced to whimpering and repeating, "Mama, Mama," and "Papa come."

"He'll come, Baby. Try to hold still so Mama can hold you."

Anna's arms were aching from holding Eva high enough to keep her head above water. Any excess movement made it hard to keep her own face clear and more than once she almost choked from unexpected water rushing into her nose. Her neck ached and her legs were going numb. If I can't hold out, we will both drown. Will we see Mama in heaven? The preacher said we would. It would be so easy to just let go and let it happen. I'm getting sleepy, and I don't feel quite as cold now. Maybe the water is getting warmer, or maybe I'm just getting numb all over.

Anna stared at the circle of bright blue sky overhead, willing something, anything, to change. Without warning, she awoke to find herself in turmoil underwater, struggling to orient herself and find Eva.

-7-

BEN

en came to the end of the last pass, winding up in the middle of the field. He drove the mules to the corner of the field where the gate was and unhitched them, leaving the harrow there. Bone had been following him all morning, around and around, seeming to think it was his duty. He wagged his tail in anticipation to heading toward the house. Ben also looked forward to sitting in the kitchen and holding Eva on his knee while Anna got the noon meal ready. He smiled to himself. Hope she don't think I'm hurrying her up, just 'cause I got done early. As he came into the barn lot he thought he heard a faint sound. Bone started barking and charged toward the house. Ben brought the mules to a stop to listen. He heard it again over the sound of Bone's barking. Someone was shouting. He dropped the reins and ran toward the house.

Anna had managed to stand with Eva in her arms. Both were coughing and choking, and Eva was crying with each breath between coughs. Suddenly, Anna heard Bone barking, then saw the dark silhouette of his nose. "Bless you, Bone, you found me again," she said weakly. Then she shouted, "Ben! Ben!" It was Bone who found her hiding in Ben's barn loft years ago, an event that turned into a blessing that time, also.

In seconds, Ben was there. Her prayers were answered.

"Anna! Hold on! I'll get a ladder!" He ran to the woodshed and brought back a short ladder he'd made to get on the roof to fix a leak. Dashing back to the cistern, he lowered it gently beside Anna. Eva increased the volume of her crying, a welcome sound to Ben. Anna's upturned face was white in the dark water.

"Can you get on the ladder?"

Anna moved toward it and grasped an upright with one hand. "I'll try," she said in a weak voice. She managed to step on the bottom rung, at last getting her head above water. "Can you get Evie?"

Ben climbed down and was able to reach with one arm to envelope Eva as Anna held her up with the last of her waning strength. "It's all right now, Baby. I've got you." As he drew her up, Eva clutched him tightly around his neck.

"I'll get her out and I'll come back for you, Anna. Hold on." Ben climbed out and disentangled himself from Eva's clutches. "Lay down here in the grass, Baby. Got to get Mama."

Bone laid down next to Eva and licked her face. Ben climbed down, and gave Anna his strong arm to cling to, and virtually lifted her out of the darkness and into the sunlight. He held her close and she began to shiver violently. Eva rose and ran to them. Ben picked her up and they both held her.

"Let's get you inside and get you warmed up," Ben said. Anna was streaming water and her hands and face were wrinkled and white. Her mass of red hair was plastered to her face and down her back.

Ben undressed Eva and toweled her dry. He dressed her in a winter flannel nightgown. She was still coughing, but had stopped crying. She clung to Ben, grasping his shirt or wherever she could reach during the process. Anna did the same for herself and he helped them both into their bed. He got out quilts that had been put away for the summer, and soon they were able to stop shivering.

Ben knelt by the bed and kissed Anna on the cheek. "Darlin', I've gotta go take care of the mules. Then I'm gonna kill a chicken and boil it up for some soup. Now you two rest easy."

Anna reached out with her cold, wrinkled hand and touched his face. "Thank the Lord you came for us," she whispered.

Ben felt the prickle of tears in his eyes. "I thank the Lord for you, Anna. I couldn't carry on without you."

At Sycamore on Bull Creek, George Zinn patted the muscled neck of the black draft horse, then ran his hand down its foreleg and grasped just below the fetlock. "Up, big boy," he said, lifting the great hoof onto his knee as the horse shifted his weight. Sometimes they were slow to take the weight off, or would doze off and forget. Made for heavy work. He had several horses waiting their turn, so it would be a busy morning. Pa still shod some, but he was getting less able to handle the heavy or cantankerous ones, so George did most of them. George enjoyed it and was good at it, sometimes putting right the work done by less capable farriers, and sending his charges away with a perfect set of new shoes.

Horses in the wild were designed by God, he mused, to naturally wear away their hooves just at the right pace. When man came along and put them to work, however, it became evident that shoes were needed. Nailing on iron shoes worked great, but the rim of the hoof continued to grow beneath the shoe. His process, if the shoe had not been lost, was to pry off the worn shoe and trim off this rim of growth. Then he would take a rasp and smooth and shape the hoof before fitting a new shoe. He smiled to himself. *Just like the manicure them fancy people get that I read about.*

What am I gonna do about Margaret? She's beautiful and she's educated, and from a family with money. I like everything about what I do, but it just doesn't measure up to what she is and where she grew up. Sure, I heard what the marshal said about where his money might have come from, but that don't change anything about Margaret. She had nothing to do with it. She's good to the core. She says she loves me, but I don't know why. I

try my best to educate myself and be the kind of man to deserve
her.

As he thought about his situation, he moved from hoof to
hoof around the horse, fitting each shoe as necessary, heating
them in turn in the forge and shaping them on the anvil. He
would briefly hold the hot shoe against the prepared hoof to seat
it properly. Smoke would rise, with the scent of burning horn.
Then he would cool it and nail it in place, carefully aligning the
nails to come out the side of the hoof at the right place without
hitting the quick. He'd bend the nail ends down, clip them off,
and clench them with the hammer and clenching iron.

I have to figure out a way to talk to her without sounding
like a whiner. I'm not ashamed of who I am and what I do. It's
just...just...I don't know what it is—or where we're goin'.

He slapped the horse on the rump and led him back to the
hitching rail, lined with others in the shade of the great sycamore
that gave the community its name. He led the horse's teammate
to his work space and began the process anew.

Margaret opened the schoolhouse as usual that morning and sat at
her desk to plan for the day's classwork. She could hear the
welcome noise of the children gathering and playing outside. A
slight noise startled her and she looked up. Lester Coggins was
smiling down at her.

"Didn't mean to give ya a start, Miss," he said.

"I'm afraid you did so, Mister Coggins," she said. "Maybe
you might knock on the door or come in the front entrance next
time."

"Yes, Ma'am, I'll shore do it. And you can call me Lester if
you wish." Coggins was dressed in clean clothes, and except for
his dramatic mustache, clean shaven. There was a little crust of
dried blood on one temple where he had nicked himself. He was
carrying a burlap bag, and it appeared to be moving.

"Mister Coggins, what is it you have there?"

"Brung you a live hen, Miss. You can either eat it, or keep
it to lay eggs, your choice."

"Well, I'm aware of the uses of a chicken, Mister Coggins, and I don't want to disappoint you, but I can't accept it."

"Oh, it's just fine. I got plenty chickens."

"It's not that. It's because if parents bring me gifts, it will look like they want special treatment for their children—"

"Oh, no, no, that ain't—isn't—it at all!" His weathered face reddened.

"I know it isn't, Mister Coggins. I didn't mean to imply that at all. I know you meant it out of generosity, and I thank you for your kindness, but it's a general rule I made for myself. All of my students are equally important to me and I don't want anyone to think otherwise."

"Well, then, I reckon me and my hen will bid you good day, then," he said, and he lifted his hat, turned and departed.

-8-

FERDINAND

Ferdinand Harvey sat brooding on his front porch. He and his remaining sons Bob and Buford had managed to get in the corn crop, but it wasn't up yet. Hope it keeps rainin'. He missed Clint, his favorite, who had some gumption. Reminded me of myself, back during the War, he mused, back when me and Clyde was ridin' with Alf Bolin and the gang. Now Clint's in the ground, thanks to that Ben Archer, who got off. He and his pa need to pay for what they did.

His daughter, Rose, came out onto the porch, the screen door slamming behind her. "Pa, I want to ride down to see Aunt Rebecca. It's her birthday and I haven't seen her for months."

"You ain't goin' nowhere. Git back in the house and help your ma. Better yet, the garden needs hoin'."

"Pa, you can't keep me a prisoner here forever!"

Ferd rose from his rocker and raised a threatening hand, "Don't you lip off at me! We'll see about that."

Rose retreated into the house, nearly tripping over the hound lying on the porch.

"Damn female," Ferd muttered. Growin' too big for her britches. Needs to be taken down a peg. And that damn Tom Archer has went and sold that Friedrich place to his renter, the Stotts. Took advantage of me when I was wounded. Brought a damn deputy out to stand guard while they completed their damn fence. 'Course mine is rottenin' in the ground. What's the point if they want to build the whole damn thing, let 'em...devil's lane growed up in weeds between 'em.

His face grew red just thinking about it. He gave a hard shove to the sleeping hound with his booted foot. "Git, you worthless good-for-nuthin'!'

The spotted hound yelped and leaped to his feet, then slunk off the porch, giving a baleful look back with deep wrinkles between his eyes.

"Yessir," he said aloud. "They need to pay. Maybe when things settle a little more...when they least expect it."

Anna had slept the night through, conscious at times of Ben leaving the room. When she awoke, Ben was there. "How is Evie?" were her first words.

"She's still coughin' and I think she has a little fever. How are you feelin'?"

"I don't know yet, but all right I think. I had bad dreams. You rescued me again. You're my everything." She squeezed his hand.

"I don't deserve it. I never dreamed she could slide that lid off. I already nailed it shut, but too late...too late."

"We didn't know, but thank the Lord we still have her."

"You're the hero, jumping in, holding her up. If not for you, she'd be gone."

"Let's not beat ourselves up over it. Let's learn from it and go forward."

"You're right, Anna. What can I get for you?"

"Coffee later, but right now I have to go to my baby."

Anna, still in her long gown, went into Eva's room. She was thrashing about on the bed and coughing. Anna picked her up and held her close. "My sweet girl! Don't you feel good?"

"No, Mama," she said between fits of coughing. Eva's little body shook violently with chills.

"Ben, she's so hot. Like a stove! We'd better get some cold water and a washcloth, see it we can cool her off."

"But she's shivering."

"I know, but she's hot at the same time."

When they attempted to sponge her with the cold water she cried and tried to push their hands away. "Cold," she said.

"Ben, I don't know what to do! She's panting like a dog."

"I'll hitch up the team. We got to get her to a doctor. There's got to be one in Aurora." Ben rushed out of the room.

Soon they were on their way, Anna holding Eva, now bundled in blankets. She had dressed hurriedly and concluded it was better to try to stop Eva's shivering if she could, despite her hot brow. Oh, what to do?

Ben slapped the reins on the backs of the grays, and urged them to a trot, harness creaking and trace chains jingling. The dirt road was in fair shape with some ruts from spring rains. In some places, creek gravel had been added to keep the road passable. They were on the south side of Honey Creek so fording wasn't necessary. Ben figured they could be in Aurora in less than an hour.

Anna held tight to Eva with her left hand and clutched the side of the spring seat with her right. She looked over at Ben who had a grim expression on his face. Should I tell him? She decided it was time. "I hope I didn't lose it."

Ben glanced at her. "Lose what?"

"The baby."

"You're not makin' sense. You got her right there."

"The other baby. I meant to tell you sooner…"

In spite of his distress, he gave her a big smile. *"Do you mean it?"*

"I'm pretty sure."

"All the more reason to get that sweet girl to doctor! He'll need a big sister."

"He?"

Ben laughed, "Can't blame me for wishin'."

As they entered what appeared to be the outskirts of the town, they crossed a railroad track, then met a man going the other direction in his wagon, loaded with sacks of grain.

Ben drew back on the reins and called out, "Howdy, Mister. Can you tell me where the doctor is? Got a sick girl."

The man reined in also, then seeing Anna, lifted his battered hat in her direction and clapped it back on his balding head. "What you do is, you foller the tracks to the center of town and turn left on the street that runs into the depot. Go up three streets, I believe it is, and turn right. He has a house about four down on the right. They call 'em streets, anyway."

Ben thanked him and hurried the horses forward on the rutted dirt street. The directions proved accurate and they soon drew in front of a house, painted white, with a sign out front stating it was the office of Doctor Fisher, Physician. The house had a wrap-around porch and reminded Ben of delivering his wounded father to a similar house in Forsyth over a year previously.

Anna handed her feverish daughter down to him before dismounting herself, stepping carefully on the wagon wheel spokes.

No one was waiting on the porch, but when they entered the waiting room they found others before them, seated in rows of wooden chairs. They approached a middle-aged woman wearing a gray dress with a white collar seated at a desk. She was wearing wire spectacles perched on her nose and looked up at them. "Yes, what it is?"

Anna spoke quickly, "Our daughter is very sick. She fell into the cistern—"

"What are her symptoms? How is she ailing?"

Eva coughed as Anna replied, "She is stopped up with a cough, and she's real hot with a fever."

"Have a seat and wait your turn," the woman replied, looking back down at the papers on her desk.

Anna and Ben looked around the room and saw empty chairs at the back. They noted the other patients. There was an older man with weathered face set in pain, holding his left arm across his lap. Sticks protruded from the cloth wrapping the arm. A tiny old woman sat with her head down, reading from an open

Bible on her lap. A younger woman was holding the hand of a teenage girl seated beside her. Their thoughts were interrupted by a door opening and a young woman emerging, her face flushed. The woman bent beside the gray lady and whispered something, then hurried out the front door.

The lady at the desk looked up, and said, "Mr. Williams, the doctor will see you now."

The man with the bundled arm cleared his throat, "Elvira if it's all the same to you, let the baby girl go ahead of me."

"Well, if you're sure, but there are still others."

The small lady in black looked up. "Same with me."

Elvira looked around the room with uncertainty, facing nodding heads. "Well…if no one objects." She rose from her desk and led the way toward the door in back. Anna and Ben rose and followed, but Anna, feeling tears start at the corners of her eyes, turned to the waiting room and said, "God bless all of you."

They were surprised when the doctor, clad in white coat, entered the examining room. He was young, slight of build, and already beginning to go bald. He smiled and extended his hand to Ben. "Hello, I'm Doctor Fisher. What seems to be the problem?"

"It's Eva," Anna said. "She fell into the cistern and swallowed some water. It was cold, so now she's all stopped up with the fever."

"Let's see what we can do. You can put her down on the examining table."

Anna found it not so easy to do. Eva clung to her and cried. "It's all right, Evie, the doctor will help you feel better. I'll be right here."

Doctor Fisher spoke soothingly as he adjusted his stethoscope and bent over her. "Mama's right, sweet girl. I won't hurt you. I'm going to listen to your heart, then I'll let you listen." Eva stopped crying and looked at him.

He held up the stethoscope bell. "See? I'm going to warm this in my hand and put it against your upper tummy and listen."

Anna opened the top of Eva's gown and held her hands while the doctor listened and moved the bell from one position to another, his expression unchanging. "Can you take a deep breath for me, sweetheart?"

Eva tried to do so, began coughing.

As her coughing subsided, he said, "Now I'll let you listen like I promised." He placed the earpieces in Eva's ears and held the stethoscope in place. Eva's eyes opened in wonder. "That's your heart beating inside you. Now I'll talk to your papa and mama, see what we can do to make you feel better."

He turned to Ben and Anna. "She has serious lung congestion and high fever, as you have said. I have boiled some willow bark and we need to get her to drink some of the water. It's been known to reduce fever. At the same time, I'll ask you to sponge her with cold water to get that temperature down as soon as possible. She won't like it, but it must be done. Can you stay here? We have a few rooms in the clinic and I'd like to keep an eye on her."

They looked at each other. "For how long?" Ben said.

"Overnight, I would say."

"Yes," Ben said. "Anna, if you can stay, I'll bring back anything you need and take care of the chores."

It was done. Ben milked the cows and fed the livestock, then made the trip back with extra clothing, a quilt, a robe, and other needs for Anna. It was to be the first of three, long anxious nights and the days between, until the third morning when Eva was able to breathe deeply again.

Ben arrived early as usual and was grateful for the good news. "Thank you Doctor Fisher. It don't seem enough to say, but I think we owe you for her life."

Fisher smiled, "It's reward enough and I wish you all the best. Say...may I ask if you were a little worried when we first met—"

Ben looked uncomfortable. "I haf'ta admit, I thought doctors was all old guys."

"I thought so. Not the first time. But you know we all start out young."

Ben smiled. "I reckon you're right. What brought you here?"

"I'm from here. I trained for years in Boston, but wanted to come home. That's my mother out front. I'm all she has left."

"Good for you."

As they drove the team back home, Anna held a pale and sleeping Eva on her lap. "She's all wore out," Ben said.

"Yes, but thank God she's going to get well. I will never, ever let anything happen to her again."

"I know you'll try, but we can't control the whole world. Don't blame yourself. It was me, shoulda' not let it happen. By the way, you look awful tired, yourself. Did you say anything to the doctor about bein' ya know…"

"No, I didn't. I feel just fine. No sickness this time like it was with Eva. And I don't want a man looking me over, even if he is a doctor."

"Well, there'll come a time—"

"We'll get a midwife."

-9-

MARGARET AND GEORGE

Marshal Joshua Lambert was driving himself and others crazy with inaction. The telegraph operators dreaded seeing him coming, often two or three times a day. Finally one morning he was rewarded with a nod of the head. The operator seemed to breathe a sigh of relief after he said, "Got one for ya, Marshal."

Lambert rushed across the plank floor and snatched the yellow paper from his hand. He almost ran into the door on his way out, trying to read the message in a hurry on his way to his horse. It was from New Orleans. It read:

MAN FITTING DESCRIPTION SOLD TWO
HORSES SAME THING STOP WHEREABOUTS
NOT KNOWN BUT LOOKING STOP RU
COMING DOWN STOP MARSHAL PEABODY

Lambert sent a message to Washington saying he was headed south. He sent the same message to Marshal Peabody. Back at the sheriff's office, he studied railroad maps. It would be a long ride by horseback, but it looked like he could ride north to Jefferson City on the Missouri River, catch a train to southern Illinois, then a train to New Orleans. It would still be a long trip, but he could take his horse with him and not wear both of them out.

He left in the early darkness the next morning, coffee and adrenalin making him wide awake. Had to be the man; one of my best guesses which way he would go.

George Zinn drove the light buggy upstream along the east bank of Bull Creek until he came to a shallow ford across to the other side. He then drove down the west bank to pick up Margaret. It was a Saturday morning, just past sunup. School was out, and she had agreed to go with him to a new trading post over on the White River, past Forsyth. He thought it best to have an honest talk about the future. He didn't know what direction that talk would go. He couldn't decide how to open the conversation and he had no idea how she would react. He knew only that he couldn't go on like this, tortured by doubt and indecision.

She was waiting on the front porch of her new log house. The older house behind, where Etta and Ike now lived, had belonged to a woman named Azalea Ward, not welcomed by some, visited in secret by others. She'd appeared out of nowhere a few years ago, and left just as mysteriously after selling the place to Margaret. George was aware of Ward's profession, of course, but not as a customer. Older folks in the community, if they acknowledge her existence at all, whispered the label, "the bad woman." George's musings disappeared at the sight of Margaret. I wish things were different, he thought. I don't know what to do.

Margaret looked forward to spending the day with George. This will be the most significant trip we have taken together. I wonder if he plans to propose to me. He's been acting strangely of late, not like the calm, self-assured man she had come to love. We both enjoy being together and have a lot in common, despite our completely different upbringing.

Margaret descended the steps and ran down the flagstone walk as George brought the buggy to a stop. "Good morning, George," she said. "I've missed you the last couple of days."

George jumped down and came around to hand her into the buggy. "Me, too, Margaret. We've had a lot of work lately and I've been traveling around shoeing horses. Ready to go?"

"Ready! This should be fun."

They drove along at a brisk pace, down through Sycamore, fording Bull Creek again and heading along the wagon road toward Forsyth. Conversation never lagged. Margaret spoke of her school children and the progress they had made. She told about her plans to take a correspondence course or two. George told her of his travels about the community, how new settlers were moving in. However, he said, there was more talk of vigilantes wanting to organize because of the lack of law enforcement. "Doesn't seem to be a lot of serious stuff, since that dispute over the fence line, but you be real careful about being out after dark."

"I always am, George."

"I know, but you can't be too careful, you being a woman alone."

Here it comes, thought Margaret. There *is* a way to correct that 'woman alone' situation. But pursuit of that subject did not happen. He changed the subject to the beautiful spring weather and the way the hillsides and coves had looked in bloom with dogwood and redbud, and now the blackberries blooming.

They talked and laughed together as always and discussed a book George had recently read. The miles went by and it was just before noon as they passed through the busy streets of Forsyth and headed toward their destination, the new trading post.

"I guess you've heard about it," George said. "Man named Rueben Branson started it to give Forsyth a little competition. It's a steamboat stop on the White at a good deep place. It's got a good big wharf. I saw it at a distance, but didn't get to stop. They have a trading post for all the stuff they bring in and ship out. Even have a café, which I'm plannin' on."

"Sounds interesting," Margaret said. "I can tell my students all about it."

"Folks say it's changing things. People are starting to settle in the area."

As they neared their destination, down a long grade toward the river, they met other wagons and buggies headed opposite their way. As was customary the men lifted their hats in Margaret's direction and George nodded or did the same if a woman accompanied them. The trading post was an impressive size, but a simple clapboard barn-like structure. There were only small flat boats tied along the bank, but as they approached the large parking area, a steam whistle blasted in the distance. As they were tying the trotter to one of the posts, they saw a steamboat coming up the river.

Margaret had seen the great ships in New York harbor and larger steamships of all descriptions coming in to Washington when she was a young girl. Now those days were long gone; of a different life. Margaret had left that life behind and saw it as through misted glass. That Margaret lived in a false family who pretended to aristocracy. Now her father was a fugitive accused of murder, her mother was out of touch with reality, and she had no contact with her brother and sister.

She was now a citizen of a real community, among the hill people living along Bull Creek. In the context of her new life, she found herself excited to see the steamboat coming, with its three decks, smoke rising from twin stacks, banners flying, and the sternwheel churning the clear water.

"Pretty, ain't she?" George said, as they walked toward the wharf.

Margaret took his arm and smiled at him.

The captain of the steamboat brought it expertly into the dock, reversing the paddlewheel to stop momentum. Members of the crew and workers on the dock tied it to pilings and a broad gangplank was lowered.

George and Margaret made their way to the trading post and were seated at a plank table on the broad porch under the roof overhang. Margaret realized it was her first restaurant meal, if it could be called that, since Benjamin and Tom Archer's trial in Forsyth. Only one meal was offered, fried catfish, fried potatoes, and canned peas. They were able to continue watching as the steamboat was unloaded. There were few passengers; three or four men and one young couple with two children in tow. The dock crew began trundling crates and barrels of supplies off and into a storage building. A team of mules and one cow were brought off from an enclosure near the stern of the boat. George guessed they might belong to the young couple.

Another bit of cargo caught his eye. A farm wagon was lashed to the foredeck. The crew untied it and wheeled it off the gangplank. He hadn't thought much about it before; just assumed everyone who came to settle in the hills came in their own wagons from wherever. He and his father were constantly repairing broken wheels and other parts of wagons and buggies that were worn or broken. He realized he was staring in silence and brought himself back to the present.

"How's the fish, Margaret?"

"It's just fine, George. Thanks for bringing me here."

"Well, I guess it's not much, considering where you've probably been."

"No, it's good. Don't say that. The past is in the past. I'm here, now."

On the long drive home, George lapsed into long periods of silence. For the most part, Margaret allowed him to do so without interruption, herself in thought, enjoying the passing scenery of the woods in spring. After they had passed through Forsyth without much comment, she decided to see if she could find out what he was thinking.

"George, you're awfully silent. Is something bothering you?"

"Uh, no. Not really. Just thinking about stuff." *Oh, no. How do I say what needs to be said?*

"What kind of stuff? ...If you don't mind sharing."

"I just don't know how to say what I need to say."

Margaret smiled. "We've always been open with each other. Don't be bashful. You know the answer will undoubtedly be 'yes.'" She moved closer to him and laid her head on his shoulder.

Oh, God! He thought. This is worse than I thought. She's taking this the wrong way. I should have had more sense than to have brought her on this outing.

"Margaret, you're not going to like what I have to say...or maybe you will, I don't know."

She sat up straighter, "What is it?"

He couldn't look at her. "I just as well come out with it. I don' think I'm the right man for you, so maybe we should stop keeping company."

"*What?* Look at me, George. What on earth are you saying?"

"Margaret, you know how much I care for you, but we're from completely different backgrounds. You're beautiful. You came from wealth and education—"

"But—"

"Wait, hear me out. You have your own place. I still live with my parents. You have a worthwhile job; I just work with my hands—"

"George, you're talking nonsense! None of those things matter. We love each other...or I thought we did." She looked down at her hands folded in her lap, her expression clouded.

"We do, or at least, I do. But it's more than that."

She looked at him and finally he looked at her. "Well, what is it, really?"

He looked away again. "What am I supposed to do? Leave my folk's home and just move into that nice cabin of yours? What will people think? Here's a man can't provide a home, so he marries one?"

"Oh, for heaven's sake, George! Male ego? I thought you were above that!"

"How we see ourselves and how the community sees us is important to me."

"Good grief! We should do what we want to do and what we know is right for us and to *hell* with the rest!"

58

"*Margaret*, I've never heard you swear before!"

"Right. But this situation calls for it. If you won't ask me, I'll ask you. Will you marry me, George?"

George's face turned red. "I'm sorry to say, I can't. Not now. Not until I make something of myself, and I don't expect you to wait for me."

Margaret looked down again and said quietly. "I will not beg. Maybe if I got rid of all my worldly goods and quit teaching, got a job as a field hand, I'd be suitable material. Or maybe not...."

George said nothing.

"I think I have another possibility," Margaret continued. "Lester Coggins has been coming around lately. He lost his wife, you know. He even brought me a live chicken. So far I've discouraged his attention...."

"You don't need to make fun of me. It's painful enough as it is."

"I'm sorry, George. I apologize. I'm not thinking too clearly. I thought you were bringing me on this outing, which I enjoyed for the most part, to propose to me. It's been a shock to my system and it's going to take some getting used to. I had the future all figured out, and now it's...I don't know what it is."

They rode in an uncomfortable silence for the rest of the return trip. George leaped down and ran around the buggy to steady Margaret as she stepped down. Ignoring their earlier conversation, Margaret rushed into his arms, pressing herself against his muscular chest. George responded by holding her close.

"I'm sorry, Margaret—"

"Don't say that. Just kiss me and go home thinking of me. When you come to your senses, I'll be here."

After he drove away, Margaret stood in the gathering dusk and thought about the feel of his strong arms around her and his rough cheek pressed against hers. When she was with George, who was always a perfect gentleman, she admitted to herself that she had thoughts the uptight finishing-school teachers claimed women didn't have, or weren't supposed to have.

She sighed and turned to go into the log house, where Etta would be waiting with supper for her.

-10-
THE RETURN

Anna awoke to the sound of rain on the roof. It was so peaceful that she wanted to stay there in warmth and comfort, listening to Ben's heavy breathing. How lucky I am, she thought, after all of the trying times when I was a girl. Maybe God lets us have trouble to make us appreciate it when life is good. If that's his plan, it works for me. Yet, I'm ashamed to say there is something missing. Maybe whatever we have, we always want more. I should be perfectly content with how things are, at least in almost everything. I wonder if Ben would understand if I talked to him about it. Would he think I'm not grateful for all he has done for me?

She had gotten up a couple of times in the night, as usual, to check on Eva since that scary sickness. Eva seemed to be over it and doing fine. Now the rain might keep Ben at home today; after chores, of course. Anna slipped out of bed, donned her robe, and went into the kitchen to start a fire in the cook stove. She set the coffee pot on and built a fire in the Franklin stove to take the chill off the house. She and Ben didn't need it, but she wanted to make sure Eva didn't catch a chill. As she went back into the kitchen, she was intercepted by a small figure running up to meet her.

Eva was barefoot, wearing a long flannel nightgown, her red tresses tangled from sleep. Anna scooped her up and held her close. "How's my sweet girl?"

"Good, Mama, 'cept I'm hungry." She put her arms around Anna's neck and held her tight.

"Hungry? Don't want some pancakes, do you?"

"Yesss. I like pancakes."

"I thought so. With some butter and that maple syrup Grandpa gave you?"

"Yesss."

"It's settled, then. I'll get started and you can go wake up Papa." She put Eva down, who promptly scurried into the bedroom.

After breakfast, Ben went out in the rain to let the cows in for milking and took corn for the chickens. Grass was up so he didn't need to do anything for the horses and mules. They'd get a rest day, as would he. Oh, there was always something to do, but maybe he could slack off a little until the rain stopped. When he got back in the house, the kitchen was all cleaned up and Eva was playing on the floor in the living room, all dressed and her hair brushed and braided. He loved the way she seemed a tiny copy of her mother. Thank goodness it went that way and not after that miserable other branch of her parentage.... Ben tried to put that episode out of his mind.

He'd hung his wet coat on the porch, but some dampness had seeped through to his shoulders. He went into the bedroom and changed his undershirt and shirt and went into the kitchen. "Whatcha doin', Babe?"

"Making a couple of pies."

"Man! What did I do to deserve you?"

"Ben, you know it's the other way around."

"No it ain't!"

Anna sighed. "Sit at the table and have another cup of coffee. I want to talk about something."

"Sounds serious."

Anna concentrated on twirling each pie in turn, trimming the crust then pinching the edges around the rim. Finally, she slid them both into the oven, rinsed her hands, and sat across from Ben. She glanced into the other room where Eva was still content to scribble on a slate.

"Ben, I don't know how to say this. It'll make me sound ungrateful, and I'm not. I thank God every day for my life. But I have a yearning. Maybe it's because of my condition. I find myself day-dreaming about our first times together, back in the hills along Bull Creek—"

"That's all it is? I think about it, too."

"Do you think we'll ever go back?"

"Thought about it some...we have it pretty good here."

"I know." She reached across and put her hand over his. "Forget I said anything. I was just thinking about the new one to come, and about Margaret and your—our family. I miss Etta. She was kind to me when I needed it most and she was like a mother to me."

"No, no. I understand. Did that time in the cistern have something to do with it?"

"I don't really know. Most of my thoughts were about you, and it was so painful to think I might not see you again in this life...." Anna stopped, her voice choked with emotion. "Also, I thought about all of the people we left behind, and those hills we love. Could be that's what pushed me over the edge." She wiped tears from her cheek with her finger and smiled at him.

Ben reached his other hand to cover hers. "It would do us both good to go for a visit. I could get a neighbor to milk the cows. We could take a few days. The corn's in and the beef cows have all calved. I'm sure Mister Coleman will be all right with it."

It was getting on toward late afternoon and Anna was weary but on edge with excitement at the prospects of seeing their friends and family. They had started before daylight and travel was easier to begin with in the flatter country. After they rode a ferry across the James in Galena, though, the terrain was more rugged and progress slower. Bone had been trotting along faithfully, but Ben coaxed him into the wagon for a rest. The wagon road was little more than a trail, twin tracks with grass between. At places, it had been carved into the hillsides with slip-scrapes and mules. Ben stopped and rested the horses every two hours so he and

Anna were able to climb down and stretch themselves. They had made a bed of hay and blankets in the back for Eva, but most of the time she wanted to ride on the spring seat with them, excited about the adventure.

As daylight began to fade, Ben said, "I reckon we're about halfway. I'll see if we can find a place to camp for the night."

They dropped into a valley beside a small stream, so they camped there for the night. The horses were unharnessed and taken to water, then hobbled so they could graze. Ben built a fire ring of stones and built a fire as dusk settled into darkness. Anna got out an iron skillet and prepared a hash of ham, potatoes, and onions. She set the coffee pot on the coals to boil. She'd brought along two apple pies she'd made. Bone waited impatiently for his food. He worshipped Anna and would follow her anytime she appeared outside. Ben was amused by his devotion, ever since Bone had discovered her hiding in the barn loft at their former home in the hills.

"I haven't camped out for a long time, Anna," Ben said, as he wiped his tin plate with a curst of bread. "And I never ate like this."

"You deserve it. And I never camped at all. It's what Papa used as an excuse for leaving me behind. When I look back on it now, I should be grateful he did. But it hurt at the time. Still, we'd never have found each other." She smiled at him in the firelight.

"Beggin' pardon, but he was a fool to ever leave you."

They awoke in the early dawn, awakened by the calls of the birds and the snuffling of the horses as they began to graze. The wagon had made a cozy bed with the hay and quilts to keep them warm in the cool night air. Eva had slept soundly between them.

After breakfast, Ben watered the horses and hitched up. He carried a bucket of water to kill the campfire and they departed.

Toward the end of another long day, a repeat of the day before, Ben said, "I think it may be close to dark before we get there. I hope the folks will be home."

"Hope so, too. Nobody goes anywhere much except church on Sunday."

"Right."

The sun was beginning to touch the western hills when they finally crossed the mail road that ran straight south from Springfield to Little Rock. Familiar territory at last! Only a few short miles later they were fording Hansen Creek and driving up the lane to the Archer farmstead. Horses whinnied and Ben's team answered. Just as they drove up to the hitching rail in front, the door opened, spilling soft gold light onto the porch. A large shepherd dog jumped down off the porch. Oren looked out, then gave a yell and came running down the steps. Bone and the other dog approached each other, stiff-legged and sniffing at both ends.

"Ben! Ben! Is that you?"

Ben climbed wearily down from the wagon and was staggered by Oren leaping up into his arms. "Oren! You're a lot bigger!" He hugged Oren and put him down. "You're a head taller."

"I shore am. I already been to school."

"Good for you. Now let's get Miss Anna down with your niece Eva."

Anna was weary also, but happy to have arrived. For the last several miles she had been holding a sleeping Eva on her lap, and her arms ached.

By the time Ben had walked around the wagon, the rest of the family had surrounded them.

"Oh, Ben!" Rebecca said. "Let me hold that baby girl." She hugged him quickly, then reached up to take Eva from Anna's arms. Jenny and Essie rushed to their mother's side and Jenny pulled the blanket aside to look at her sleeping niece. Essie was jumping up and down trying to see, so her sister lifted her up.

"Look, Jenny," she whispered. "She's bigger." They hadn't seen Eva since she was an infant.

The others stood back until Ben assisted Anna down. Then they came forward to exchange hugs and handshakes; Josephine first with Anna, then Ben. Tom came forward to shake Ben's hand, then embrace him. Jimmy finally came to shake Ben's hand, and shyly approached Anna to do the same, but Anna folded him in an embrace. "You don't get by with a handshake, Jimmy," she said. "My, my! You're all grown up. You're taller than I am!" Jimmy looked away in embarrassment.

"Let's all go inside," said Tom. "Becky has a big pot of soup ready, with some of her cornbread. Then we'll put the horses away and figure where to put everybody."

"I hope it's not a problem," said Ben, as they all climbed the steps and started inside. "We slept in the wagon just fine on the way down."

"No, no, no," said Tom. "Not a problem at all. We'll sort it out."

"Oren and me'll sleep in the barn," said Jimmy.

It was a loud and happy meal, questions flying to Ben and Anna from all the siblings and from Tom and Rebecca. Ben and Anna in turn asked about the school year just completed and Anna asked about her friend Margaret. Eva had awakened, bewildered at all of the unfamiliar people, but soon basked in the attention of everyone, performing from her perch in a high chair.

"She's just a great teacher, and now I'm all finished," Josephine said.

Later, Rebecca said, "I hope the loft is all right for you and Anna, Ben. I'll turn the mattresses and put on fresh bedding. Jimmy can fetch the little folding bed Essie used to sleep in for Eva."

"That'll be fine, Becky. It's where I used to sleep."

After all the children except Josephine were in bed, and the boys gone to the barn, the five gathered around the kitchen table.

"So glad you're here," Tom began. "Bit surprised, I reckon, but so happy to see you."

Ben smiled, "Surprised us, too. We was just gettin' a bit homesick, I guess. Anna said something first, but I realized I felt exactly the same way." Anna put her hand on Ben's forearm and smiled at him.

"Everything is all right, I hope," said Rebecca.

"Oh, yes, it's just fine," Anna said. "Ben works hard and has the spring crops in, the garden's planted, and the beef cows have all calved. We did have a terrible scare a while back. Eva, the little rascal, managed to fall in the cistern and could have drowned—"

"Mercy!" Rebecca said. "How horrible! She seems just great, now."

"She is," Ben said, "But Anna jumped in and held her up for a long time until I came to the house. Bone raised a ruckus. If it hadn't been for Anna, we would have lost her." He looked down for a moment and continued with a catch in his voice. "And if the water had been deeper...." He put his other hand over Anna's and looked at her with the shine of a tear in his eye.

Josephine said, "Oh, Anna, how brave you are." The rest murmured assent.

Anna looked embarrassed, "Thank you, Josie. It's what anyone would do."

"That's not why we came to visit," Ben said. "We miss all of you and we miss Bull Creek and the hills. The country up there is pretty, too. Nice rolling land with lots that's good to plow. There's a creek close by, too, but it ain't the same. Here, Bull connects to the White, and in the spring the suckers and redhorse make their run. I miss grabbin' 'em and I miss trappin' in the winter...well, you know how it is, Pa."

Tom smiled, "I guess I do. I don't ever want to leave here. Uh, don't suppose you'd think of comin' back?"

"Well, we feel awful obliged to Mister Coleman. He helped us get away from a bad situation. What do you hear about the Harveys?"

"Not much. They keep pretty much to themselves. There's still stuff goin' on around here, but nothing anybody can prove. You may not know; we sold your home place, Anna, to the folks we'd rented Becky's place to. The Stotts, remember them?"

"What about Becky's farm, now?" Ben said.

"We're doin' the best we can to keep it up." He and Ben looked at each other. "Let's talk some more in the mornin'."

"Good," Ben said. "Josie, haven't heard much from you. What are you doin' these days?"

"Just the usual here on the place. Finished school. Don't know what comes next."

"She's a great help," Becky said, and she reached to take Josie's hand. "Some fella will snap her up one of these days."

Josephine blushed.

-11-
ETTA

B en found it strange to wake up in the bed he occupied as a young man. Tired from the journey, he had slept soundly and it took a moment to realize where he was. When he was that young man, his wildest dreams never included the miracle of the woman and child beside him. Anna was still sleeping soundly, but not soundlessly. He smiled at the vision of her with mouth slightly open, snoring softly. Usually she was up before him, starting a fire, brewing coffee. Rebecca was now fulfilling that duty downstairs with the assistance of Josie, judging by the whispered conversation he heard.

He slipped silently out of bed and put on the clothes he had worn yesterday. He ran his fingers through his tangled hair and crept downstairs in his stocking feet, carrying his shoes. Rebecca met him with a cup of coffee. "Good morning," she whispered and he returned the greeting, taking a seat at the table to watch them work.

Anna awoke with a snort when Eva shook her shoulder. "Oh, my, sweet baby. Mama was really sleeping." She got quickly out of bed and dressed Eva, then herself. She combed Eva's hair and braided it, then twisted her own into a bun at the nape of her neck. Then she carried Eva down the steep stairs to the others waiting below. She was embarrassed that everyone was there, awaiting their arrival.

"Good morning everyone," she said. "So sorry I was such a slug-a-bed."

All returned her greeting with added reassurances, "Just got here," "No problem," "Glad you slept good."

Rebecca and Josephine served all of them biscuits and sausage with sausage gravy. It was a happy gathering but Anna felt uncomfortable with her role as guest. She felt better about it when she was able to dive into the cleanup and dish-washing. Afterward, Eva was surrounded by her three aunts and was happy to entertain them. Oren focused on Anna as soon as she was free, telling her of his success in catching crawdads in the creek. It was an emotional feeling for Anna, being a part of a loving family. Now I know why I wanted to come, she thought.

Ben went with his father and Jimmy to feed the stock and milk the cows. There were only two milk cows, so Jimmy insisted on doing his usual part, leaving Ben to stand and talk while they worked. "Ben, back to our talk last night, would you be interested in comin' back?" Tom said.

"I believe I would, if you think it's safe. After being basically alone, it was such a good thing to be together last night and this morning. I know Anna loved it. What family she had just run off and left her after her ma died. She got a taste of it before that mess at the fence, but you could see what a pleasure it was for her, bein' back."

Jimmy stayed quiet, but enjoyed hearing the conversation. Tom continued, "Well, what are your plans for today?"

"I know Anna's dyin' to see Margaret and Etta. If it's all right, we might do that this mornin'."

"That'ud be fine. Maybe sometime today or tomorrow mornin' we could go walk the Tate place and see what you think of it."

Ben wheeled the buggy up the east bank of Bull Creek to cross the ford above Sycamore. He glanced over at Anna, with Eva sitting on her lap. Anna had brushed out her hair and braided it. She was wearing a fresh dress she'd brought along and he smiled at the two of them: same red hair, flowered frocks, and expressions, Eva a little copy of her mother. Pa had insisted he take the new buggy; give his own horses a rest. They had invited Josie to come along and she sat in the back seat. Pa must be doing pretty well, he mused. The roan trotter with white mane and tail was a new addition, also.

"Maybe it ain't my place to say," said Etta, "But Margaret, girl, you been havin' the mopes the last coupla' days. Somthin' wrong?" The two had finished cleaning the kitchen after breakfast, and Margaret was mostly silent, deep in thought.

Margaret put the last of the dishes in the cabinet and took off her apron. "You're right, of course, Etta. You know me well."

"Shouldn't be a surprise. Knowed you since you was a babe. You been so happy for a year or more...ever since you been seein' that fella of yours. That it?"

"Right again. Let's sit and have some coffee. Can you stand to hear my troubles?"

"If it'll help. Don't want to be nosey."

"You're all I have, Etta, and I'm grateful. You sit and I'll get the coffee."

Etta looked uncomfortable at the role reversal, but did as she was bid.

"It took me completely by surprise," Margaret began. "I thought everything was wonderful. You know he is a really good man."

"What I hear, yes."

"He thinks he's not good enough for me, that I'm above his station, that he doesn't have a place of his own...stuff like that. Can you imagine?"

Etta smiled with a flash of white teeth. She put her hand on Margaret's. "You know how I feels about you. No man really good 'nuff, but he comes closest, of those I know about."

"What am I to do?"

"I'd say, give him some time to come to his senses."

"I guess you're right, but it's hard. I thought I had it all figured out. Can I ask you something? I really have no right—"

"Ask me anythin' you want."

"Did you ever have a fellow? Were you ever married?"

"Yes and no." Etta stared in the direction of the front window, her face set in a sad expression. "I put it out of my mind a long, long time ago."

"I'm sorry—"

"No, it's all right. You have a right to know." She paused to gather her thoughts. "I was a house slave on a plantation in Virginia, you know, and we wasn't supposed to mix with the field hands, but young people, well they figger out a way. We had some chances to get out and about. Wasn't too strict. It was at Christmas one year, we was allowed to have a bonfire and a singin'. Well, there he was, name of Moses. Tall, strong, handsome. We took to sneakin' out at night, meetin' under a tree on the river bank. We talked of jumpin' the broom...gettin' married. One night he didn't show...." Etta looked down at her clasped hands and swallowed.

"Etta, please. I'm so sorry I asked."

"No. Jest part of life, like all things. Found out later he been sold. Never found out where he went."

"So sad. Makes any problem I have seem trivial."

"Don't think that. I'm an old woman now. Jest left it behind me. Never had thoughts about a man after that. Had a pretty good life, 'cept for a thing two." She flashed her smile again. "You prob'ly know about that."

They were interrupted by the sound of a horse trotting and iron wheels on the road outside. They rose and went to open the front door as a buggy rolled to a stop out front. When they saw who was in the buggy, they both ran onto the porch. Margaret shouted, "It's Anna!" Etta echoed, "Anna! Anna! My sweet Anna!"

They both rushed down the steps and down the flagstone path, Etta following Margaret as fast as her aging body allowed.

Anna barely had time to dismount from the buggy in time to be engulfed in their combined embrace. Tears of joy flowed freely all around. Even Ben and Josie found themselves feeling the same way, watching the three of them. Ben was holding Eva, and Margaret and Etta soon turned to them.

"Let me see that sweetie!" said Margaret.

Eva turned away and buried her face in Ben's shoulder.

Ben spoke softly to her. "Evie, don't be bashful. These here are people who love you."

At last Eva turned to face them and gave Margaret a bashful smile.

Soon all were inside the house, with coffee served and Eva once again the center of attention. Anna was flushed with delight and Ben was pleased to see her have the chance to enjoy the reunion.

Back at the Archer home, Rebecca took Tom aside and whispered to him. "I have something to tell you. You're going to be a grandpa again. You think you can handle that?"

Tom's face lit up. "Really? Anna told you that?"

Rebecca nodded. "She was bashful about telling me, but it makes me feel good that she sees me as a sort of mother figure."

"I wonder if it has something to do with them payin' a visit?" Tom said.

ROGER MEADOWS

-12-

THE FARM

George and Homer Zinn were working together reassembling a wagon wheel on their rotary work table. They had taken the wheel apart to replace two broken spokes and one of the felloes that had cracked. George had made the new spokes out of ash, and the curved piece out of seasoned white oak. They were getting ready to install the wheel rim, now heating to expand it. George thought it was a good time to bring up what was on his mind. He waited until they had dropped the rim in place and centered it carefully, and they had paused to let it cool and shrink to a tight fit. As they took off their heavy gloves, and stood back, George spoke. "Pa, there's something I been thinkin' about."

"Yeah? What's on your mind?"

"Well, I keep thinkin' I can just keep on like I am, which is just fine—I like what I do—or I could reach out, try to make something of myself."

Homer took out his pipe and lit it, taking tongs and using a hot coal from the forge. George waited.

"Anything to do with the way you been mopin' around lately?"

George smiled. "I reckon so."

"Well, I think you've already made somethin' of yourself. Everybody in the country wants you to shoe their horses, or make things."

"I hope you won't shoot it down, but what if I built a shed on the north side, and see if I can build buggies?" He hurried on with his idea before Homer could interrupt. "We already repair them and wagons. Seems as more people get prosperous, they'll want a buggy to get around in instead of the old farm wagons. There aren't many buggies yet on the Creek. And as to buggies, I've written to a couple of suppliers in Springfield and Saint Louis where you can get parts you need, like the steel hubs and axles. We really need to get a lathe to turn wooden hubs for wagons, then we could make them too." His father was staring at him, puffing on his pipe.

"What do you think?"

"You caught me off guard. Need to let it sink in a bit. What about this business?"

"We could bring Hiram back. You know he's good with his hands."

"Your brother might not want to. There wasn't enough for three of us before. And Jensen might want to keep him at the mill...of course that could all be worked out...."

"Nothing has to be decided right away. This is way out, but there has been talk of replacing the horse with a steam engine or other such thing. Who knows where things might go? Has no bearing on us, of course, at least not now. Just something I read about."

"Doubt I'll live to see it. Anyway, let's sleep on it. I know if you set out to do something, it will probably happen." He smiled at his son and clapped him on the back.

"Thanks, Pa," George said. Well, he didn't kick me out of the shop!

As they turned toward the entrance, a tall figure appeared silhouetted against the bright outside sunlight.

"*Ben, is that you?*" shouted George.

"In the flesh!"

Homer and George rushed forward to shake hands and George gave Ben a hug. "Man, it's good to see you! What brings you home?"

"We got homesick, I guess. Didn't realize how bad until we got to see the folks again. And you should see that love fest going on right now up at Margaret's."

"I can imagine," George said. "There was a special bond between Anna and Margaret...and Etta, too, in fact, after what they all went through."

"I didn't have a chance to ask Margaret, bein' outnumbered by females—Josie's there, too—but I figured you two would be hitched by now."

George's face clouded, and he looked at his father.

"Uh-oh, did I step in somethin'?" Ben said.

Homer said quickly, "Why don't you fellers go outside and catch up. I'll take that wheel down and remount it on the wagon out back. It's cool by now.

George led the way to the benches under the sycamore.

Ben spoke first, "Well, are you goin' to tell me about it?"

"Not much to tell. I guess I'm the one slowed things down a little."

"Are you crazy? You two are really right for each other."

"No, that's not true. True, we do like each other—"

"I thought they called it *love*."

"Call it what you wish, there's a practical side of things. She comes from money and society; I grub around with my hands—"

"You think she cares about *that*?"

"I care. What kind of man would everybody take me for if I was to marry her and move into her nice house, directly out of livin' with my ma and pa, like some little boy...."

"I'd say, don't worry about shallow people who want to snipe about others."

"Easy for you to say. Not how I'm put together."

"What are ya goin' to do about it?"

"Well, I have a plan, and if it works and she's still there, I'll see if she'll forgive me and take me back."

"I hope it's a good plan, then. Mind tellin' me about it?"

"I don't mind, but I don't want you to tell anyone else, particularly not her. If you're ready, here goes...." George laid out his plans while Ben listened without interruption. "Well, what do you think?"

"If anybody can do it, you can. But won't it take quite a while?"

"Not if I work night and day and every day, which I will."

"When will you start?"

"Tomorrow, if Pa sleeps on it and gives me his blessing. And we have to see if Hy will come back to work in the shop, which I think he will."

Ben reached to shake hands, "Good luck, George. I hope it works great. If I can scare up the money, I'll buy your first buggy."

When they were driving back to the Archer's after a noon meal at Margaret's, Anna put her hand on Ben's arm. "How was your visit with George? Margaret wouldn't say much since others were there, but it seems things have cooled off."

"That's about it. George thinks she's too good for him." Ben smiled, "Maybe he's right."

"Maybe so, if he's acting like that."

"He knows she came from a fancier background. Of course she ain't like that."

"Of course not. What's he going to do?"

"He swore me to secrecy, but I think he's startin' a business. Wants to be more important."

"Well, I hope it works. I like both of them and they belong together."

Tom was waiting when they arrived. "I hung around here for a while, thought you might want to take a ride up to the Tate farm and have a look. Don't want to hurry you, but I don't know if this weather will hold."

Ben noted the clouds were gathering in the west, with a warm breeze springing up. "I'm ready if you are," he replied. Then to Anna, "Will you be all right here?"

"Sure. Let me know what you think."

Tom led the way as they rode up the wagon road on the east bank of Bull Creek. He had provided a tall sorrel gelding for Ben to ride, and Jimmy rode with them on his new pony, a sorrel and white paint. As they rode along, Ben listened to the music of the crystal water flowing over limestone ledges and plunging over small waterfalls into deeper pools. He scanned those deeper places shaded by overhanging willows and wished for the chance to fish again.

At their quick pace it took less than an hour to reach the ford across Bull Creek to the Tate farm. As they rode up the lane toward the house place, Tom discussed the lay of the farm. "Charlie's pa homesteaded the original hundred and sixty acres, then he bought an eighty off the place to the south. The eighty is 'most all timber and it ain't been logged much." He waved his arm at the surrounding fields. "As you can see, it has some good bottom land along the Bull. Plenty of water for the stock, of course. You've been to the house and barn, so you know about what's there."

"It's a good place; better'n the Friedrich place." Ben liked the way the house was set up on the gradual hillside with a spring on the north side, shaded by a couple of large oaks. A Tate ancestor had built a stone springhouse and scooped out a pond below the spring that looked like it might keep full during dry times. And the barn and barn lot were on the south side so it wouldn't contaminate anything. Really a good layout. There was even a dug well with a windlass to draw buckets of water.

"It's for sure a nice place, all right."

"Seems to have about everything. Got a chicken house, smokehouse, pig pen. Is that an extra shed on the barn?"

"Yeah. Charlie's old man had him a sort of tack room and shop in there. Charlie said he used to joke that it was to hide from his wife, though she wasn't like that. As you know, Rebecca certainly wasn't."

"What do you plan to do with the place?"

"Well, it's still in Rebecca's name, so it's up to her. As you know from the trial, I didn't want there to be any doubt I married her for *her*, not to get the farm. We rented it to the Stotts at your suggestion, I recall."

"So what now?"

"She said she'd love for you and Anna to live here, take over what's left of the mortgage, and eventually own it. She said she doesn't need it for security with you and Anna as family here."

"Pa, that would be most generous and I feel sure Anna would jump at the chance. She's all right wherever she is, but you know, after she lost her whole family, it left her yearnin' to be among her new family. She don't complain, but I could tell this visit meant the world to her."

"Poor girl. You know we love to have her."

"We'll talk it over, but I know what she'll say. And we have to make sure we don't leave Mister Coleman hangin'. Might take a little while to get everything in order."

After they had ridden over more of the farmland, they headed back down the lane to the ford. They rode through the shallow water, their horses' hooves throwing sheets of water ahead of them. The bank of clouds had become darker and rain threatened. They urged their mounts to a faster pace.

As they turned south along the wagon road, a man standing in the woods on the hillside above them observed their progress. He narrowed his eyes and shifted the shotgun to his other hand.

Anna was relegated to sitting at the kitchen table while Josie and Rebecca made preparations for the evening meal. She'd tried to help, but they insisted on her taking it easy because that's what a guest is supposed to do, they said. Jennie and Essie had taken over Eva, seeming to consider her a live doll to play with, and all three were laughing and playing. Anna was brimming with feelings of contentment, as she participated in conversation with part of her mind to talk about the community. At the same time, another part of her mind traveled to the Tate place with Ben, wondering what the outcome would be.

I had a family, I guess, when my mother was alive. But then, I didn't really know what a family was supposed to be. Well, Mama was good to me and took care of me, but Papa was distant and didn't pay much attention to me except to order me about and punish me at times. Evan was good, but quiet. Mostly he tried to avoid trouble from Papa—it's what we all did, when I think about it. After Mama was gone, and Papa put me to work for that horrible Colonel Madison, I thought all was lost. But Margaret and Etta made me realize that there are good people in the world, and then Ben. Oh, Ben! Thank God for Ben and for Eva!

"Anna?"

"I'm sorry. What?"

"You were a hundred miles away," Rebecca said.

Anna stood and saw Rebecca and Josie smiling at her. "Oh, you're right. I apologize. I was thinking about Ben and where they've gone, but mostly about *family* and how I finally know what the word means." She went over to them, standing by the stove, and embraced them each in turn.

They heard rumblings of thunder, and rain began to fall. Then they heard the sound of horses galloping up the lane and saw their men riding past the window toward the shelter of the barn.

ROGER MEADOWS

-13-

THE MOVE

The steam locomotive labored up the flank of a mountain in southwest Wyoming approaching the border with Utah. It pulled a string of cars; two passenger cars, two sleepers, four boxcars, two flats, three cattle cars carrying horses and cattle, and a red caboose. It left in its wake a trail of smoke and cinders, mixed with spurts of steam at each stroke of the pistons on each side. In a few hours it would climb over the last pass and cruise through Sacramento toward San Francisco and the Pacific.

In the second passenger car, halfway down the left side, Marshal Joshua Lambert shifted in his seat and wished he had booked a sleeper. He'd been riding the railroads for days and days after leaving New Orleans. Sleepers cost a lot, however, and he considered himself tough enough to ride in a seat. By now, he didn't feel quite so tough. This long trip would have been hard on his horse, and he was glad he'd boarded him in St. Louis at a place that would exercise him.

He hoped he had made a correct guess about his quarry. Marshal Peabody had assured him it was a good gamble. The two of them had canvassed all the horse traders and stables in New Orleans and surroundings, and had finally hit the jackpot at a small stable on the northern outskirts. They were satisfied that they had stared the horse, Devil, in the eye after the grizzled stable owner nodded when he stared at the picture on their wanted poster. He further confirmed that his stable boy had ridden with that man to the docks on the Mississippi after the purchase was agreed upon, and brought the horses back. Three more days and nights tracking down ticket agents for the several shipping companies turned up a man who recognized the picture. "T'warnt his name, though.   Man called hisself Jefferson." Peabody and Lambert gave each other a look. Madison, Jefferson? Simple enough. When they located the passenger manifest, a John Jefferson had purchased a ticket for Panama.

Lambert could see why Madison might have chosen the longer route. He could blend into a larger population by ship; less likely to be remembered. He shifted in his seat and counted the hours until he could get off the damn train.

Anna mopped her brow as she stood at the kitchen stove. August was drawing to a close and she and Ben had been working hard the past week to prepare for their move back home to Bull Creek. Their belongings were packed up and ready to go. It had taken longer than they expected to find a family to take their place on Mister Coleman's farm they were tending. Ben refused to leave him without a good replacement after Coleman's kindness to them.

The delay had its advantages. They had been able to harvest and preserve a winter's supply of produce from their garden and they would have plenty of time to settle in their new home before the breath of winter. Eva seemed to have a good understanding of what was about to happen and was excited about seeing her young aunts and uncles again.

Anna smoothed her apron over the bump in her stomach that was becoming more prominent. Baby was kicking pretty hard and felt like he was turning little flips in there. She didn't know why she thought of it as "he," but Ben would like it if that turned out to be true. She was grateful that she had no morning sickness this time. Rebecca had told her it sometimes happens that way.

Ben came in behind her and put his arms around her. "Hey, Babe. Smells good. Pa should be here pretty soon from what he said in the letter."

"I'm hoping. I'm cooking extra and maybe we can hold supper if he's late."

"Good idea. I'll go on out and milk a little early."

Ben had finished milking and was pumping fresh well water into the wooden barrel around the milk can containing the results, when he looked down the lane to see a wagon approaching. Two horseback riders followed it. He hurried to finish and ran into the house. "Anna, they're comin'!" He shouted.

She went to the window to look. "He's bringing help to herd the animals, looks like."

"I thought he would." As they drew closer, he added, "It's Mark Johnson and Jimmy...and he brought Oren."

Eva had heard their excitement and waited on the porch with them to see the arrivals. "It's Paw-Paw!" she shouted. She had made a strong attachment to Tom during their short visit earlier in the summer.

They were soon wheeling into the back of the house, harnesses jingling and wheels crunching on the gravel. Ben's horses whinnied from the back lot and Tom's answered. There was a flurry of activity as the riders dismounted and Anna and Ben rushed to greet all of them. Mark was a bit shy in the middle of the family greetings.

Tom Archer approached Anna and said, "All right if I give you a hug? You're my daughter now, you know."

"By all means. We're glad to have you." She went on to say, "I'll get supper on while you tend the horses."

As she was doing so, Oren came into the kitchen. "Since Pa said you're my sister, kin I call you 'Anna' 'stead of 'Miss Anna'?"

"You may certainly do so, Oren." She gave him a quick hug.

"Uh, Anna, I caught a wood lizard on the way up. Would you like to hold him?" He held out the creature in his hand, its head peeping out, and its tail dangling. Eva looked on with great interest.

"Thank you, Oren, but I'm kinda busy with supper. Let me give you a jar to put him in while you wash up."

They traveled down the east bank of Bull Creek in the golden light of a full moon. It was well past nightfall and all were weary—two wagons, two riders, two milk cows, five calves, and a dog. Two mules and a saddle horse were on lead ropes. Anna was tense with anticipation as they neared the ford back across the creek to approach her new home. The journey was longer in time than their earlier trip in the spring, thanks to the yearling calves and the complications of making camp the night before and getting organized this morning. They had stopped in the same little valley by the stream where they stayed on the previous trip. Ben and Tom had put up a lean-to for her and Eva, while the men slept by the fire, under a canopy of stars glittering through the tree branches overhead.

They hobbled the horses to graze, but Jimmy and Mark took turns keeping track of the cows and calves during the night. It amused Anna to see the two of them herding the unruly bunch yesterday to begin, but eventually they got them sorted out. Bone had no heritage as a shepherd, but he soon caught on and helped. The four young heifers were of beef stock as was the bull calf, from a different herd of Coleman's.

"You ain't asleep, are ya, Babe?" Ben said, as they jostled along the road.

"No, but I'd like to be. I'm really tired, I guess, but excited at the same time."

"I know what you mean. We're close to the ford back across the creek, so we'll be home in just a little bit."

"That word 'home' sounds good to me."

"Me, too. I hope it's a place I can spend the rest of my life with you. It'll be a little rough to start with, so I don't want you to kill yourself—you take your time and let me help."

"I promise."

Tom was in the lead and turned right to cross the creek at a wide expanse of shallow water. He stopped far enough forward to let the horses drink, including Ben's horse, Charger, on a lead rope behind. Ben pulled alongside for his horses and the trailing brace of mules. The cows and yearlings splashed in to drink, scattering around the wagons.

They were soon pulling into the side yard between the house and barn. The first order of business was to get the cattle herded into the barn lot along with the two mules.

"It's late, Pa. Why don't we unhitch the teams and leave the wagons for me to unload tomorrow. You can either bed down here, you and Jimmy, or take my horse and ride on home. Mark, you can decide what you'd like to do."

Tom spoke first. "If it's all right with you, we'll put down a pallet in the house. Better than last night. That way we can sort it out in the morning."

"I reckon I'll head on home," Mark said. "It ain't far."

"That'll be just fine, Mark, and I'm much obliged. We couldn't have done it without you."

Ben heard a slight noise and awoke to see bright sunlight blazing through the front window. He saw Anna, already dressed, putting the coffee pot on the stove. She had a fire going and had found what she needed in the kitchen box they'd packed. This log house was a little bigger than the Friedrich place and it had a similar shed bedroom off to one side where Anna and Eva had slept. Tom had insisted they set up the bed for Anna last night because of her "delicate condition," he'd whispered.

"All right," Ben had whispered back, "But 'delicate' is a word she ain't too familiar with."

The two men, Oren, and Jimmy, who would have rankled not to be included in the 'men' category, all stirred and rose from their corners in the main room. They'd all slept on the floor in their clothes.

"Morning, everyone," said Anna. "Now I can make some real noise. If you want to find me a table to work on, I'll make some biscuits."

"It's a deal!" Tom said.

The wagons were almost unloaded and furniture carried in by the time the biscuits came out of the oven. A short time after breakfast, the unloading was completed, and Ben urged Tom and Jimmy to head home, with his gratitude.

At last, Ben and Anna were together in the kitchen area, with Eva playing on the floor. Ben embraced her and said, "Well, what do you think?"

"It's just great to be here. This is a better house than my old home, and it just feels different to be back on the Creek."

"I feel the same way. Old man Tate was a good man with wood, if he's the one that did it. These logs are longer and squared better than most, and the barn looks good. First thing after I milk, I'd better saddle up and ride all the fence lines and make sure they're good before I let the stock out."

"I'll start cleaning up in here and get our stuff put away."

Remembering his father's statement, Ben said, "Now you be careful and don't work too hard." He reached down and caressed her stomach. "Don't forget what you got in here."

She smiled. "Believe me, it's not something I forget."

Ben was saddled up and on his way a short time later. Anna set about organizing her kitchen and storage areas. Ben headed west up the slope toward the ridgeline behind the house place. This was pastureland, without a doubt. Too much slope to plow easy and some scattered trees for shade. Bone trotted along behind, taking an excursion after some animal scent. The sun was beginning to make its late August heat felt.

He eventually hit the rail fence line, figuring that was the west boundary of the farm. He headed south, now through denser woods. The fence looked in fair shape, a rail here and there looking like it should be replaced. After a half-hour or so, he encountered a square crib of rocks, which must be the corner of the original tract. That must be the eighty on the other side of the fence ahead of him. Sure enough, the timber in there looked good. No fence around it. Apparently Charley Tate never let livestock in that part.

As he turned east to follow the south boundary, Bone jumped a rabbit and took chase, causing Charger to shy. Bone soon returned, tongue hanging in the heat. Ben made mental notes as he rode, passing a gate into the timber, continuing on until he hit the bank of Bull Creek. The Creek formed the east margin of the property, so he would always have plenty of water. Had to have a fence line along the bank, but there was a part of the fence built out into the water to allow cattle to drink. Ben rode Charger knee-deep into this entry to the Creek so the horse could drink. Charger pawed the water, then drank his fill. Bone took the opportunity to do the same.

Ben continued his ride northward in the heat, along the west bank of Bull Creek. He passed through gates for the cross fences that set aside the hayfield and cornfield. The corn looked to be maturing nicely. He crossed the lane that led to the farmstead and continued to the northeast corner of the property. As he proceeded, he picked up woods and brush on his right that separated him from the Creek, and the land began to slope upward. Bone took off into the woods to explore and Ben heard him trailing something.

He couldn't recall being to this part of the Creek. The corner of his property terminated on a rock outcropping overlooking Bull Creek. There was a sturdy rapid below, almost a waterfall, that cascaded into a deeper pool. The pool was deep and long, full of clear water. He took off his hat and mopped sweat from his brow with the sleeve of his shirt. Oh, man, he thought. Why not? He rode back off the rocky point and dismounted. He hobbled Charger and removed his saddle and bridle, turning him loose to graze. He climbed down to the rocky bank by the flowing pool and removed all of his clothes, folding them carefully, setting his boots and hat beside them.

He jumped into the cool, deep water. How refreshing it was! He dived underwater and swam the length of the pool, then back upstream, coming up for air. He enjoyed swimming underwater with his eyes open, repeating several laps. On one cycle back upstream, he burst through the surface in time to hear loud spoken words:

"Wel-l-l-l! Lookee hyere!"

-14-

THREAT

Ben whirled around in the water and looked up to see three men on the rock above him, one sitting a horse, one standing, and one sitting on the rocks. He recognized the voice, last heard at his trial, and the last voice he would want to hear—Ferdinand Harvey.

He brushed back his wet hair and treaded water, deciding to take a direct approach, "Good mornin' Mister Harvey. What brings you out on this side of the Creek?"

"Just checkin' for vermin. Heered there was some moved into the area."

"That's interesting. I'll be on the lookout. How are you, Bob? And you, Buford? You've grown up some since I saw you last." Buford was on the horse, Bob standing, and Ferd sitting on the rock.

Both boys stared back in silence. Bob's eyes were downcast but Buford was grinning in anticipation. He had managed a thin, scraggly beard in keeping with family tradition.

All three men were armed with shotguns. Ferd turned his head and Ben heard him give orders, "You boys go un-hobble that horse yonder and chase him out in the pasture, whilst me and him have us a talk."

Ferd climbed down and squatted on the bank above Ben and spoke in a low voice, "If the boys weren't here, I'd just go ahead and take care of you with this-here shotgun right now, for what you did to my Clint. But I'll wait 'til a proper time."

"Ferd, you know as well as I do that it was self-defense. More killing won't change that. We need to let him rest in peace."

"Ain't no peace for me or his ma. You'd better just watch your back and watch your family." He rose and started to leave, then stopped. "That water's kinda cold. You might need a little fire to warm yourself when you get out.'

He gathered Ben's clothing into a pile on the rock surface, got out a match and set fire to the shirt, then as the flames caught, added the rest of the clothing including the boots and hat. He cast about for some dry limbs and brush and added them to the fire.

There was nothing Ben could do but tread water and watch. Ferd dusted off his hands and walked away, chuckling to himself. He climbed back up the slope to join his sons. Ben heard them ride away.

Anna was on her hands and knees, scrubbing the plank floor in the kitchen area. Her face was red and wet with sweat, and damp tendrils of hair had escaped the bun at the back of her head. Thankfully, Eva was taking a nap, a rare event, perhaps still tired from their trip. Ben was later getting back than she expected. It was past noon and she was keeping his dinner warm in the oven. She heard a knock at the door and rose to her feet. She'd pulled the latch string as Ben had told her to do when she was alone. As she approached the door, she called out, "Who is it?"

"It's me, Babe. Is Eva out of sight?"

"Yes," she said through the door as she prepared to open it, puzzled by his question.

There stood Ben, holding a bushy limb in front of him. In spite of herself, she blushed and put her hand over her mouth when she saw his condition. "You're naked!"

"Yeah, I noticed that. How about you stop starin' and let me in."

She jumped out of the way. "Sorry. You surprised me. What on earth—"

"I'll explain once I get some clothes on."

Anna stifled a smile and shyly turned her head. Ben hurried into the bedroom to put on clothes and came back out.

"You got some sunburn," Anna said.

"Well, there's quite a bit of my skin that don't see the sun much."

"I would hope not." Anna waited.

Ben went to sit at the table. "Have a seat, Anna. We might'a made a mistake, comin' back. I had a clash with the Harveys already. I rode the whole fence line and was all hot and sweaty; wound up by a nice deep pool of water, so I decided to take a dip...." Ben told her the whole sequence of events.

"Oh, Ben. He could have killed you!"

"I thought about that. May have helped that the boys were along. Still, we're dealing with a crazy man. All I thought about, walking barefoot through the fields, was how to keep you and Eva safe. I'm gonna go have a talk with the sheriff tomorrow, just to let him know about the threats. You and Eva can stay at Pa's where you'll be safe."

They got around early the next morning and headed down the Creek in the wagon, Charger on a lead rope behind. Tom Archer had finished his chores and greeted them from the porch, a cup of coffee in his hand.

"Hey, you-all. Come in. What brings you out so early?"

Ben got down and helped Anna descend. "We need to have a talk. I'll explain."

When they were seated inside around the table, the children listening in, Ben told all, or almost all, about his encounter with Ferd Harvey and his sons. He left out the naked part in deference to the children. "He's crazier than before, and he's served notice that he wants to do us harm. I think that stands for the whole family; mostly me, of course. I aim to ride in to Forsyth and let the sheriff know, not that I think he can do much."

"I'll go with you," Tom said. "Rebecca, I don't think anything will happen this soon, but I hope you and Jimmy can watch the place while I'm gone. I'll get the shotgun down."

"We'll be fine, won't we, Jimmy?"

"Yes, Ma'am," Jimmy said.

As Tom and Ben approached Sycamore, Ben said, "Pa, when we moved back, the first thing I wanted to do was come down and see how George was makin' it with his buggy business, but it looks like we'd better sneak by and do that later."

"Yep, but as to that, he seems to be gettin' after it. He pitched right in and built a space to work, and I understand he has three orders already. None built complete yet, of course."

"I told him I wanted to buy his first one, but don't look like I could afford it anyway. Especially now, I got a few other things to worry about—well really one thing."

"You're right. We'll see what the sheriff says."

They were able to ride through Sycamore and bypass George's shop, since the door was closed. His father, Homer, was out front of the blacksmith shop in his leather apron, and waved a greeting as they went by.

They reached the streets of Forsyth near noon and went straight to the sheriff's office. A deputy they knew, Henry Jeffrey, was on duty at the front desk, and greeted them. "Howdy there, Archers. What brings you here?"

"Sheriff Horton in?" Tom said.

"Naw. He's chowin' down up the street at Mabel's. Anything I can help you with?"

"We need to eat anyway. Maybe we'll see if we can catch him there. C'mon Ben."

They did find him, seated at the counter joking with the proprietor herself, Mabel Long. She was as sturdily built as the sheriff, but thankfully not equipped with a mustache. When she glanced up as they approached, the sheriff looked over his shoulder. "Well, look who's here," he said. "I hope it ain't more trouble." He rose to his feet to shake hands. "Mabel, you know these two? This here's Tom Archer and his son, Ben."

She leaned over the counter and smiled as she shook hands. "Pleased to meecha. You havin' dinner?"

"Can we have a word, Sheriff, or do you want to wait 'til after you finish?"

"I just got started. Mabel, if we can have that corner booth, we'll move over there."

"That's fine. We're doin' meatloaf, mashed spuds, and peas."

"We'll do two of those," Tom said, "and coffee if you've got it."

When they were seated, the sheriff continued to eat while they waited for their food. They were far enough from other patrons for Ben to tell his story, speaking quietly. The sheriff listened without comment until he finished. By then their food arrived, and he shoved his empty plate aside and began to explain what he might do. A young waitress refilled his coffee cup and retreated.

"I hoped it wouldn't happen, wuz you to move back here. Ferd is a stubborn sonofabitch, and half crazy, so I cain't say I'm surprised. Here's the thing—I can go out there and look him in the eye and try to put the fear a'God into him. And I'll do that tomorrow mornin'. But I cain't guarantee it'll do any good. Problem is, in most things, the bastard has to do somethin' before you can arrest him. You understand?"

"I'm afraid we do," Tom said. "But we appreciate anything you can do."

The sheriff sighed and shook his head. "I'll tell him that if he keeps this up, somebody's goin' to shoot his sorry ass. Best thing I can recommend is, take every step you can to watch things and be ready to defend yourselves. He's served notice he ain't gonna put it behind him." He looked down in silence, then continued. "Here's another thing I just as well share with you. You know from your own experience the legal system don't work like it should around here. Even if I catch 'em, crooked juries sometimes turn 'em loose. And the opposite, we've got some folks now thinkin' they can take the law into their own hands. Some of it, you cain't blame 'em, but it's a dangerous thing. It's the kind of thing could get out of hand."

"Has it so far?" Tom said.

Horton shrugged, "Matter of opinion. Feller came to church meetin' drunk from the night before. Next night, men in masks drug him out of his house and whipped him with switches. Bad thing? You be the judge...or let me say that different. Do you have the right to judge? Remember when that mob came here and wanted to bust you out of jail? Headed that off, but can you imagine what woulda happened if they'd got you?"

"Afraid so. We thank you for that," Ben said.

"I believe your jury was tainted and it left you in limbo. There's a sayin' that time heals all wounds, but we know that ain't true. There was a worse case over the line into Arkansas. Folks decided they knew a fella had stole some horses. One night they took him out and hanged him. Sheriff over there tried to find out who did it, but didn't get anywhere. They all clammed up like Bob's your uncle."

Tom started to rise. "Well, Sheriff, we thank you for listenin' to us. At least we all know we need to watch out. Let us know if you find out anything."

"I shore will," he replied as they all rose and went to pay.

When they were back on the street, Ben said, "Pa, there's another stop I need to make. I'm gonna teach Anna to shoot, and I need to find the right kind of guns."

They crossed the street to a large hardware store that advertised guns on the sign hanging above the door. After some negotiations, they walked out with what they sought. Ben had selected a short-barreled twelve-gauge shotgun that folks called a "messenger" because guards protected stagecoaches with it. He also purchased the smallest pistol they had with any reasonable firepower. It was a Colt New Model Police, not too heavy, so he felt she could manage it. It had a shorter barrel and was designed for concealment. He bought ammunition for both.

-15-

SAN FRANCISCO

L ambert felt a great sense of relief and anticipation as the train at last pulled into San Francisco at mid-day. After a brief stop earlier in Sacramento, he had managed an uncomfortable sleep sitting in his seat. He awakened with a stiff neck as he rose and stretched himself after the train jerked to a halt. He looked forward to see a great cloud of steam released from the cylinders. He got his bag out of the overhead bin, clapped on his hat, and filed off with the other weary passengers. They stepped off onto a long wooden platform shaded by an overhanging roof. Lambert stood and looked around him at the crowds bustling about, carrying luggage. Porters wheeled carts of boxes and luggage. Among the crowd he got his first look at people he'd heard about—Chinese. They had been brought in to help build the railroads and now had stayed. They were quite different to his eyes; smaller, and wearing long shirts and with hair in long pigtails.

No one was meeting him. He had decided to arrive unannounced before contacting any local authorities. In his experience there was a chance for things to go cockeyed, even if intentions were good. An over-eager law officer might jump the gun and spook the quarry before Lambert got there. No, best dig in and get the lay of the land himself before contacting anyone.

He made his way through the station and out on the street. He was amazed at the buggy and wagon traffic traveling both ways. There was a lot of shouting back and forth as the drivers fought for space, sometimes bumping hubs and threatening to run over pedestrians. As he looked around him he was surprised by the steep hillsides above, covered with multistory buildings, and beyond, residential housing. He'd been through Saint Louis recently, but it was at night and since it was flatter, not as much of it was visible at the same time. Way out here he'd expected to see a dusty, smaller city. Just the opposite. Might be tougher than I thought to find this bird, he thought. He saw a line of hacks along the curb and travelers like himself queued up behind a rope. He joined them and waited his turn, finally climbing aboard.

"Where to, Mister?" the driver said.

"I want you to take me to a decent hotel not too far from the docks."

"You interested in women? I can—"

"I'm here on business, so get me someplace handy, not too fancy and not a dump either."

"Yessir. I know just the place. It's right on the cable car line." He slapped the reins on the hackney pony and pulled out into traffic. "You ain't from here?" Lambert nodded. "You may not know about the cable car. You can hop on and it'll take ya all the way up the main drag to the top of the hill."

The hack dropped Lambert off in front of new-looking four-story brick hotel at the foot of a steep street. He walked across a brick sidewalk and checked in at the front desk. He fought off a uniformed bellman and climbed the curving staircase and on up to the third floor to find his room. He dropped his carpet bag on the floor and went to the window to look out over the bay a short distance away. It was crowded with shipping; forests of masts on sailing vessels and numerous steamships with smokestacks and auxiliary masts.

He looked around the small room. The white-painted walls were bare except for a framed print that appeared to be a layout of the city and the bay. There were two single beds and a wash stand with a large pitcher of water and a bowl. He looked longingly at the beds and shook his head. "Nope," he said aloud to himself. Getting in that bed would be a mistake at this time of day. I'll make myself get out and walk, stay awake, then get some supper and go to bed when these folks do. He visited the toilet at the end of the hall and descended the staircases and to the street outside.

It was surprisingly cold with a chill wind blowing in off the bay. He was thankful for his long coat for two reasons; for warmth and the concealment of the long Colt reversed on his left hip.

Seems to me, he thought, I'd best just start walking the waterfront, get the lay of things. Madison, now Jefferson, is bound to be in some kind of business with all this cargo coming and going, unless I miss my guess. That big bay out there and this city with its railhead appears to be a big mouth gobbling up all the stuff coming in from China and them other places over there, then sending it east. Same thing the other way; stuff coming all the way across the country to go the other direction. I'll bet the colonel is dipping into it both ways.

He walked a short distance north to the docks and turned east to proceed along the waterfront. There were long piers, supported on pilings, fingering out into the bay with ships tied up along both sides of each of them, loading and unloading cargo. Flatbed wagons were queued up to proceed onto the piers to receive the cargo. The piers were wide enough to allow a turnaround at the outer end. The ships themselves had derricks to hoist stuff out of their bowels and load it directly on the wagons. Lambert stood and watched the operation for a while. Pretty neat. It dwarfed anything he had seen inland on the rivers with steamboats.

As he walked along the waterfront, he noticed most of the buildings on his right were painted with various signs: "Warehouse No. 23", "Thomas Forwarding", "Sydney Enterprises", and so forth. Guess it would be too much to expect to see "Jefferson Imports." Life don't work that way.

After a half mile or so, he came to one pier that looked a little different. More of it was covered with a long, tin-roofed wooden structure. Smaller boats were tied up to that one. As he approached, he saw what was being unloaded: great nets of silvery fish. Out at the far end he saw a fish as long as a man, being hoisted out of a boat with boom that reached out over the boat. He walked out in that direction and stopped a Chinese man rushing by. "What kind of fish is that big one out there," he pointed.

"Tunny," the man said, then looked up a Lambert with a smile. "You long fella!" he said, and hurried on.

Lambert walked on until he felt he'd seen most of the commercial docks and no place said anything about a Jefferson. He moved inland a couple of streets to head back. This street appeared to be taken up by saloons and eating places. Everybody seemed in a hurry so he attracted little attention, just an occasional quick stare. Must be the scar, he thought, a souvenir of the Oklahoma territory. Not a bright fella, that one had been, bringing a knife to a gunfight.

Nearing his hotel, he stopped in at a prosperous-looking saloon. It had a wide, arched doorway with the two halves of the door folded open. The top halves of the door were stained glass. Lambert noted that if they were closed, the glass depicted a fancy lady reclining on a couch, wearing a gown and a plumed hat. With the doors open, she looked like a magician's trick, her two halves separated.

Inside, he noted a pressed tin, paneled ceiling, with shaded lamps hanging on chains for the evening hours. There was a long bar to his left, crowded with late afternoon drinkers. Tables were scattered in the middle, with booths along the wall to his right. He went to an empty booth and sat facing the entrance to observe the crowd coming and going and passing by on the street outside the plate glass window. In moments, a waitress appeared, leaning over him to provide a view of her bosom. She was dressed in a short skirt fluffed out by petticoats. The blouse was ringed with a ruffle at the neckline, but the neckline could hardly be called that as it was off the shoulders.

"What can I get ya, Darlin'? She said. She was wearing heavy makeup, and was missing an eyetooth.

"Bring me a double shot of some decent bourbon with a beer chaser. And can you get me a beefsteak?"

"Shore can!" she said, and hurried away.

The bourbon and beer arrived quickly, and he sipped it, deep in thought, tuning out the crowd noise and the tinny piano playing in the far corner on a raised stage. This town is bigger than I expected, based on what I saw on my walk around the docks. Better go ahead and contact Marshal Bean. There's bound to be some way to find out the names of all these businesses. I'll send him a note when I get back to the hotel.

He attacked his steak as soon as it arrived and went wearily back to his hotel. At the front desk, he wrote out a note on the hotel letterhead, asking Hubert Bean to meet him at the hotel at nine the next morning. If he could not, let the messenger know. If no reply came back, Lambert wrote, he'd have to do his best on his own. He folded the note and sealed it with wax and a seal from the hotel. A bellboy was happy to hand-deliver it for four bits.

Lambert awoke from a deep sleep, refreshed after a night's sleep in a bed after many days without the luxury. He splashed his face and washed his hands in water from the washbowl, and made his way down to the lobby. Shaving could wait for finding a barbershop. There was a note for him at the front desk. It said simply, "I will be there," and was signed with the word "Hube."

He seated himself and waited. As the Regulator clock over the front desk started to strike the hour of nine, a man walked in the front entrance. I wonder, Lambert thought, if we're all so easy to recognize for what we are. He, like Lambert, was a tall man, dressed in a black, long frock coat, black pants and boots, and black hat. Only thing missing was the scar. Well, he has a mustache and I need a shave. Bean immediately headed toward Lambert, who rose to shake hands. "Josh Lambert," he said. "Thanks for coming."

"Hubert Bean," he replied, "But I reckon you guessed that. They call me 'Hube', or sometimes 'Hubean'."

"Pleased to meet ya.   What say we find us some breakfast?"

"Man after my own heart, or should I say 'stomach'?"

Over breakfast of eggs, bacon, fried potatoes, and sourdough biscuits, Lambert quietly filled Bean in on the fugitive. He paused as the waitress came to pour more coffee. "I don't know what he calls himself out here, but I bet he's involved in trading goods or something like that. He was in Army procurement during the war. Problem was he procured for himself while he was at it. What do you suggest?"

"There's gotta be some kind of licensing of business, and most cities have chamber of commerce, whatever they call it."

"My thoughts, too. I was dumb enough to think I could walk around and spot something, but after I saw this place, I knew I was wrong. Besides, I'll need help when we close in on him."

"What I'm here for."

"Breakfast is on me," Lambert said, and he reached for his hat and rose. "Might as well get at it!"

-16-

BUGGIES

As Marshal Lambert began his search to find a fugitive believed to be in San Francisco, the pattern of life along Bull Creek continued as it had been for years: completing the harvest and preparing for the upcoming winter season. Leaves were beginning to turn and the heat of August turned milder with cooler nights, good for sleeping. It was a busy season—as all were.

Anna was in the garden digging potatoes with a spading fork, brushing them clean and stowing them in baskets. Some former tenant, probably the original settler, had dug a root cellar, a pit in the hillside behind the house with a roof to shed rain and snow. Potatoes, turnips, and carrots would be wrapped in straw and would keep for most of the winter. The turnips would stay in the ground a little longer. Eva was helping, mostly in the way, but she liked to pick up what she called "ta-toes," getting herself grubby in the process.

Anna heard the sound of hoof beats and wheels on gravel. She glanced at the small basket she had moved along as she worked. It contained the Colt revolver, with a checkered napkin covering it. Ben was working in the cornfield with his pa and brother Jimmy, and had given strict orders for her to have it with her when she was outside alone. No need this time, however. She was delighted to see Margaret Madison coming up the lane. She dropped her fork, picked up Eva, and hurried to intercept Margaret as she drove up in front of the house.

She waved and shouted, "Margaret! What a nice surprise!"

Margaret set the brake and jumped down to embrace the two of them.

"I just couldn't stay away. I missed meeting on Sunday and had to come see my favorite people."

Anna put Eva down and Margaret knelt to talk to her. "How's my girl?"

"I'm workin'. I'm helpin' mama dig ta-toes."

Margaret smiled. "I bet you're a big help, too."

"Yes'm. Mama says she couldn't do it without me."

"I bet that's the truth." Margaret said. She glanced at Anna and the bump in her apron. "And how are you, Mama-Anna?"

"I feel fine. Now and then someone's doing hand-springs and cartwheels in there, but otherwise all right." She smiled. "Let me go get my stuff out of the garden and we'll go inside and have some tea. Can you eat dinner with us? The men will be coming in from the field in an hour or so."

"I'd be glad to. Let me help you get it ready."

"I was about to get started. I also have to sponge a pound of dirt off a little somebody."

They were soon working together in the kitchen. Anna was preparing fried potatoes, steamed cabbage, and baked ham. Eva was cleaned up and playing with a doll in the corner, so they were free to talk. "Tell me, has anything changed with you?" Anna said.

"I assume you mean a certain carriage builder."

"Yes."

"We're cordial when we see each other on occasion, but it's an uncomfortable politeness. He's working long hours and I'm told he's making headway. I'm too stubborn to go see for myself."

"What about you?"

Margaret shrugged. "I finally get to start preparing for the school year. This summer has been a lonesome drag in many ways. God bless Etta. She's my best company. I did take some courses by mail out of Missouri University to keep from going insane—and it will help my credentials. I've been teaching Etta and her brother to read, too. They're coming along."

"Good for you. Anything from your family?"

"I've exchanged letters with Gertie, but we're as different as sisters could be. She says Mother hardly knows what's going on. And I really don't know my brother Reggie anymore. Been years since I've seen him. We await any news about my dear father. How about that marshal? Real man, or what?"

"I wouldn't want him after me! Er...maybe if I didn't have a husband." Anna blushed.

"Anna! Such talk!"

They both giggled. "I was making a joke. You know that, Margaret."

"I know, but you surprise me sometimes. Now for *me*, in my present situation...."

They laughed again.

"What's that little basket you were carrying, Anna?"

"I'll show you." It was on the table beside them and she pulled the napkin aside.

Margaret's eyes went wide. "You have a *gun?*"

"I do. I have my own shotgun, too. See it over by the door? Ben got them for me and taught me how to use them. The pistol is pretty heavy and I hold it in both hands. And he had me hold the shotgun against my shoulder real hard because it really kicks."

"Anna, you're sure not any little delicate flower."

Anna smiled, "I guess not. Ben shot them first so I wouldn't be surprised, then taught me how. It's a little scary, but he said the man on the other end would fare worse."

"I'd say he's right, but why all this? Are you in danger?"

"We might be. It's that crazy Ferdinand Harvey. I'll tell you what happened." She proceeded to tell Margaret about the incident, concluding with, "Can you imagine Ben completely naked with nothing but a little tree branch held in front, sort of like Adam at the first sinning?"

Margaret, with a solemn expression, said, "Well, I *could*, but I won't since he's your husband." Then she burst into laughter and Anna followed suit.

"I don't mean to make light of it, Anna, but I couldn't resist. It does sound bad." She nodded toward the basket. "Would you use it?"

"Yes I would. What happened that other time will never happen again. The sheriff went and talked to that crazy man and came by here afterward. He said there's not much he can do besides threaten him; that we'd best be careful."

They heard the sound of the men talking outside as they washed up at a stand beside the house. They were soon clumping up the steps and came inside.

"I see we got company!" Ben said. He came forward and gave Margaret a hug. He smelled of the outdoors and the cornstalks.

Tom shook hands, and Jimmy blushed as Margaret hugged him.

They enjoyed the meal together, catching up on happenings around the community. Ben managed to avoid asking about George. After they were finished, the three men picked up their long corn knives off the porch and headed back to the field. Margaret headed home and Anna resumed her work in the garden.

George Zinn was preparing to paint the first of the three buggies that were in various stages of completion. All this one lacked was paint and the installation of seat cushions and the canvass top. He'd found a saddler in Ozark that could make the horse-hair stuffed leather cushions. He had decided on two-seaters for his first production, believing his first customers would be families. Turned out to be true, as all three were spoken for. They'd be black, but he had ordered some yellow paint for decoration.

He didn't count his own labor cost, but it looked like he would make enough margin to get the materials to expand the next run to twice as many. Maybe he would include some light, sporty models for those courting, or for couples with no children. These thoughts and plans continued to run in his mind as he worked, but in spite of everything, thoughts of Margaret intruded. Will all these efforts rescue me from my stubbornness? He thought.

His new venture attracted a lot of attention. Visitors would drop in to watch him work and marvel at his craftsmanship. It did slow him down a bit, but he realized it was good for the future. He stopped work when Ben came for the first time. George proudly showed him all the features he was incorporating. He had come up with double wheel brakes that clamped onto the inner part of the rear hubs, rather than a shoe against the wheel rim. The brakes were controlled by a lever beside the driver's seat and could be applied while moving, or ratcheted in place at a stop.

-17-

ROSE

A late hurricane in the Gulf called a temporary halt to the march toward October's blue weather. A cold front approached out of Canada and moved swiftly to the southeast, driving a wedge that lifted the moist gulf air swirling in from the south. The citizens did not know all of these faraway events that caused it, but some had seen the threatening dark bank of clouds in the northwest. A line of violent thunderstorms swept through during the night pouring heavy rains on the hills along Bull Creek. Families were awakened by the vivid flashes of lightning and the crashing thunder. Some went back to sleep, thankful for being in the dry, while others rose to place pans and buckets under leaks. Eva climbed into bed with Anna and Ben until the storms passed over.

George Zinn arose at daylight, as the front had passed through, bringing cold, clear air. He and his father, Homer, and brother, Hiram, drank a quick cup of coffee and headed to the shop to check for damage. There were some limbs down, but everything looked all right as they walked around the building, so Homer and Hy proceeded to open the double doors of the blacksmith shop. George opened the sliding door of his carriage shop in preparation to begin his day. Esther had told them to come back in a half hour and she'd have breakfast ready.

George had a small, open shed along the north side where he stored some of his materials, particularly the lumber. Most of it was covered with a tarpaulin, so he thought he'd better make sure it was still covered. As he approached, he was startled to see a shape that shouldn't be there move beneath one end of the tarp. Some kind of animal? A coon? A bear? He went back to his shop and came back with a pick handle and jerked the corner of the tarpaulin back. No need for a weapon. It was a woman, huddled and shivering, wet dress and stringy hair clinging to her. She turned her startled white face to look at him. It was a mass of bruises.

"My God!" George said. "What happened? Who are you?" He whipped off his coat and bent to cover her.

A weak voice responded, "Rose. It's Rose."

"*Rose?* I didn't recognize you. Let me help you up."

"*Don't tell nobody,*" she whispered.

"I won't. Let's get you over to the house. Can you walk?" He saw that her feet were bare and bloody.

"*I don't know.*"

George didn't stop to find out. He picked her up and hurried around to his father's shop. As Homer turned around, he said, "Pa, I found her out by the shop. I'm takin' her to Ma to get her fixed up and warm."

"*Gracious me!*" Homer said. "Let me help."

"I've got her, but Hy, you might go ahead and let Ma know we're comin'."

Hiram ran ahead and they were soon inside the house. Esther was there with a quilt to wrap around Rose as George helped her to stand next to the wood cook stove. Esther took charge. "You men help yourself to breakfast and I'm takin' her back and gettin' dry clothes on her."

Rose stood mute and trembling.

Esther led to a back bedroom and helped her sit in a rocker. "You wait here, Hon, I'll get some things."

She was back in moments with some clothing and a towel. "Now here, stand up if you can, we'll get you dried off."

Rose did as she was bid. Esther was shocked at the ragged undergarments and the bruises on the pale arms and other parts of her body, in addition to her black eye and swollen left cheek. She gently dried the slender girl and helped her dress. Rose remained silent at first, but then began to speak in a soft voice, "I don't want to cause you no trouble. We can't let him know where I am."

"You're talkin' about your pa?"

"Yes."

"You want to tell me what happened?"

"It was 'cause I kept wantin' to see my Aunt Becky. He makes Ma and me stay in the house all the time, except to work outside when he's there. We don't ever see nobody. I waited 'til he was asleep and I run away."

Esther was drying her hair, and stopped to hold her. "I'm so sorry. I once had a daughter, my first-born, but she died of the fever. I kept this one dress in a trunk. Didn't know why but now I do. It's yours now. We'll take care of you until we decide what to do." She draped a woolen shawl around Rose's shoulders.

"I'm sorry about your daughter, Ma'm."

"Thank you. It's a long time now."

"Pa can't know. I didn't go to Aunt Becky's, 'cause he said if I did he'd kill us all."

"My, my! We'll be careful. Now let's go in and get you some breakfast."

When Esther led her in and sat her at the table, the men avoided staring. George saw a battered but pretty woman he remembered from years past when she was just a girl. She must be eighteen or nineteen now, he thought, still a slave to Ferd Harvey.

Rose kept her head bowed. "I'm ashamed," she said, "but I thank you for your kindness."

"Don't think a thing of it. Not your fault," Homer said gently. "We'll do what we can."

As the Zinn family was having breakfast, Tom and Rebecca and their family were doing the same. Tom and Jimmy had checked the livestock and milked the cows, then they had come back inside. Rebecca heard it first, the sound of hoof beats coming up the lane at a fast pace.

"Keep your seats," Tom said, and he went to the front window to see who was coming. "It's Ferd and his boys. You kids stay back where you are 'til I see what's up." He opened the door and stepped out on the porch as the three riders yanked their horses to a halt.

Ferd shouted, "Get her out here and I mean right now!"

"Simmer down. Get *who* out here?"

"You know damn well *who*! *Rose*, that's who!"

"Ferd, you're not makin' sense. Rose isn't here and she hasn't been here. We haven't seen her for months."

"You're lyin'. She was comin' here. I know it."

"Ferd, if you'll calm down and put your guns away, you can come in and see for yourself. You can have a cup of coffee and visit with your sister and your nieces. You can check the outbuildings. But Rose is not here and she hasn't been. When did she leave?"

"Sometime last night." Ferd looked less sure of himself.

"I'm sorry. I hope she wasn't out in the storm."

"Bound to be if she ain't here."

"Come inside. You and the boys have some coffee."

Ferd handed his shotgun to Robert and dismounted. "No coffee, but I want to come in."

Tom opened the door and stepped aside as Ferd came in to face his sister. He stopped and stared, keeping the space between them.

"Hello, Ferd," Rebecca said. "It's been a long time. I heard, and I'm sorry."

Ferd nodded and stroked his grizzled chin.

"What happened?"

"She's been gettin' cantankerous lately. Won't mind. Talks back."

"Did you fight?"

"No. But this mornin' she was gone."

It had been a year since Jennifer and Estelle had seen their uncle, and they and the three Archer children stayed at the table and stared.

"Look around all you want." Rebecca said. "But Tom told you the truth. Come with me and you can look in the bedrooms if you like."

Ferd mumbled. "I reckon not." He turned around and hurried out the door and down the steps. He mounted his horse and all whirled and galloped away.

Tom turned to Rebecca. "What do you make of that?"

"I'm really worried about Rose. No telling where she is. I suspect Ferd beat her. I just know he does his wife. Can't get her to say so, but I just know it."

"I'll go out and see if I can find out anything," Tom said. "I'm worried about her."

"Would you? I've been so sad we couldn't be closer. I hope she's all right."

Tom and Jimmy spent the day riding to all of the neighbors and into Sycamore asking about Rose and getting the word out. They talked to the Zinns, Henry Guthrie at the store, and Jensen at the mill. They rode up Bull Creek as far as Ben and Anna's. They went by and talked to Margaret. No one seemed to know anything about Rose. Some had seen Ferd Harvey riding around. Jensen, who was the preacher for the community, promised to put the word out at Sunday services.

ROGER MEADOWS

-18-

THE DISCOVERY

Marshals Bean and Lambert found there was indeed a directory of businesses licensed to do business in the city. They were given access to the listings which included dates of startup and the owners' names. With a rough estimate of the time period, they scanned the names involved. There were no Madisons or Jeffersons, nor any other presidential names. They developed a list to investigate, at first rejecting hotels, saloons, haberdashers, and the like. Lambert got a trim haircut and purchased a derby hat and a foppish plaid suit to make himself look less like a marshal, not an easy task. Bean began staking out the most likely candidates and observing from a distance while Lambert would go inside them, pretending to be a businessman.

They concentrated first on the six businesses in the right time frame that were involved in imports and exports. After observing each for a day or two, with Lambert going inside and pretending to be interested in a business arrangement, they had no success in finding anyone resembling Madison. They moved on to warehousing establishments, but with similar results. It was only after some weeks of effort, and they had moved on to cartage companies, that a possibility appeared.

The second cartage company they staked out was called "Golden State Carters." It was one of the companies supplying wagons and drivers connecting the wharves to the railhead, in addition to general hauling in the surrounding area. The current owner had owned the business for only about six months, buying the business from the heirs of the original owner after he had simply disappeared months before.

It was located just west of the business district in a large clearing in a wooded area. It was on a slightly higher elevation, but not like the steep hills behind city center. The two marshals observed from a distance, and it appeared to be a prosperous enterprise, with extensive stables and corrals and a front office and warehouse building. Drivers and other workers were coming and going, night and day. After observing from the cover of the surrounding woods for a day, Lambert drove up in a buggy late in the afternoon of the next day.

He entered the small office and asked a male clerk, "May I speak with the proprietor...Mister O'Reilly, I believe."

"He's not in at the moment, sir. May I help you?"

Lambert seemed to be in thought. "No offense, my good man, but I always like to start at the top. When may I have the pleasure of his attendance?"

"Well, sir, he should be in first thing tomorrow. He's across the Bay and expects to return this very evening."

"Very well, I shall return tomorrow morning. Here's my card." Lambert presented a business card that read, *R. T. Dugan, Precious Metals.* "I have need of a reliable hauler. I assume you also provide extra security?"

"Oh, quite so, sir."

Bean and Lambert met in the evening at the back booth of a saloon. Lambert had changed out of his businessman attire.

"What do you think about this one, Josh?"

"Don't know, Hube. Just like all the others. We'll just have to see what the boss looks like. Seems a little suspicious that the original owner disappeared at a convenient time."

"We're gonna run out of places to look, eventually."

"Yep. Might be I got it wrong and he ain't here."

In keeping with their plan of the night before, Bean arrived early at a vantage point in the woods at the edge of the clearing. The business appeared to have a shift change around seven in the morning, although there was overlap of departing and arriving workers. Around nine o'clock an impressive coach arrived out front and a man got out and went into the office. Bean's view was partially blocked, but he suspected it was the owner. He kept his station and waited.

In a short while, Lambert arrived in Bean's buggy and went inside the office. It was Bean's signal to maneuver to a position behind the business where he could watch the back entrance. It was their usual routine. They had no intention of making any sudden moves, but never could tell what a fugitive would do.

Lambert greeted the clerk with a hearty "good morning" and said, "R.T. Dugan to see Mister O'Reilly, my good man."

"Yes, sir. I'll see if he's in."

The clerk led the way down a short hall and rapped gently on a door.

"Enter!" was commanded.

Lambert saw a man seated at the desk. He was wearing a dove-gray three-piece suit with a silk cravat at his throat, held in place by a diamond pin. Lambert's fake card was lying in the center of the desk blotter. The man had longish dark hair and a full beard. He looked at Lambert over a pince-nez perched on his nose.

"Mister Dugan, I presume." He rose and reached across the desk.

Lambert nodded and shook hands. "Mister O'Reilly, a pleasure."

"Please be seated. What can we do for you?"

"I'm a commodities broker and I deal in gold bullion and silver. On occasion I have need of secure shipments and I need security and secrecy—even some sleight of hand, if you will."

"We can fulfill your needs. Tell me, this 'sleight of hand,' as you put it, is that versus the outlaw population or other entities?"

"Well...let's just say, I keep my business to myself."

O'Reilly picked up Lambert's card and squinted at it. "Let me give this some thought, and I'll get back to you. Where can you be reached? I hate to hurry this conversation, but I have another appointment in a few minutes."

"Not at all, not at all. I took a chance to meet you without an appointment. Thank you for seeing me." He gave the name of his hotel, shook hands, and left.

Lambert drove away in the buggy and Bean moved back to a position to watch the front entrance. An hour later, Lambert rode through the woods and joined him.

"Well, Josh, what do you think?"

"I think it's him. Take away the hair dye and lose the beard, and it looks like him. He's the right age."

"How're we gonna tell?"

"Easy. We arrest him and take off his left shoe. He's missing the little toe. Horse stepped on it when he was a kid going barefoot."

"Are you *serious*? How the hell did you know that?"

"When I was in Missouri, sendin' out telegrams and waiting and waiting, I read his Army file several times. Memorized the damn thing. It was in his physical when he applied for the Point. Didn't disqualify him. But they should have examined his integrity."

"You ready to take him?"

"Think we'd better. He might have spotted me for a phony. He ain't dumb. How about if you go get the two deputies and let the sheriff know we might need a room reservation. I'll stay here in case he bolts."

Bean left and Lambert settled in to wait. He moved to a position where he could watch the back and still see the road out front. He saw a few wagons coming and going, and wranglers putting hay into racks along the corrals. It had been long enough that Madison should be making a move if he was going to. Just as he had that thought, he saw a saddled horse being led out of the back of one of the stables. Lambert raised his field glasses. It was him. He was wearing a black hat and long black coat. The man

118

threw saddlebags across the rear skirt of the saddle and tied them down. Lambert hurried back to his own horse.

The road made a bend around the brow of the hill and circled behind Lambert's position. He could ride down the way he had come and be there well before the man arrived unless he took off through the woods, which was unlikely.

Lambert waited behind a clump of small pines bordering the road. As expected, he heard the approach of a horse at a canter. At the right moment, Lambert spurred his rented horse into the road. The other horse almost collided with him and reared back, the rider grabbing the saddle horn to keep from being unseated.

"What the hell!" the man shouted, as he brought the horse under control. *"What's the meaning of this?"*

Lambert held up his badge. "U.S. Marshal Joshua Lambert, sir. Like to ask you a few questions." He dropped the badge into his pocket, and cleared his coattail from his Colt.

"I have no business with you *Mister Dugan*. Now get out of my way."

Lambert watched the man's hands as he gave him a choice to make. "We're in need of some information about the former owner of your business, Mister O'Reilly, so I'm asking you to accompany me to the sheriff's office."

"I have no information. I'll not do that."

Lambert sighed and pulled out his Colt. "Then keep your hands where I can see them, sir, and dismount." Lambert moved his horse forward to keep the other horse from shielding his captive.

As the man complied, Lambert dismounted also and commanded, "Turn around and keep your hands in the air."

Lambert holstered his revolver, and holding the reins of his own horse, pulled the man's hands behind him and handcuffed him.

"You'll hear from my lawyer about this!"

"That's all right. We need you as a material witness and you refused. Had to do it."

Lambert searched him, removing one derringer from a waistcoat pocket and a second from an ankle holster. After that, he managed to get his captive aboard his horse, then mounted his own and started toward the city, leading a man he hoped was Colonel Perry Madison.

-19-

THE SHOOTING

The Ozark hills were ablaze with fall color and the days were blessed with blue skies and cool nights. School had started in Sycamore with the completion of harvest. In the evenings, a scent of wood smoke filled the air as fireplaces were lit to take off the night chill. Ben Archer had resumed work in the wooded eighty acres south of his house and Anna was pleased when she viewed their shelves loaded with winter's food. George Zinn had delivered the first of his buggies. The event drew quite a crowd as the gleaming new coach was rolled out. It was black with yellow spokes and yellow pin-striping. All agreed it was one of the prettiest they'd seen.

Rose Harvey continued to be a willing prisoner inside the home of the Zinn family, under the loving care of Esther Zinn. Rose's bruises and black eyes had healed and she had blossomed like her namesake flower. Esther had been busy making clothing for Rose, who had escaped with nothing. Henry Guthrie had expressed his curiosity at her many purchases of fabric. "Working up a new wardrobe are ye?" He's said, between puffs of noxious pipe smoke. "Yes," she'd replied, with no other explanation.

Now as she worked at sewing another new dress for Rose, she pondered what to do about her. She loved the company while the men were away. Rose was a good helper, but there were those two young men living there. She had raised them right, but you never know about young men. She remembered when Homer was that age…and her face colored slightly. We'll just have to see.

As George worked in his shop, he thought about Rose also. I don't see any way she can live in this community as long as her pa is alive. He keeps roaming around like a madman asking about her. I don't think he cares a whit about her. It's an affront to his control. She can't stay hiding in our house forever, going outside only at night…. His train of thought was interrupted as one of his frequent visitors stepped into the shop. He had a sudden inspiration.

"Morning, George," said Abraham Phillips. "How are you this fine morning?"

"Very good, Professor. And you?"

"The same. I hope I'm not being a pest."

"No, no. Always glad to have you." Abraham Phillips was a retired college professor out of Springfield who had chosen to live in the hills. He had taught for a time in the one-room school as an act of grace and had helped Margaret get her start there to replace him.

The wheels turned in George's head and he paused in mid-stroke of his spoke-shave. "Professor, can we sit a minute and talk about something?"

Phillips took his pipe from his mouth. "Of course, if it won't interrupt your work."

"Time for a break." He led the way to some chairs in the corner.

"What I have to tell you is a secret, maybe life or death," George began.

"You can trust me," Phillips said, with a look of concern.

"I know I can. What it is, we're hiding a fugitive in our house; not from the law, but from her pa. He beat her and he's a violent man. It's Rose Harvey."

"Oh, my! I know her from my first year at the school. I wondered what happened to her."

"She's been with us a few weeks, but we don't know what's next. She's helpin' Ma and she's a good worker, but…."

He searched for words. "I even carried buggy wheels over to the house and let her paint the spokes. When you came in, I got an idea."

"Yes?"

"Do you have contacts back in Springfield that might need help? Say, a maid, or somethin'?"

Phillips drew on his pipe and puffed a cloud of smoke. "Don't know, but I'll sure be happy to find out. Yes, we still write back and forth."

"How about this? You can think about it and I'll float the idea with Ma and Rose. And how about you come to our house for supper around five or so tomorrow? Whether it flies or not, we can have a visit."

They rose and shook hands. Phillips left to look in on Margaret, and George went happily back to work, pleased with the prospect of a solution. He could hardly wait for noon so he could see what Rose thought about it.

Rose was thrilled at the prospect, "I've been wanting to escape for as long as I can remember," she said.

"Well, there are no guarantees, you know, but we can hope. I invited him to supper tomorrow night, so you can see what he thinks about it."

Supper the following evening left Rose glowing with hope. Abe Phillips was amazed at how Rose had grown up from the gangly young girl he remembered. Esther had worked her over with a curling iron to provide a cascade of shining brown curls, and she was dressed in one of her new dresses. George started to think he would hate to see her leave.

"I've already posted two letters of recommendation, based on George's reports," Abe said, embarrassing George in the process as Rose gazed at him.

"I won't disappoint you," Rose said.

Now that crops were laid by and sorghum cooked out of the cane at his father's place, Ben could concentrate on working the untouched timber in the south eighty. George had given him some specific cuts of wood to harvest and season for the future of his business. Mostly it was white oak and ash. Ben also had the usual fence rails and railroad ties to produce and there was a cooper in Ozark that paid good prices for stave bolts, also of white oak. For George's logs, he stacked them in a shed and coated the ends with tar so they would cure without checking. They'd go to a sawmill next fall.

He used the team of mules for this type of work, so the team of dappled grays that he had inherited from Rebecca got a vacation. He seldom saw King and Silver as there was still pasture until into winter. They made themselves scarce. They knew what was coming if their master came after them.

Early one morning, before daylight, he heard a horse whinnying several times out behind the barn. Anna had just made coffee and was handing Ben a cup.

"What's going on, Ben?" she said.

"I don't know, but it don't sound good. I'd better go see."

He grabbed his hat off a peg and got the Winchester off the wall. Still carrying his cup of coffee, he went outside. As he came around the barn, he saw Silver, obviously agitated. His eyes were wild and he reared and whinnied again. He whirled and galloped a few yards away, then stopped and whinnied again.

I've never seen such a thing, Ben thought. Looks like trouble. He took a slurp of coffee and set the cup on a post. Better see what's happened. He climbed over the fence and followed Silver. The horse would gallop a few yards toward the fringe of wood at the back of the hillside pasture, then stop and wait for Ben to approach before taking off again. It was nearly a quarter mile before Ben would arrive at what he dreaded. Silver had disappeared around a screen of brush and was standing in a small clearing over the inert figure of his teammate, King.

Oh, my, Ben thought. Silver trotted over to him and nuzzled his shoulder, with a soft whicker. Ben stoked his neck. "I'm sorry, big guy. Let's have a look."

Ben could see that the great beast was dead. There was a wound in the ribcage that looked like a bullet hole. Blood had dried around it and in a thick black stream down his side. In his death throes, his hooves had cut wide, arcing grooves in the sod. His normally dark liquid eye was clouded and there was a flood of dried, bloody froth coming out of his nostrils.

As he stood staring, his mind filled with sadness and anger, Silver came up behind him and put his head over Ben's shoulder. Ben put his arm around the massive head, stroking the long nose. "I'm really sorry, big fella. I just don't know what to do about it right now." He decided the only thing he could do was go for the sheriff.

Silver seemed to know that there was no hope, so he plodded along behind Ben all the way back to the barn. Ben opened the corral and put some new hay into the rack and made sure the water trough was full before going inside to give Anna the sad news.

She met him at the door, with Eva now up and holding to her skirt. "What is it?"

Ben shook his head. "King's dead."

"Dead! What happened?"

"Looks like somebody shot him."

"Why on earth?"

"Could be an accident, but I doubt it. Could be somebody besides who I suspect, but I don't think so."

"What can we do?"

"Probably nothing, but I'll go see the sheriff. It was a sad thing, Silver comin' for me. Poor thing followed me back to the barn like a puppy, head hangin' down."

Ben hurried through his milking and a quick breakfast, then insisted on hitching the wagon and taking Anna and Eva to stay with his parents while he rode on to Forsyth on Charger, who he'd led behind the wagon.

Tom offered to go with him, but Ben declined. "I'd as soon you'd look after my brood. We're reachin' a boiling point with that man. Somebody's goin' to kill him if they catch him in the act of somethin'."

The sheriff shook his head with a grim expression on his face. "We prob'ly cain't prove a damn thing, but I'll see what Ferd has to say about it. Meanwhile, I'll send Deppity Jeffery back with you to see if he can get the bullet out. Might not help, but we'll see."

-20-

THE ESCAPE

Margaret walked across the swinging bridge over Bull Creek in the early dawn, humming to herself. She loved to start the day early, getting the school building open and having some quiet time at her desk before the students arrived. It would be another hour before the sun cleared the eastern ridge, but the sky was bright. She carried a bag with her lunch and the papers she had graded the night before. It was also weighed down with a book, *Les Miserables* by Victor Hugo, lent to her by Professor Phillips

As she started descending the ladder on the Sycamore side, she heard hoof beats out on the dirt street. A buggy came into view with the top up, but she could see clearly that it was George driving. Seated next to him was a slender, well-dressed woman. She was wearing a tailored red coat and a hat with a veil that hid her face. Margaret stopped on the ladder, gripping the rail. The woman could not possibly be Esther Zinn. Who could it be? And at this early hour? Where did she spend the night? And where are they going? George was dressed up, too. Thankfully, he did not look in her direction. He was too busy talking to that woman.

As the buggy drove out of sight, Margaret shakily finished her descent and made her way to the school house with her mind in turmoil. I can't get George out of my mind, and with his apparent success with his buggy business, I thought it was time for us to talk again about the future. Apparently his thoughts are in a different direction.

She opened the school house doors and swept the steps, making herself keep to her routine. Still, when she might have done some lesson plans and focused on her work, she found she could not. Instead, she immersed herself in the novel, taking herself to the streets of Paris and the plight of its people. The title could not have been more fitting to her mood.

She managed to get through the day, forcing herself to normalcy in her relationship with the pupils. They were their usual boisterous, happy selves, and were the best antidote one could have to combat negative thoughts. She kept the front door open all day so she could see the road. The weather was nice and they were past bug season. There was some traffic, but no George.

Later in the afternoon, Margaret called Luke Johnson to come up front. She spoke quietly, "Luke, you're doing well, so I need to ask a favor of you. Would you take a message to Miss Etta at my house?"

"'Course I will, Miss Madison. Be glad to."

"All right. Just tell her not to expect me for supper. I have work to do here and I'll be late getting home."

"Yes, Ma'am. No supper and late home."

Margaret smiled. "Correct. And thank you."

Luke whirled and exited the front door, grabbing his hat on the way out.

After all the students had gone home and twilight was approaching, Margaret closed the doors and moved to a bench out front under a tree. She had donned her coat and hat against the chill of evening. In the beginning it was still light enough for her to read her book.

Homer Zinn closed up the blacksmith shop at his usual time, and noticed Margaret sitting over there. He was puzzled, but decided it was none of his business.

Darkness began to fall, and still no George appeared. Crickets and tree frogs began their songs. As the darkness grew, the moon was visible through the tree branches to the east. Margaret had closed her book and sat staring at the moon. Then she heard a sound behind her. When she rose and turned to look, there was Etta approaching, carrying a basket.

"What are you a-doin' girl?" Etta said.

Margaret rose. "Oh, Etta, you shouldn't have come."

"Cain't have you sittin' in the dark by yo'self!"

"Well, come and sit with me, dear Etta." They moved to the bench and sat side-by-side.

"What kinda work is this?"

Margaret laughed. "It isn't work. I lied."

Etta patted her hand. "I brought you some supper. You want'a eat and tell me the truth?"

"I guess I'd better. You're all I have." She proceeded to tell Etta all about her arrival at the school that morning and who she saw in the buggy. "It's driving me crazy," she said.

"Don't let it do dat," Etta said. "Maybe it's nuthin'. Wait 'til you know what's what."

"You're right, of course. I'm being silly."

Etta put her arm around Margaret's shoulders. "Not silly. Jest love, sounds like. How about we go home?"

Margaret spent a sleepless night, her mind racing with thoughts about her past with George; remembering that first meeting at the burying of Anna's mother, the pleasant times together, the unexpected revelation on their expedition to Branson. When the time came to get out of bed and get ready for her school day, she thought that she hadn't slept at all, then recalled a few strange dreams she could not retrieve.

At breakfast, she told Etta that she might "work late" again unless something happened earlier in the day. She said it with a smile, but Etta returned a look of disapproval.

"You cain't change nuthin' by sittin' out there in the dark. Find out in due time."

"I want to know as soon as I can."
"Well, I don't see you, I be there, too."

Margaret's second evening unfolded as a repeat of the day before, but this time the results were different. She read her book, Homer Zinn closed his shop, and Etta appeared with a basket. The moon came up, sending silver fingers of light through the trees. Then there was the sound of hoof beats of a trotting horse. A buggy appeared from the left and passed by. There was a lone occupant. George was back. She felt some sense of relief, but still could not explain the mystery to her satisfaction.

-21-
THE CAPTURE

Marshal Lambert had gone no more than a mile back toward the city, leading his prisoner he had labeled a "material witness," when he met Marshal Bean and two deputies. Bean grinned and said, "Couldn't wait for me, huh?"

"Was up to him when to run for it. Maybe you took too long. I told him we need to ask some questions about the former owner of his business."

"Got it." Bean and the deputies fell in behind them and the five rode in silence the rest of the way to the county sheriff's office and jail.

The jail was not far from the hotel where Lambert was staying. It was inland a few streets and therefore up hill. Seemed to be some overlap between the county and city forces. When they arrived and went inside, Lambert met the sheriff for the first time and introduced himself.

The sheriff looked more like a city policeman than Lambert's expectation of a sheriff. He was dressed in a black, vested suit with a star pinned to the vest. He was robust and red-faced, with a fringe of gray hair and a trim white mustache.

Sheriff Weathers shook hands firmly and squinted at Lambert. "Surprised to find out we have a stranger operating in my county."

"Apologize for that. Like to get the lay of the land first."

"Un-huh. Well, whatcha got? Marshal Bean says you want temporary quarters for this gentleman."

"We want to ask him a few questions. Sit in if you like."

Weathers nodded and said, "I'll pass for now. Hank, you and Albert take this man into interview room One."

The man who called himself O'Brien stood stone-faced.

Soon they were seated in the room, Lambert on one side of the table and his captive on the other side, handcuffs removed. Bean remained standing near the door. The man said, "This is an outrage! I demand to be released. I have a business to run and a wife and family!"

Lambert nodded. "I understand. Just a few questions and we can get this out of the way. First off, what is your full name?"

"Daniel T. O'Reilly."

"What's the T stand for?"

"Trevor. Let's get on with it!"

Lambert slowly wrote down the name. "Now, Mister Daniel Trevor O'Reilly, do you have any means of proving that's your name?"

"It's all over my paperwork at the office and the papers I carry on my person! Talk to my wife!"

"Yes, but where do you hail from? Is there anyone here that's known you for a long time that can vouch for you? How long have you been married?"

"Well...I haven't lived here long. Came from back east."

"Where?"

"Uh, Philadelphia."

"Contact person there?"

"Well, I can't say for sure. People move around. Where are we going with this?"

Lambert could see that pressure was building so he decided to take the next step. He took the folded Wanted Poster out of his valise and smoothed it out on the scarred table, taking his time. "I need your help in identifying this man. I think you might be able to help." He turned it around and placed it in front of the man across from him.

It takes a good actor not to react when he sees a picture of himself on a Wanted Poster. Lambert thought the man across from him did a pretty well, but he'd played enough poker to see that all was not calm within the man. Still, he gave it a good try. Just a little twitch in the left eye.

He said, too quickly, "Never seen him before in my life."

"You're sure?"

"Absolutely."

"Mister Madison, I'm placing you under arrest for the murder of Marshal Elbert Strong. Hube, you can put the cuffs back on Madison."

"You've got the wrong man! Get me my lawyer!" Madison started to rise, but Bean was already there to hold him down.

"All in due time. We have a barber on the way to give you a shave. On the house."

"You can't do that!"

"Yes we can. Wearing a big beard is like wearing a mask. You think if you had a bandanner over your face, I couldn't take it off? Don't think so."

Despite the prisoner's protests, the barber made short work of the beard. Perfect likeness. Didn't need the little toe thing, although they found out later it was true when they changed Madison into prison clothes. Lambert composed a telegram to the Attorney General in Washington:

HAVE SUBJECT PERRY MADISON IN CUSTODY STOP NEED TO CLEAR UP LOCAL BUSINESS ENTANGLEMENTS BEFORE HEADING EAST STOP WHAT ARE INSTRUCTIONS STOP

Bean, Lambert, and Sheriff Weathers gathered in the sheriff's office to decide the next steps. Lambert began the discussion. "Seems to me we have a mess on our hands. No doubt he's the right man, but here's the thing: He still has a wife back east, so if there is one here, she ain't legal. Got to feel sorry for her. Then there's the business he bought, all with ill-gotten money. I've got to take him back, but that may be the simple part."

"Here's what I think," Bean replied. "We'll need a judge to appoint a solicitor to sort out his local business, with oversight from the Attorney General. The business will belong to the government, seems to me. The second wife, if she's really a wife, will have to be apprised of the first wife and family, after proof she's still living. Second marriage, if there was one, would then be annulled. She wouldn't have no claims. Anyway, a bunch of legal stuff out here, but you'll be long gone. But you know, I feel sorry for her, taken in by a skunk like that, so I don't think I'll even bring it up."

Sheriff Weathers said, "I ain't a lawyer, but it's all right by me. And based on what you said, Lambert, Madison goes back to face murder charges in Missouri and embezzlement in D.C., right?"

"Right. We'll see what the AG says, but I think me and the prisoner will be headed east. I suppose my man can be a guest here for now? If so, Hube and I will head back to my hotel and look for a telegram."

"Sounds good." Weathers stood and they all shook hands and the two marshals departed.

Lambert and Bean spent several hours in the saloon of their choice, discussing the capture and making plans for Lambert's journey.

"Do you need any help takin' him back?" said Bean.

"I don't think so. I'm plannin' to get a sleeper this time. The trip out here plumb wore me out. And I think it would work to get a sleeping compartment for Madison and have any windows screwed shut and a hasp for a padlock on the door. I can't see handcuffs twenty-four hours a day. Think the railroad people will do it?"

"We'll see that they do."

"And the local wife, if there is one, needs to know."

"I'll take care of that this evenin'.

When they returned to his hotel, Lambert had a telegram from the Attorney General:

TRANSPORT MADISON TO TANEY COUNTY MISSOURI FOR MURDER INDICTMENT STOP WILL SEND PROSECUTOR FROM DC STOP ADVISE ETA WHEN KNOWN STOP OTHER INDICTMENTS DC WILL FOLLOW STOP GOOD JOB STOP

"Sounds good," Bean said.
"Yeah. I'll send one back about working with you on the local stuff."

Two days later, in the morning, the prisoner was brought to the train station by two of the sheriff's deputies. He was turned over to Marshal Lambert, who had made all the arrangement with the railroad for a modified sleeping compartment. Standing at a distance observing the exchange was an attractive woman dressed in a long black dress and veiled hat. She made no move to come forward and turned to walk away without waiting for the train to depart. Another loser, she thought to herself...and he seemed so sincere. No wonder he kept putting off marriage, but at least now I know he's gone. I'm glad that nice marshal didn't ask questions.

Lambert boarded behind Madison who was dressed in business attire, but was handcuffed. Lambert ushered him to his compartment and told him how they would operate. "I'm going to take the cuffs off and you will be locked in this compartment. When we are underway, I'm going to allow you to go without them as long as you are beside me or locked in here. When we approach a station, or you are not by my side, you go into the locked compartment. Understand?"

Madison nodded, looking down.

"You will also be allowed to wear regular clothing Marshal Bean brought from your house. Any false move, you go in prison coveralls and handcuffs. Understood?"

Madison nodded again.

"Good. We've got a long way to go." Lambert exited the compartment and locked it behind him. He went forward to a lounge car and took a seat. In a short time, a loud whistle sounded and the car jerked into motion as the slack was taken out of the couplings.

-22-

THE NEWS

The next day after Margaret's second evening vigil, she finished the school day and walked over to Guthrie's store to pick up a few things for Etta. As she walked past George's shop, the doors were open and he was in there working as though nothing had changed. He looked up and waved as he usually did and Margaret waved back, but kept walking.

When she checked the mail pigeon-holes, she saw a yellow envelope, the kind telegrams came in. She nervously dialed the combination and took out a couple of letters and the yellow envelope. She quickly tore it open and read a surprising message:

LEAVING SAN FRANCISCO TRANSPORTING PERRY MADISON TO TANEY COUNTY SHERIFF STOP FELT YOU SHOULD HAVE NEWS FIRST STOP JOSHUA LAMBERT US MARSHAL STOP

She was shocked, despite knowing in the back of her mind that this day might come. She found it difficult to know how she should feel about it. He was her father, after all, but for some time she did not consider him worthy of a daughter's love and respect. She was thankful that the next day was Saturday so she could have time to come to terms with this latest news...on top of her last two days of worrying about George. When he is brought here, will I go visit him? I suppose so, if for no other reason, to see what he has to say to me. If he's to be tried here, will I have to testify?

She hurried home, across the swinging bridge and up the footpath. She went inside to find Etta busy at the stove.

"Etta, I got a telegram. They're bringing Father here!"

Etta turned from her work. "Merciful heavens! They found him?"

"In California. That marshal that was here is bringing him. I don't know what I'll do."

Etta walked across the room and put her arms around Margaret. "It'll be all right, girl. You'll know what to do when the time come. The good Lord will tell you."

Sheriff Horton had also received a telegram and he was not too happy with the news. "Hell's bells," he muttered. He was seated at his desk. He took off his hat and scratched his head. "Bobby Joe! Henry! Get your asses in here!" he shouted up the hall. They came clumping down the hall and found their boss sitting behind his desk, red-faced.

"We got us a God-damned circus coming to town!" Horton shouted.

"You mean with elephants and stuff?" Bobby Joe said, full of hope.

"No, dumb-ass! Worse than that. That-there P. T. Barnum fella don't even come close to this."

Henry Jeffrey and Bobby Joe Duke stood frozen in place, afraid to say anything else.

"Sit your asses down. That marshal whatshisname that was here has caught good ole Colonel Madison and is bringin' him here. They're gonna bring a fancy prosecutor here from Washington to guide us hicks through a murder trial for off'en that other marshal. I reckon they figger it's cheaper to send him here than to round up a bunch of yokels and bring them somewheres else. Go lock the front door and get Jake in here too."

When they were all seated, Horton began. "We better get goin' on findin' anybody who might know something about what happened and let them know they'd better stick around. Off the top of my head, there's Hank Green, his overseer; that hired hand that found the body; Miss Margaret Madison and her maid and her horse fella. They prob'ly won't let the colored actually testify in open court, but they should. Least they can tell us how it went." He paused to look at the ceiling and stroke his mustache. "Was Miss Anna there then? Don't remember. Missus Madison was there, but she really wasn't, if you know what I mean. Besides, she's back east. Oh, there was that fella in Ozark rented a horse to the marshal that was kilt, and Ed Bain, Christian County Sheriff. You fellers know him. Doc Stevenson took a look at the body....

"We'd better get crackin'. I'll let Shelby know. He prob'ly won't get to do much when that fancy prosecutor comes in, but he'll be involved. Well, let's get on it, decide who does what."

Horton found Moses Shelby in his office in the court house. When he walked into Shelby's office, the county solicitor was turned toward a roll-topo desk contemplating a rat's-nest of pigeon holes stuffed with paper. Shelby's bald spot, striped with oiled strands of hair, was exposed. He whirled around on his swivel chair.

"Sheriff Horton, to what do I owe the pleasure?"

"Ain't gonna be pleasure when you hear what I got to tell you."

"Please have a seat." He indicated the chair on the other side of his paper-strewn work table.

Drawing on his deputy's misunderstanding, Horton said, "We got us a circus comin' to town, and it don't involve elephants."

"Sir?"

Horton showed him the telegram and laid out his plans to contact his list of possible witnesses, which he provided to the concerned Shelby. "Anything else we ought to be doin'?"

"I will give it some thought. We should hope to hear from Washington soon and it will be of interest to talk to this marshal when he arrives, not to mention Madison himself."

Horton rose. "I'd better get after it."

Shelby stood also and they shook hands. "Thank you, Sheriff. Going to be interesting."

Sunday morning dawned cool and clear. Margaret had slept deeply but was troubled by dreams she could not reconstruct in the light of day. She decided to attend Sunday meeting at the schoolhouse, serving as a church on Sundays. She needed to talk to Anna and Ben if they were there, and possibly Tom Archer and Olaf Jensen for their mature guidance. Oley, the miller, was the nearest the community had to a spiritual advisor.

Etta agreed to accompany her, and dressed in her best dress. She also wore a stylish straw hat with a flat crown and upturned brim. She had woven it for herself from a bundle of sweetgrass Margaret had gotten for her. They chose to walk down the path and cross the swinging bridge rather than get the buggy out.

As they descended the ladder, Margaret saw Ben and Anna leading Eva, and the Tom Archer family streaming toward the schoolhouse door. The building was full when Margaret and Etta entered, but there was one available desk, which they shared. Several of the men stood at the back and along the side walls. Anna saw her, smiled and waved. Margaret saw George out of the corner of her eye, but did not make eye contact.

Jensen began the service with the singing of "Nearer My God To Thee," accompanied enthusiastically by Jewel Bowman on the piano. Margaret could not concentrate and remembered nothing of his sermon, eager to talk to Anna about her troubling news. The service was finally over, concluded with "Abide With Me" which always brought tears to Margaret's eyes.

Oley Jensen was allowed to exit the front door first to greet everyone as they streamed out; first the women and children, then the men and older boys.

Margaret rushed to find Anna. She picked up Eva first and hugged her. "How's my sweet girl?"

"Mama says I'm sweet, too," Eva said, then squirmed to be put down. "Mama says I'm her big helper."

"That's probably true!"

"Yesss. Mama says so."

Next she and Anna embraced. "Anna, she whispered, you have your bustle on backwards again," triggering that musical laugh.

"Yes, I've let someone come between us."

Ben had stood by, but now came to hug Margaret. "We miss seein' you, Margaret."

"Well, school's started, you know."

Tom and Rebecca came over, trailed by Jenny and Essie. Jimmy and Oren had sought out their friends.

Rebecca said, "Margaret and Etta, we're all gathering at our house. We'd love to have you join us. I have a ham in the oven and there's plenty."

"Please come," Anna said. "We have a lot to talk about."

"We'd be happy to," Margaret replied. "I just need to catch Oley for a few minutes."

"We have a bench in the back of the wagon. You can ride with us, then we'll take you home," Ben said.

Margaret was able to catch Jensen alone for a few minutes. "May we speak privately, Mr. Jensen?"

"Of course, Miz Madison."

Margaret glanced around her before speaking softly. "I have just received a telegram with surprising news. Apparently my father has been captured and is being brought here for trial."

"That's amazing! And I can see how it could trouble you."

"It does. How does one break the bonds of family in order to do what is morally right?"

Jensen scratched his bristling brown beard. "I can see your problem."

"I know I shall be called to testify."

"Well, from my view, you have to follow your conscience and just tell the truth, no matter how much it might hurt your father's cause. I don't see any other way. You'll be swearin' on the Bible."

"I know that, I guess. Thank you for putting it into words for me."

"Good luck, young lady. I wish you the best." Jensen patted her shoulder as she turned to go.

Controversial subjects were left unsaid until after the meal. Tom Archer gave thanks for the gathering and the food. A warm family dinner followed with input from everyone present, most of the focus being on the children. Everyone wanted to hear from Margaret about how the new school year was progressing. After the dinner was over, Etta and Josephine insisted on clearing and wash-up while the other five adults gathered at one end of the table for more serious discussions.

"Margaret, would you like to go first?" Tom said.

Margaret drew a deep breath and began. "I received a telegram on Friday. Marshal Lambert was in California and wrote that he had taken my father into custody and was bringing him here."

There were expressions of surprise all around, but Tom spoke out first. "Oh my goodness! I can only imagine how torn you are." He looked over his shoulder. "And you, too, Miss Etta. There'll be a trial, I suppose?" Etta nodded.

"Without a doubt," Margaret said. "There's the trouble about that other marshal, and there seemed to be a problem in Washington form the war effort."

"I beg your pardon," Anna said, "but I hope I don't have to see him."

Margaret put her hand over Anna's. "Not a problem. I don't blame you. Now what's happening with you and Ben?"

-23-

DISCUSSIONS

Anna looked around her and said, "We are truly blessed in so many ways, but we do have a problem. I never should have asked Ben to move back here. It's that Ferd Harvey."

Ben quickly squeezed her hand. "Don't say that, Anna. Nothin's your fault."

"What happened?" Margaret said. "You told me about that incident at the creek, but—"

"Somebody shot our horse, King!" Anna said, her face clouded with anger. "And we know who it had to have been."

"How horrible!" Margaret said.

Ben said, "The sheriff went and talked to Ferd, but that's about all it is, *talk.* A deputy came and cut out the bullet, but it was a 12-guage shotgun ball. Didn't prove a thing. So here we are, just tryin' to guess what he'll do next."

Tom said, "We all just have to be on guard all the time, which isn't the way to live, but I suspect it's just what he wants. By the way, does anybody know anything about Rose? Rebecca's worried sick about her."

Ben and Anna shook their heads. Margaret said she'd heard nothing.

Rebecca said, "She was such a comfort to me after Charlie died. Ferd let her stay with me and help me with the girls. I don't know how my brother got so hateful, but after Tom and I started seeing each other, I scarcely saw her again. She used to yearn for a way to escape that house. You remember, Josie."

"That's right," Josie said. She us'ta wonder if there was anything a girl could do to get away. Her pa treated her like a slave."

"I pray that we won't find her dead somewhere," said Rebecca.

"Hard to figure," Tom said, "how he could be so different from Becky. It must have been all that nonsense around here during the war."

Margaret and Etta were soon riding toward home with Ben and Anna in their wagon. Eva was going to sleep sprawled across Anna's lap. The wagon was pulled by the team of mules. Ben hadn't yet gotten a replacement for King. The conversation was general until they neared the driveway beside Margaret's cabin, then she said, "Ben, I hate to ask, but could I have a few minutes of 'girl talk' with Anna before you go? I'll make you some tea or coffee. We won't be long."

"It's all right. I don't need anything. I might go check on your brother, Miss Etta, and see what he's up to, or I could just sit on the porch."

Etta smiled. "Ike ain't up ta much, now the corn's laid by, but he'd be happy to see you."

The plan was put into effect. Anna carried her sleeping child in and gently laid her on a daybed in the corner, then came back to the kitchen table to sit across from Margaret. She smiled and said, "Now, what kind of gossip am I about to hear?"

"I'm afraid it is gossip, but I want to know what you think. About daybreak one morning last week, just as I had crossed the swinging bridge, I saw George in the family buggy headed north with a woman by his side."

"Oh, my! Wasn't his mother?"

"Not a chance. She was slim and well-dressed; had a hat with a veil. It's killing me!"

"I understand. Where'd she come from?"

"I don't *know*!"

"Why don't you walk over and ask him?"

"I couldn't do that!"

"I guess not."

"The next day after dark he came back, and he was by himself."

"How do you know? Did you wait for him?"

Margaret colored slightly, "I'm afraid so. Two nights. Etta kept me company."

"What did she have to say about that?"

"When I said I was being silly, she said, 'just sounds like love.'"

"I agree. Do you want me to ask Ben to snoop around a little?"

Margaret squirmed and sighed. "Well...if it comes up naturally sometime."

Anna rose. "We'd better get along. I'll collect my girl." She patted Margaret's hand. "I don't know when Ben will be back down to Sycamore, but we'll see. There's probably a good explanation."

On their ride back home, Anna told Ben of Margaret's concerns about George. "She wants you to see what you can find out next time you're down to Sycamore."

"Don't know if that would be proper for me to ask. I'll listen, of course."

"What do you think?"

Ben shrugged. "Who knows? There's folks movin' in and out all the time. I never heard George speak of relatives, but sounds like he was just takin' whoever it was to catch a train or something, since they was dressed up."

Anna, not satisfied, said, "I guess we'll wait and see. Oh, another thing. Remember that gold piece I had that Missus Madison gave me? We still have it, you know. Why don't you use it to get another horse to go with Silver?"

He patted her hand. "That would be generous. Maybe we ought to save it 'til spring plowin'. What if he was to just keep kilin' our horses?"

Anna looked down at her hands and mumbled, "I wish somebody would catch him in the act."

Acts were continuing to take place in the hills and valleys of Bull Creek and Swan Creek. Evidence occurred of an occasional calf being stolen and butchered, or missing chickens from henhouses. Nothing rose to the level of the killing of a horse or a human, and nothing could be traced to Ferdinand Harvey or anyone else.

There was a move afoot to exact vigilante justice for lesser infractions, such as a man beating his wife, or for public drunkenness. The rise of this kind of activity was almost as disturbing to the community as the original acts, as no one seemed to know who was deciding guilt and punishment. Reports were that a small group of men on horseback with masks over their faces would appear at night and take the accused out and whip them with hickory rods. Granted, the sheriff couldn't be called out for everything, but this kind of thing could get out of control.

Citizens soon had another kind of law and order development to consider. A large headline appeared in the weekly *Forsyth Beacon* announcing the impending trial of Colonel Madison, a former prominent figure in Taney County. The *Beacon* used the largest lead type-slugs available, not used since the paper began printing ten years after the war was over. It had begun as a broadsheet, but had now worked its way up to four pages. The article went on to say that he was to arrive within a week and that a prosecutor was coming all the way from Washington, D.C. to participate. Colonel Madison was accused in the disappearance of a U.S. Marshal, it said, and that further details would be forthcoming. Sheriff John Horton had declined to comment.

Sheriff Horton did not decline to comment in his office after he saw a copy of the paper. He called his deputies into his office and, red-faced, shouted, "Which one of you assholes talked to the paper!"

They stood facing the sheriff across his desk. All three were identically dressed in denim, with leather vests and wide hats. All carried Colt Peacemakers on wide gun belts with a row of brass cartridges in loops all around. They also, despite differences in size and appearance, sported handlebar mustaches. Townsfolk joked that the 'staches were issued at the same time as badges and opined that it wouldn't be a good idea to hire a woman in the department.

Henry Jeffrey, being senior and the largest of the three, felt it was his duty to speak first. "John, no way I ever talk to the paper and I doubt these guys did." The other two shook their heads.

"Somebody did!"

"Well," Jeffrey continued, "I did tell the missus. Didn't think it would do no harm."

Bobby Joe Duke quickly spoke up in his high-pitched voice, "I did mention it to Sam down at the saloon. Figgered he'd need to get ready for the rush."

Jake Sloan said nothing, which was a habit of his.

Sheriff Horton sighed and looked out the window. He leaned back in his chair, and without looking at them, said, "All right, get the hell out'a here."

The paper did not have wide circulation, but did not need to have. News traveled up the valleys and hills on a swift, but unexplained grapevine, the speed in direct proportion the sensationalism of the subject. The capture of Madison ranked high, because he was well-known and universally disliked. Ever since the discovery of the dead marshal, Madison had been tried and convicted in most minds, the subject of many conversations back then and again after the news of his return leaked out.

Grandpa Ned Bowman could make a trip to Guthrie's General Store last most of the morning when his daughter-in-law Jewel sent him for supplies. He would spend the time rocking on the front porch of the store, whittling, and jawing with the other idlers while they waited for their corn to be ground or for a horse to be shod.

On this particular morning the subject was, of course, Colonel Madison. "I hope he gets his neck stretched," said Ezekiel Peake. "He thought we was all a bunch of dumb hicks and let everbody know it. He was right, a'course, but that don't make it easy to take."

There was general laughter and Hannibal Montgomery added, "Zeke, you're right. He was just downright high and mighty. I worked for him once't hoein' weeds ough'a tha corn. He was on us all tha time."

"You probably needed it," said Preston Stewart.

"You did too, Press," Hannibal replied.

Grandpa Ned spoke up. "Do y'all think they'll hang him?"

"I doubt it," Preston said. "Rich folks have a way of gettin' off."

Henry Guthrie had come out on the porch to hear the last few comments. "I worry these days how the court is going," he said. "Used to be, you could predict a verdict pretty well. Not anymore. There's talk he might be in trouble back in Washington, even if he gets off here."

"He'd better not get off here," Preston said.

-24-

FORSYTH JAIL

The Greene County sheriff in Springfield had gotten word of the approaching high-level prisoner and dispatched two deputies to meet the train. It was a cold fall morning, gray and raining, with mists rising from the streets. The deputies were driving a police wagon, recently acquired. It had a full-length hard top with canvas side curtains that could be drawn to keep out weather such as was currently happening. It had two full-width bench seats for the drivers and passengers, and a barred cage at the back to house up to a half-dozen prisoners. Since it was a heavy rig, it was pulled by four Belgian horses, beautifully matched chestnuts with white stockings and blazes, and white roached manes.

The sheriff was quite proud of the rig and lived for opportunities such as this. If he was unfortunate enough not to have some criminals to capture, he liked to show it off to the community at fairs and parades. Helped get the folks ready for the next election.

The train huffed into the station on time and disgorged its weary passengers. Marshal Lambert waited until the conventional passengers had left before entering the compartment that had housed his prisoner.

"All right. Time for the cuffs," he said to Madison. "Behind your back this time."

"Why?"

"We didn't come this far to take any chances."

When they stepped off the train onto the platform, Lambert behind with one hand on the cuffs, the two deputies were waiting for them.

One of them spoke, "Marshal, I reckon you're lookin' for a ride to Forsyth."

"Right. Hey, I remember you two."

They immediately reached in turn to shake hands with Lambert. Their names were Goode and Dade. Lambert was a big man, but they were both larger than he was. Since they worked as partners and were always seen together, in the department they were referred to with one phrase, "Good 'n Dead". They formed a moving wall in front as they worked their way through the crowd toward the wagon.

Some of the crowd knew who had arrived and they started hooting and jeering. Lambert heard shouts such as "String him up!," "Welcome back!" At one point a man pushed his way close to Lambert and shouted, "I'm a reporter. What do you have to say, Colonel Madison?"

Madison said nothing, and Lambert pushed the man aside, saying, "No comment."

When they were safely on their way, Lambert said, "That went well. Thanks."

"Didn't get to bust no heads, though," said Goode.

"Maybe next time," said Dade. "They wasn't stirred up enough."

The mail road headed south was in good condition, being packed gravel with a crown for drainage, but it was a long, long ride reaching into the early morning hours before they reached Forsyth. The misting rain continued throughout the day and into the night.

For the first few hours they talked. Lambert sat on the bench behind and was able to lean forward between them and talk in a low voice about his journey. They'd thrown a couple of quilts in the back so Madison could wrap himself and lie on one of the benches back there.

Dade said, "I recollect you mopin' around the office back then. Drove the telegraph office crazy."

"Gotta do what ya gotta do," said Lambert. "Didn't know if it would work, but didn't know what else to do. Lucky break somebody remembered him in New Orleans. After that it came together pretty straight."

He talked at length about all the steps taken with the other marshals down there and in San Francisco.

"How is Frisco?" asked Dade.

"It's a really purty place and busy as Hell. All kinds of stuff comes in from China and thereabouts and stuff goes the other way off the railroad. Really something to see."

"Maybe some day."

"Get to shoot anybody or bust any heads?"

Lambert smiled, going along with the joke. "Nope. I guess when I show up, folks is just too scared to mess with me."

Goode, sitting on Lambert's left, said, "Looks like one wasn't."

"Yeah, but he was dumb as a box of rocks."

As the day passed and talk wound down, the three of them took turns dozing on the back bench. Occasionally, they would stop to rest the horses and bring buckets of water for them to drink from creeks along the way. Lambert would also check on his prisoner. The deputies had brought food along for all four.

Sheriff Horton and Deputy Sloan were waiting through the night to receive the prisoner. When the bedraggled Madison was brought in, hands cuffed behind him, Sheriff Horton said cheerfully, "Howdy, Colonel Madison. Good to see you again!"

Madison would not look at him.

"We've got a nice room waitin' for you." Still no response, not a word, as they led him back and locked him in a cell.

Afterward, back in the front office, Lambert introduced the two Greene County deputies.

"I reckon all three of you will want to get some rest. I already told Mabel over at the rooming house you'd be comin' in.

She said she'd have somebody awake to take care of y'all. They might even have somethin' to ease you into sleep."

Lambert slept past sunup, unusual for him. He went downstairs to seek breakfast. Mabel, the burly hostess, greeted him. "Howd-do, Marshal. Your buddies are already eatin' over there. Can I get you some coffee? How many eggs?"

"Yes, Ma'am!" he replied, and held up four fingers.

"Have a good sleep?" Dade said.

Lambert nodded. "What there was of it."

"Wasn't a beauty sleep, evidently."

"Look who's talkin'."

"Hope you don't mind us headin' out. We got a long way to go," said Goode.

"Not at all," said Lambert. "You get right on it. And I'm much obliged. Let me know if I can do anything for you."

They all rose and shook hands, and "Good n' Dead" left just as Mabel returned with a steak and four eggs.

For several weeks Lambert had looked forward to his next duty. It was time to go in person to see Madison's daughter. He had thought about her on the long train ride and again on the trip in the wagon at times when conversation with the two deputies had ceased. He thought about the cascade of shining brown hair down her back, about her slender waist, and the way she filled out that frilly white blouse. She had been wearing a long black skirt and high button shoes. She was damn good lookin'—and the thing was—she didn't seem to know it. She may already be taken, maybe by the blacksmith fella. But a man can dream.

He found a barbershop for a haircut and a shave, hired a horse at the livery stable, and headed for Sycamore.

-25-

MEETINGS

The morning was clear and windy after the rain of the day before. The sky was bright blue and there was a chill in the air. The children still scurried outside for their noon break as soon as Margaret gave them the word. She remained at her desk to eat the lunch Etta had prepared and began grading the papers from the morning's work.

There was a knock at the entrance door and she rose and walked through the cloakroom entry and to the door. It was a soft knock, so it was probably one of the smaller children who couldn't handle the heavy door. She gave a small start when she opened it to face a tall figure. "Oh!" she said.

Lambert whipped off his battered hat. "Sorry to startle you, Miss Madison," he said.

Margaret smiled. "It's all right. I apologize. I was expecting a little girl needing help with the door, and you're someone quite different. Please come in out of the wind."

He followed her up the center aisle, his boot heels clumping on the plank floor and his spurs jingling. She led the way to the front stage and indicated the chair to one side of her desk. "Please have a seat, Marshal," she said, as she seated herself. "I don't have anything to drink except water, but here's an extra apple and a half sandwich."

"Don't mind if I do, Miss. Kind of you."

"Please call me Margaret."

"Yes, Ma'am." She was dressed just like his daydreams of her—long black skirt and white ruffled blouse, with a large black shawl around her shoulders.

"I know why you're here." He was as tall and broad as she remembered. He was wearing tight black trousers and a once-white shirt, clean but needing ironing. His long coat was showing signs of wear. His face was weathered from being almost continually outside in the elements, and the thin scar was just the way she remembered. "You may remove your coat if you like, but we haven't started a fire in the stove yet this season."

"I'll keep it, thank you. Also, it'll cover my gun from the children."

"As you wish."

Lambert drew a deep breath. "You got my telegram?" Margaret nodded. "It must have been mixed news to you."

"It was...but I've come to terms with it. I'd ceased having any warm feelings about him a long time ago and if he's guilty of what he's accused of, it's best to get it over with."

Lambert nodded. They heard the sounds of the children playing outside contrasted with the moment of silence in the room. "What I came for...if you're willing...I'll go back and rent a buggy, come tomorrow and take you to see him."

"Let me think. It has to happen sometime...." She rose and walked over to the window, then turned to him. "I have an idea. I have a buggy we could use. You could spend the night at Oley Jensen's. He and Maybelle take in a boarder now and then, as you already know. Save you the round trip. I'll see if Professor Phillips can cover for me here."

Lambert rose and joined her by the window. He looked down at her upturned face. "That sounds good...Margaret. Call me Josh. I travel with a little stuff in my saddlebags, just in case. I'll go on over to the miller's and check it out."

She smiled up at him. "Good. If something doesn't work for me or you, we'll get in touch. Otherwise, I'll see you at daylight."

She followed him to the door and rang the bell to summon her charges back inside.

George arrived early to build a fire in the iron stove in the shop. He had delivered buggies two and three and was nearing completion on another pair. These were to be the light, sporty models with an upholstered seat for two people. Business was good. Word had gotten out about the quality of his work, so demand was exceeding expectations. If he could find the right man, he was considering putting on another person full time. His brother had been helping when the blacksmith shop permitted.

Before beginning work, he went and opened the front door to look over at the schoolhouse as was his habit—see if Margaret was arriving to start the day. He heard the sound of a trotting horse and buggy wheels on the gravel road and it came into view, heading south. He immediately recognized it as Margaret's and as it drew even with him she smiled and waved. He waved back, but stared, noting that she was not driving. A large man dressed in black occupied the left seat on the other side of her. What the hell? Then it came to him…must be that marshal that brought her pa back from California. But how did he get here this early unless he spent the night? Surely, she wouldn't allow such a thing, in consideration of her reputation in a gossiping community—and her a *schoolteacher*.

With a troubled mind, he turned to go back inside. As he did so, he saw Abe Phillips descend the swinging bridge ladder and head toward the schoolhouse.

Margaret thought about George, standing there, watching her ride by. She also thought about the coming reunion with her father. She pushed those subjects aside and asked. "Marshal…er, Joshua, can you tell me anything about your search for my father? I know we were not able to tell you much when you were here."

"Sure, Miss Margaret. There's nothing secret about it. Just like any fugitive, you just have to try to put yourself in their position and think about what you'd do." As they drove along, he

155

told her about all the telegrams and wanted poster mailings, and the waiting and worrying. "Just a stroke of luck, really, getting a hit in New Orleans. Went there, and the rest kinda fell into place."

"Quite remarkable."

"Well, ya never know. Had some help from folks here and there."

"Did he change his name?"

Lambert turned to her and smiled. "Yep. He was Mister Jefferson in New Orleans and Mister O'Reilly in California. Had a beard and long hair."

"I dread seeing him again."

Margaret lapsed into silence and Lambert did not interrupt her with further conversation as they drew closer to their destination. Margaret thought about her father as he used to be. When she was just a young girl, she saw little of him. There was a war going on, although she knew nothing about that. Father was a stern figure that appeared infrequently and had little to do with her. In those days her mother also did not spend much time with her and her sister, Gertrude. Etta was the constant in her life as she grew up, always there, always kind to her, always making her feel secure. Her brother, Reginald, was eleven years older and seemed almost of a different generation. He was away most of the time at boarding schools and university. He didn't make the move to Missouri with the rest of the family.

She hated to acknowledge it, but people said she and her father must have some of the same traits, as they were always at odds. There was little warmth between them and conflict increased as it became apparent Margaret was determined not to follow a path of making an empty-headed "lady" of herself, devoted to idle pursuits. She openly defied him to become a school teacher and she never regretted the conflict, as she loved what she was now doing.

Gertrude, on the other hand, played up to him with flattery and following his every direction. Naturally, she became his favorite, and he often openly ignored Margaret. And her mother also, for that matter. Father was a controlling, unpleasant man and there was little connection between her parents, at least in recent years. Gee, I have a really fouled-up family, she thought.

"You seem deep in thought, Margaret."

"I was. Sorry. I was just thinking about what a mess my family is. Getting in the mood to meet the worst part of it."

Lambert smiled at her. "I hope it won't be too bad. You know I'll do anything I can to help."

She reached over and grasped his forearm and said thanks.

She soon found herself escorted into the entry room of the sheriff's office connected to the jail in back. Sheriff Horton had seen them approaching and met them there, sweeping off his hat and nodding at Margaret. "Howdy, Miss Madison. I reckon you remember me?"

Margaret held out her hand. "I certainly do, Sheriff. I should apologize for my family."

Horton looked embarrassed. "No need, no need. Nuthin' you could have done. I suppose you'd like some time alone with him?"

"Not really, but it's something I must do. I'll leave my pocketbook with the deputy, so you can check it for guns, files, and so forth."

"Not a problem. He'll keep it safe." He turned to Lambert. "I'll take her back, then I'll see you in a few minutes. Just make yourself at home. There's coffee."

As he unlocked the door leading to the jail cells, he said, "You know, Miss, your pa is the only one back here. We've got four cells, but the rest are empty, or I wouldn't take you back. Got rid of an overnight drunk already this mornin'."

"I understand." Margaret followed with some trepidation. She had not seen what the cells were like when Ben and his father were held here before their trial. She followed the sheriff to the back corner cell and looked in to see an old man in coveralls, sitting on the lower bunk, staring at the floor. It had to be him.

The cell walls were exposed brick and there was a high, barred window.

"Got a visitor," the sheriff announced.

The man started, then rose, turning toward him. Margaret saw a changed version of her father. He looked tired and dispirited, understandably so. Gone was the haughty swagger of the past. "Margaret!" he said. "What are you doing here?"

"I came to see you. I still live here, you know."

The sheriff unlocked the door, let her pass through, and relocked it.

"I didn't know. You shouldn't have come."

"May we sit?"

He pointed to the single straight chair and returned to sit on the bunk.

"I'm not going to ask any questions about the case and I don't want to hear about it. I felt it my duty as the only family member nearby to see if there is anything you need."

He smiled ruefully. "Under the circumstances, the only thing I can think of is a lawyer."

"I'll see what I can do. Do you know anything of the family? Do you care?"

"I left that life behind. We'd come apart hadn't we?"

"It seemed so to me."

"I do care. How are you? Married?"

"I'm fine, teaching as before. And no, I'm not married."

"What about the rest of the family?"

"I have little contact, but as far as I know, Mother and Gertrude are living in New York with Mother's sister. Mother has dementia, which is just as well, I believe. Better that she lives in the past than to know what we've become."

"What do you mean?"

Margaret saw no need to answer.

After a long silence, Madison said, "Do you think you can find a good lawyer?"

"I'll see what I can do. Do you have money?"

"I have no idea. See what that marshal says. They might have taken it all."

"I'd better go." She shouted, "Sheriff!"

"Uh, Margaret...." He looked down at his feet. "Maybe I was wrong about you...I do have some regrets."

He made no move toward her and Margaret thought it was just as well. Too late for him to start being a real father now.

-26-

MARGARET AND JOSHUA

Anna sang a hymn as she moved along the clothesline, reducing to a hum when she had clothespins between her teeth. It was a bright clear day in late October, with a light breeze to dry the wash. She always enjoyed getting everything clean and smelling of the outdoors. Baby was moving frequently, seeming to stay especially active whenever she was moving about as she was now. She was amused how the little thing seemed to hear goings-on in the outside world. When Ben would say something or laugh, she'd feel an extra little jump.

Eva was underfoot as usual, trying to help by tugging wet things out of the basket so her mother could reach them. She was increasingly talkative and was now attempting to sing with her mother.

As she moved forward, Anna glanced up the hillside behind the house. Up there at the tree line, in deep shade, was a man on a horse. She was alarmed and glanced down at the small basket containing her revolver. He was too far away to identify and she could think of no reason for him to be there. Ben was working in the woods on the south eighty. She stopped singing and thought about what she could do. She decided to keep working and if he moved in their direction, she'd take Eva and latch them inside the house.

She kept going, glancing up from time to time, until she was almost finished. Then another glance, and he was gone. Was it Harvey? Hard to tell, but that miserable man seemed always on their minds. She'd see what Ben thought when he came to the house for evening chores and supper.

When Ben came in that afternoon, Eva came running barefoot to greet him, "Papa, Papa!" she said.

Ben scooped her up and whirled her around. "How's my girl?"

"I'm happy. I hung clothes and Mama helped."

"Well I'm happy, too. I'll have clean sheets to sleep on."

"Me, too."

Anna turned from the stove where she had started vegetable soup. "When you get settled, I have something to tell you."

Ben put Eva down. "You want to run and play, Sweetie?"

Eva ran back to her doll on the other side of the room, and Ben turned to Anna. "What is it, Darlin'?"

Anna came and put her arms around him, resting her cheek against his chest. "I'm glad you're home. I don't want to be a fraidy-cat, but there was a man on a horse up at the tree line behind the house, just watching us."

"What did he do?"

"Nothing. Just sat his horse and stared. A little later I looked up and he was gone. Too far away to see who he was."

"Did you have your gun?"

"Always."

Ben lowered his voice. "Pa told me that his pa told him that in the old days, you could call somebody out and get it over with, if it was all done fair. I'm wishin' you still could."

Anna shook her head. "I don't. I wouldn't want you to do that. I'd die if I lost you, and you know you still think about what happened at the fence. You had to do it, but it still bothers you."

"Yeah, you're right. I just wish we could do something about him. It ain't fair we have to just wait until he tries again."

"That's the way it is. We're careful, and maybe it was nothing today. I don't want you to worry. I'll always be ready."

Ben gave her a quick squeeze. "I'd better get busy. You mean the world to me and if he ever threatens to harm you two, I'll kill him without regret."

When Margaret came back into the front office after seeing her father, Lambert was waiting for her. "Let's go get some dinner and you can tell me how it went—if you want to. The sheriff says Mabel's up the street is the place to go."

"That would be fine, and I'll tell you all about it."

As they exited the office, they were accosted by reporters with shouted questions, all talking over each other. Over a chorus of *"Miss Madison! Miss Madison! Miss Madison!"* Lambert held up both hands and shouted, "No comment! Miss Madison has no comment! Now clear out and don't risk arrest for disturbing the peace."

As they turned up the board sidewalk, he said, *sotto voce,* "I doubt I could do that, but maybe it'll hold 'em off."

Margaret smiled.

The diner was busy with an eclectic mix of diners, mostly men. Every stool at the long counter was occupied and Margaret assumed the sturdy woman entertaining them was the proprietor. They were shown to a booth by a young woman, also sturdy, who she assumed was a daughter. The booths were of unfinished pine lumber and were in a row on the wall opposite the counter. In the middle were long plank tables and most of them were full. Seated elbow to elbow were men in suits, farmers in overalls, and others of unknown occupation, perhaps river men off the White.

"Well," Margaret began, after the waitress left, "He's changed a great deal. Didn't seem so proud of himself; a bit deflated."

"I reckon so."

"I didn't ask about the charges. No point. Asked him if he needed anything. He wants me to see about a lawyer. One question, Joshua: does he have any money?"

"I don't know the answer, but I'll send a telegram to Marshal Bean in San Francisco. You see, since the government thinks he stole a bunch of money from them, they feel like everything he has is subject to confiscation. They talked about a judge setting up a trustee bank to freeze his assets. Then there's the other wife—"

"Other wife?"

"Sorry. And child. Should'na sprung it on you like that. I'm afraid so. Don't know the particulars, but I suppose they'd have to be taken care of somehow. Anyway, I think you could at least start lookin' for a lawyer. They'll surely let him defend himself. Oh, I didn't talk to him about the case, either. Made it a point not to, even when he wanted to bring it up."

Their plates of pot roast and vegetables arrived, along with cornbread and coffee. As they began to eat, Margaret continued.

"They did confiscate the farm here, but let me keep the bank account to provide for Mother, my sister, and myself. As to a lawyer, I was impressed with the young man that defended my friends Benjamin and Tom Archer when they were accused of murder. I think I'll track him down. He was from Springfield, from his father's law firm. Maybe his father might take a case like this."

"Sounds good. Meanwhile, as I said, I'll find out about money."

"How much time do we have?"

"I'd say at least a month. Swift justice moves real slow. That super prosecutor won't get here for a week or so, I expect...so better make it two months."

When they got back in the buggy to return to Sycamore, Margaret said, "I don't know what I was thinking. We could have brought your horse with us and I could have driven back...saved you a trip."

"Well, I thought about that, but discarded the idea. Why make you do that? And besides, I get to enjoy your company that much longer."

Margaret looked at him. "I don't understand that last part. I don't enjoy my *own* company when all I think about is that trial coming up. But thank you, anyway."

Margaret's mood would have been further clouded if she had known about Rose's letters. George had received the first of them about a month after he had transported her to Springfield. It might have been more proper for her to have addressed her thanks to George's mother, but it was quite evident that she considered George to be the one who had rescued her.

At first she wrote about the family who had employed her. The man was a young professor and his wife was a nurse. They had two children, ages eight and six, and Rose watched over them and took care of the house while the children were in school and the adults were at work.

In subsequent letters, one every two weeks, she told of her excitement about going to school herself, arranged by the professor, while the children were in school. She would often express concern for her mother and say how relieved she was to be away from her father. At times she would say that she did miss *some* of the people on Bull Creek, without being specific.

If Margaret's thoughts were clouded, so also were George's as the letters continued to arrive and he continued to answer, keeping his subjects limited to any news along the Creek. For a couple of years now, since he had met her, George's mind dwelt on thoughts of Margaret. Now, as he went about his work, Rose would sneak in there. She didn't replace Margaret, but she did carve out a share of those inner thoughts.

ROGER MEADOWS

-27-

THE PROSECUTOR

October was gone and November was drawing to a close. The trees were barren and the hillsides dark and gray. It was a cool, rainy fall, with the creeks swollen and the ground too soggy for fall plowing. There wasn't much to do outside anyway, since harvest was over. For those who hadn't finished getting the winter's wood supply in, there was that to do, and soon colder weather would bring hunting and trapping season and hog-butchering.

Anna calculated that she was in her twenty-eighth week and was beginning to feel considerable discomfort with her unwieldy body, despite the thrill of what was to come. She tired more easily and had trouble sleeping, even though some of that sleeplessness could have been brought on by worries about Ben being in the woods alone, and the feeling she could not shake of being watched when she was outside.

George's buggy manufactory continued to thrive. His brother Hiram had joined him after their father had hired a new man in the community with skills as a blacksmith. George and Margaret continued to observe each other's coming and going, but remained separated by that space between his shop and her school.

There may have been a slackening of outside farm work in the hollows and hills along Bull Creek and Swan Creek, but night oil burned in the offices of the county prosecutor. The man from the attorney general's office in Washington had arrived early in the month, coming south out of Springfield by mail coach to Forsyth. His name was Jacob Fortner. He was a tall, distinguished gentleman in his sixties with a trim white beard and mustache. He had arrived in time to sit in on preparations for arraignment, as Judge Blackburn was due to pass through in the week following. In that first meeting, he was able to listen to the evidence, as presented by Moses Shelby. In attendance also were Sheriff Horton and Joshua Lambert, plus an assistant or two of Shelby's.

"Let us please hear what you have in brief, not as you might present it to a jury," said Fortner, being familiar with the tendency of prosecutors.

"Well, Sir," Shelby began, "We have motive and opportunity. This was the third time a marshal had come from Washington with a subpoena, and all indications are that Madison desired not to go. On that dark, rainy night, after counter orders by the defendant to the servants, both men, the defendant and the marshal, disappeared...the former to San Francisco and the latter to whatever location in the nether world he was destined to go."

Fortner sighed and rolled his eyes.

"Cause of death? Murder weapon? Witnesses?"

Shelby managed to squirm standing up. "Uh...as to the first, the local doctor determined it was a blow to the head, by something like a hammer."

"Like a hammer, or a hammer?"

"He will testify a hammer."

"Assuming most people have a hammer, was there anything special about it?"

"Not that we can determine."

"Anything else?"

"The defendant had a fifth of whiskey placed in the bunkhouse room assigned to the victim."

Fortner made no comment for several minutes. Then he turned to Lambert. "Marshal Lambert, I understand you're the one who tracked him down and brought him here. Do you have anything to add?"

"Well, Sir, I've been thinking on it a great deal, and the only thing I could come up with was the horses."

"Horses?"

"Yes, Sir. We found a man in New Orleans that took the horses off his hands, a black stallion and a sorrel mare. He also described Madison pretty good, though he gave a different name."

"And?"

"I sent a telegram to Marshal Peabody down there to find the man and send him up here."

"Any results?"

"Not yet, Sir."

"Did Madison discuss his situation while you were traveling? Make statements we might use?"

"No, Sir. I discouraged any attempts on his part, knowing it could be disclaimed later."

Fortner nodded. "Very good. Well, we may have enough for arraignment, but we will need more for the trial. Let's hope you find your man, Marshal. Now, I intend no offense to your clerks and assistants, Mister Shelby, but I would like to limit exposure to confidential information. So may we clear the room by all but the four of us: you, me, and the two peace officers?"

When they were all settled, Fortner began, "Gentlemen, I would like to have your word that nothing goes outside this room or it could jeopardize the government case against your defendant in his next trial, if it comes to that." They all expressed consent. "Mister Madison did have a motive to escape and it remains to be determined if the judge will allow it in this trial. I brought with me depositions and documents showing a pattern of embezzlement of government funds during the war and also testimony of agents from the Confederacy that he also procured military hardware for them, again for personal gain."

"My God," Horton muttered.

Shelby said, "We shall have several minor witnesses who will describe activities of the night in question, including his own daughter. We also have the man who found the body and the accompanying riding equipage."

"As I opined before," Fortner continued, "the arraignment should be all right. We wouldn't want to show all our cards anyway. But it would behoove us to find this New Orleans hostler at all cost."

The arraignment had gone as Fortner had predicted. Judge Blackburn waited while both sides, all standing before him, introduced themselves. First were Jacob Fortner whom he did not know and Shelby, who had appeared before him many times. Frederick Kilgore, along with his son, Charles, of the firm Kilgore McVey Blanchard in Springfield, represented the defendant.

Blackburn said, "Welcome back young Mister Kilgore."

"Thank you, Your Honor," Charles replied.

Then the judge listened to Shelby present his reasons for believing Perry Madison had killed Marshal Strong. Madison, handcuffed and in prison coveralls, stood staring straight ahead, expressionless.

"Your Honor, Kilgore said, "it appears that the state's case is based upon guesses and coincidence. Where is the evidence? I realize standards may be lower in arraignment, but, my goodness! They have presented no evidence linking my client to the events described."

Blackburn looked at Shelby. "Mister Shelby?"

"It would be a coincidence beyond any reasonable credulity," he said.

Fortner said, "If I may, Your Honor, I have brought with me from Washington a number of documents which will prove motivation beyond doubt."

"I move that they not be allowed into evidence unless they are directly involved with this case." Kilgore said. "Not some attack on the character of my client."

Blackburn stared at them, drumming his fingers on the bench. "Here's what we will do. Make a list of those documents and with one *short* sentence of what each document seeks to prove. Give the same list to Mister Kilgore. I do not wish to see the actual documents and neither should Mister Kilgore. I'm going to bind Mister Madison over for trial and we will consider motions at that time. We will let a jury determine the merits of the case." He picked up his gavel and rapped it on the block.

"Your Honor," said Kilgore, "Two more points. First, if there is a chance other evidence will be introduced — whether it is germane is to be decided — rules of discovery should allow us to see it in advance and prepare our arguments. And second, Colonel Madison requests a bench trial."

"A *bench trial*? Are you aware of what you are requesting, Mister Madison? The law allows you to have a jury of your peers decide your case."

Madison drew himself erect. "Your Honor, here I *have* no peers!"

"Oh, Lord," Blackburn muttered, rubbing his chin. "Mister Madison, you're sure you want to put your fate into the hands one man — *me*?"

"Yes, Your Honor. I didn't intend my statement to sound as it did. But no one around here comes from anything close to my background. My attorney has been researching local cases and finds little correlation in some of the judgements versus the evidence. I trust that you will decide based on facts and law and no other factors."

"Well, that's quite a statement, and you have the right to a bench trial. So it shall be. Now to the other point, Mister Kilgore, I believe you are in the right. If prosecution intends to present evidence, you should have a chance to prepare for it. Mister Shelby?"

"Your Honor, may we have a moment to discuss it among ourselves?"

"Yes. Let's take a short recess. Be back in here in ten minutes."

Out in the hall, Shelby looked at Fortner. "It's your evidence. What do you propose we do?"

"Well, I believe Kilgore and the judge are correct. What I suggest is that we pull a 'King Solomon' and split the baby. We can pick one piece of evidence and give it to them and hold back the rest for the future trial in Washington."

Approval was reached and a court date selected in early January, since the Christmas holiday was just over a month away. Both sides went to work to prepare their case.

-28-

THE VISITOR

Anna left Eva by the fireplace playing with her rag doll and talking to herself, while she went out into the cold rain to gather eggs. Ben, as usual, was working in the woods at the south eighty. She dashed to the henhouse with her basket and gathered the warm eggs, upsetting the hens in their boxes as they attempted to frighten her away from the fruits of their labor.

As she hurried around the front of the house she saw a dark figure on the lane in the distance headed in her direction. She bolted the door behind her, withdrawing the latch string, and placed the egg basket on the kitchen counter. Eva was still occupied on the hearth so she went to the front window. It was a man approaching, bent against the falling rain and drawing ever closer with halting steps. She took her shotgun from beside the door and continued to watch. He wore an old felt hat with the wet brim drooping to partially cover his face, and his clothing was soaked and ragged.

He looked up for a moment, then climbed the front steps and walked over to the door, now sheltered from the rain and her view. Anna waited, holding her breath. Finally there was a weak knock. What was she to do? Without Ben there it would be foolish to open the door to some derelict looking for a handout, even if her inclination was to help someone in need.

She spoke loudly through the door, "I'm sorry, I can't help you!"

His answer was muffled, but it sounded like he said her name.

"*What?*"

"Anna?"

This time there was no mistaking it. He pronounced it with an "Ah" sound, not like the flat "A" she normally heard.

"Who is it?"

"It's your papa, Anna. Will you let me in?" This he spoke with more authority.

What could she do? It was a startling development, but it did sound like him. She poked the latch string back through the hole and backed away, holding the shotgun at ready. Eva, having heard the exchange, ran up behind her and peeked around her skirt.

"All right, you can come in," she said.

The leather string tightened and the latch slowly lifted. When he entered, despite his haggard appearance, there was no doubt. His face, beneath a wet, unkempt beard was wrinkled and blanched white. He had a bag over his shoulder and he lowered it to the floor.

"I'm sorry, Anna. I had no place else to go."

"Well this is a fine thing! Showing up and expecting mercy after what you did!"

"I don't blame you. You can send me away if you wish."

A small voice spoke, "Mama, who is that?"

"He used to be my papa."

"You have a *papa?*"

"Not anymore. All right, go over by the fire," she commanded. "I'll get you some dry clothes to put on."

He took off his wet coat and dropped it by the door, then made his way across the room, shivering, dripping water. Eva backed away, watching in fascination.

Anna put the shotgun back in the corner and went into the bedroom. She brought in a towel, a blanket, wool socks, and a suit of long johns and handed them to him. "Go in the room and change. Just drop your stuff on the floor. You can wrap yourself in that blanket and come back by the fire."

I'll have to let that stuff dry then burn it, she thought. It's not worth washing and it smells terrible. But what will I do about him? He has a lot of explaining to do.

Friedrich walked back in, looking down, and seated himself in a rocker in front of the fire. Eva stayed close to her mother, clutching her skirt.

"Would you like something to eat?"

"If you will be so kind."

Anna took him a cup of coffee and went back to the stove to scramble eggs.

Eva approached him cautiously and said. "My name is Eva and I'm almost three." She held up three fingers.

"I'm Jürgen," he said, with a faint smile. "You have the name of your mama's mama."

"Yergin? That's a funny name."

"It's German."

"What's *Cherman*?"

"A country from which I come. In the old country, we call it *'Deutchland'*."

"You came today?"

"No, no, a long time ago."

Anna brought a plate of eggs and ham. "Eva, back off and find something to do while he eats."

"Yes, Mama," she said, but there was nothing more interesting to do, so she stood back and watched him eat. "He's rilly hungry, Mama."

"Be quiet, Eva," Anna said, as she went back to the kitchen area and began chopping vegetables for the stew she was making for dinner. With the rain, she expected Ben might be coming in at noon. She hoped so. She needed his support for whatever was to come.

Anna collected his empty plate and turned to go back to the kitchen.

"My thanks to you, Anna," he said.

She nodded without speaking.

"Are you going to stay with us?" said Eva.

"Be quiet and leave him alone," said Anna. "You go play by yourself. Now."

Eva slumped her shoulders and sat down on the floor, picking up her doll.

Jürgen's chin dropped to his chest and he started snoring. Eva looked up at her mother and grinned.

Anna ignored her and retrieved the pile of wet clothes from the room and carried them and the wet coat out on the porch, draping them over a bench. In the distance she saw Ben approaching, driving the mules and the wagon piled with fence rails. She went back inside, but watched from the window until he came up on the porch, then went out to intercept him before he could enter.

"What's this, meetin' your wet husband outside?"

"We have a visitor."

"Really? I didn't see a horse or wagon."

"He walked. It's my papa."

"Your pa? What on earth—?"

"I haven't talked to him about it yet. I wanted you to be here. He doesn't look good."

"That's his clothes?"

"Yes. He's wearing a suit of your underwear and wrapped in a blanket. We'd better go in."

Jürgen was still sleeping when they entered and Eva jumped up and ran to Ben. "Papa, Mama's papa is here," she whispered. "He's sleepin'."

"So I hear, Babe. Let me get my wet clothes off before I hold you."

Ben went into the bedroom to change, then came out and went to Anna at the stove and put his arms around her from behind. "How's the little one?"

She reached up behind her and put her hand behind his neck. "Jumping around as usual. Hold your hand still and you'll find out."

"Yep. He's doing somersaults...Sure smells good in here."

"Better than it did. Got beef stew and there's bread coming out in a little bit."

He smiled, "I think I might just ask you to stay around awhile."

"Maybe I will."

"What are we goin' to do about him?"

"I don't know."

"Them shoes on the porch are pitiful, fallin' apart. And his clothes...he don't look like he's had much to eat for a long time, either. 'Course, I don't remember him much."

"We'll see what he has to say. I guess we'd better wake him up and get some clothes on him before we eat."

They went to where he was sleeping in the rocker. Ben put his hand on his shoulder and shook him gently. "Mister Friedrich, better wake up and get ready to eat."

Friedrich started awake and looked up with blinking eyes. "Yes, yes. So sorry."

"It's all right." Ben extended his hand. "I'm Benjamin Archer."

Friedrich struggled to his feet, holding the blanket around himself. He took Ben's hand. "Jürgen Friedrich. You are the husband? Yes?"

"That's right. I'm Tom Archer's son."

"Yes, yes. I remember him."

"Come back in the bedroom and we'll see if we can find some clothes for you until we get sorted out. Anna's got dinner ready."

After they were seated at the table, Anna and Ben in their customary places at the ends of the table, Ben asked for them to bow their heads and he gave thanks for their food. Eva, across from their visitor, began to ask questions, "Yergin, are you hungry? Yergin, where do you live? Yergin—"

"Hush, Eva," Anna said. "Be quiet and eat your food."

Eva stuck out her lower lip, but did as she was told. 'Yergin" did not have to be told. He dug into the stew and fresh bread with gusto.

Ben rescued the moment. "Mister Friedrich, after we all enjoy our dinner, maybe we can have us a talk by the fire."

Friedrich nodded and continued eating.

After the midday meal was cleared away, the three adults sat before the re-banked fire in a semi-circle with Anna in the middle. Eva got her blanket and climbed into Ben's lap, a rare treat for her in the middle of the day.

Friedrich cleared his throat and stared into the fire. "Is not a *gut* story," he said. "But tell you I must." He turned to Anna. "I owe it to you."

-29-

FORGIVENESS

The day outside was dark and raining, but they were enveloped in a circle of flickering gold light from the fire. For a few moments there was only the sound of the rain on the roof and the crackling flames while Friedrich gathered his thoughts.

"We were not doing so well," he began. "Crops were not *gut*, no money coming in to pay for the farm...and then we lost your mother. I didn't know what to do."

"You said nothing to me! You wouldn't talk! I lost my precious mother, who loved me!"

"I know, I know. But what was I to say? I know nothing about little girls or their feelings. I don't know how to talk of such things."

"You could have said *something* to me! You could have said you were sorry for what happened. And then you left me behind. You took me to that horrible man and made me stand there like a heifer to be sold!" Anna's face was set in pain, and tears began to course down her cheeks. She swiped them away with her fingers.

Friedrich shook his head from side to side. "Yes! Yes! I *was* sorry, but I thought it best for you...at least I thought you'd be safe...have food and shelter. I did not know horrible of the man. Excuses don't make it right, but it would not have been *geeignet*, suitable, for you to go. But you are now well?"

She looked at Ben and reached for his hand. "Oh, yes. But you have no idea what happened to me before Ben rescued me."

"What did happen?"

"We won't discuss it. Where is Evan?"

"Last I know, he was working as a cowhand on a ranch in Texas."

"And you left him also?"

"There was no choice. Too old, they tell me. Clear out. We won't feed you if you can't work cattle. Got a little work in town, sweeping floors, hauling night soil, things like that, but not enough."

"What happened to your money, our possessions, the horses?"

"The worst thing. We had gone across most of Oklahoma Territory, when we were robbed by highwaymen. They beat us and took everything. We walked and we walked...."

They lapsed into silence again. Anna took a deep breath and dried her eyes. Ben had been silent throughout and Eva had fallen asleep on his lap. Anna looked at the broken old man her father had become and felt some of the resentment she had carried slowly begin to melt away. She looked at Ben and Ben looked back at her. What if I had never met you? She thought.

She turned to her father and addressed him with a title she had vowed never to use. "Papa, what now?"

He looked at her. "I do not know. All this time, I wonder how you are. I told you I come back for you, but not to be like this. Still, all I have are you and Evan. Now I know that you are well, you have a family, so I go away again."

Ben spoke at last. "We'll talk some more. We have to wait for the rain to go away."

Anna nodded. "Yes. Ben and I will talk. You need to get rested up, let me wash your clothes, feed you a few good meals."

"I am most grateful for already what you have done."

Ben went out as usual to do the evening chores. The heavy rain had abated, but light drizzle continued to leak from the dark clouds. As he milked the two cows, fed the pigs and Silver, who had continued to remain close by, he thought of Anna's father and what they might do with him. Anna warmed up left-overs from the noon meal and Jürgen ate again with gusto. Already his color was better, but he was subdued except to express his gratitude again.

When they were at last together in their bed, Ben began their whispered conversation. They could hear Jürgen's snoring from his pallet in the other room. "Anna, I've been thinkin'. You know that tack room off the barn? It's pretty big and has a little King heater. Charlie's pa had him a sort of workshop in there. We could—"

"Wait a minute. Are you thinking—?"

"Yeah, I am. It's up to you, but I could get a little work out of him. He could help feed and he could pile brush when I'm workin' wood. I could clear out some stuff and put a bunk in there...."

"I don't know...I'd put him out of mind, or tried to...."

"Well, let me kiss you two good night and you can sleep on it."

Anna was first up as usual, before dawn, but the rain had stopped and there was some weak light in the east. She padded barefoot to the fireplace, dressed in a quilted robe Margaret had given her. Her papa was still snoring on his pallet in the corner of the room. She lifted the fire screen, raked through the ashes, and put some kindling on the exposed embers. Next some dry wood on top, then a tendril of smoke and a tongue of flame appeared. Satisfied, she went to the cook stove, carefully removed the round lids with a handle and built a fire in the firebox.

All through this routine, she continued sorting the troubled thoughts that had kept her awake for much of the night. What am I to do about him? What will it serve to continue to hate him for leaving me behind? I know I'm stubborn, but in spite of everything, I *am* better off that I didn't go with them. And when I was in a desperate situation and Ben found me in his barn, what did he do? He took me in and treated me with kindness. Tears formed in her eyes and her throat closed up. She was barely able to stifle a sob.

She heard movement and Jürgen coughed and sat up.

"Coffee will be ready in a few minutes," she said.

"I thank you."

Ben came into the room, fully dressed. "Good morning,' Mister Friedrich. How'd you sleep?"

"Much better than the trail," he said. "I am grateful to be warm and in the dry."

Ben walked over to Anna at the stove, and kissed her cheek. "Are we a go?" he whispered.

Anna looked at him, and slowly nodded. Then she said, "The kettle is hot for washing, then we'll have coffee."

Friedrich had slept in his borrowed clothes. He got up and followed to the washstand where Ben fixed him a basin of water.

After they finished breakfast, Ben said, "Mister Friedrich, let's you and me take our coffee over by the fire and have a chat."

Jürgen got up from his chair and followed. "Yes, yes. And I would be pleased if you would use my given name, not so formal. I don't deserve such respect."

"Well, it was how I was taught, but I'll do as you wish." As they both seated themselves in rocking chairs, he continued. "Anna and I have talked and I wanted to ask you a few questions."

"Yes?"

"Did you have any plans for what you were to do next?"

"No, no...I only thought about trying to make it back...see if she is all right. Because, you see, I thought of it a lot...leaving her here. I was frustrated and angry at *Gott* in that time and I realized I may not have done what was best."

"Are you able to work?"

"Yes, yes. I am old, but I can still do many things. Could not handle cattle ranching, on a horse all day, but yes, doing work again would be a blessing."

"Well, there's always plenty to do on a place like this, working in the woods feeding the stock, shelling corn, and so forth. What would you say about staying on, helping out for your board?"

"*Oh! You would do this?*" He looked over his shoulder at Anna. "Anna, *you would do this for me?*"

Anna was drying a dish, listening. She solemnly nodded her head. "Yes, I have forgiven you."

Friedrich's face contorted with emotion and he began to weep. After he regained his composure, he said, "I will do anything to justify your kindness."

They both rose and Ben held out his hand. "Let's shake on it, then I'll show you around and we can fix a place for you."

Jürgen's ragged coat had been dried over a chair by the fire and he had turned up the sleeves and pant legs of his borrowed clothing. The two men went out to the barn, where Ben showed him the tack room where he might fix up a bunk. After the morning milking, they went to work together, organizing the room, removing the clutter, and building a bunk in one end of the room. They took a short break for the noon meal, then sawed some stove wood to the proper length for the little stove. It was much more efficient to use the two-man crosscut saw instead of the one-man that Ben had been used to using. Both split wood, Ben for the fireplace, Jürgen for the King heater. Jürgen filled the wood-box in the house with fireplace wood and promised Anna it would always be so.

While the men were getting the tack room set up, Anna washed clothes. Ben and Jürgen carried water to the big black iron pot for heating water and to the tubs for rinsing. Jürgen picked out the best of his clothing for washing, admitting some should be destroyed.

Toward the close of the day, they carried a tub into the tack room and warm water for him to take a bath, admittedly the first he had had for months. He was able to come to supper feeling almost a new man.

The next morning, Anna cut his hair and trimmed his beard for him, preparing him for a trip to Sycamore with Ben for new shoes and work clothes.

Ben dropped a sack of shelled corn at the mill to be ground, then pulled up in front of Guthrie's store. Grandpa Ned Bowman was holding forth from his usual rocking chair and Preston Stewart and Hannibal Montgomery were on the bench, whittling and sending occasional steams of tobacco juice at the spittoon. As Ben and Jürgen climbed the steps, Pres said, "Well, lookee who's here! That really you, Jergen?"

"Yes, it is I," Jürgen replied.

"Made your fortune out west, did ye?" said Hannibal.

"No, was not so good," Jürgen mumbled, walking past and reaching for the door.

"Morning, fellers," Ben said and followed him into the store.

Henry Guthrie came to meet them and held out his hand to shake with Jürgen. "Back, are you?"

Jürgen shook his hand and nodded.

Ben spoke quickly, "He's gonna be helpin' us out at the place. Let's fix him up with some stuff and put it on my bill."

-30-
CHRISTMAS

December weather along Bull Creek was typical of the season; frost at night, some days of sunshine, some cloudy days with chill winds. No snow yet, although children were hoping for a good one by Christmas to let Santa Claus and his reindeer have an easy time of it. Anna's body continued to expand, stretching her skin and causing it to itch. She, unlike the children, looked past the potential gifts at Christmas to that day, perhaps in early March, when she would get a gift of her own, another child and a return to a normal body. She thought of that young girl named Mary, so long ago, anticipating her gift of a child.

It surprised her that her father had been such a help to her. She no longer carried water or fireplace wood, and he was always quick to help in any other way. Who was this stranger? She thought. Did all of his trials out west change him? Apparently so. It made her realize the great dividend of granting him forgiveness. Ben had not known him before, but was pleased to have his help around the place. She remembered him as being a man of few words, inward-looking, unhappy, but now he seemed to be patient with Eva, listening to her chatter, answering her endless questions. Anna didn't know what they talked about, but they often did so at times when Jürgen was by the fireplace awaiting a meal.

Margaret was busily preparing one of the major events of the year in the community of Sycamore—the school Christmas program. It was a time of great excitement for the children, as it was a break in the routine of lessons and school work. Some lessons continued, but a couple of weeks before the program, Margaret gave out assignments for the reading performances and they all began to practice Christmas music. Jewel Bowman managed to join them to play the piano for their practice sessions. A week before the Friday program, the older boys got to go into the hills to cut a cedar Christmas tree of the proper size. It would not take long, as cedars were abundant, but they managed to make the expedition last at least a half day before they triumphantly carried it in on slender poles they had cut.

George observed them from his carriage shop, and grabbed a saw to go over and help them erect it, as he and his father had always done. Margaret seemed surprised to see him, but quickly said, "Hello, George. Thanks for coming. Luke already brought the stand over from the woodshed."

George nodded. "I'll get right too it, then, if that's all right."

The stand was made of ornate wrought iron, one his father had made years before. With the help of Warren, Jimmy, and Luke, they soon had the tree standing in the corner to the right of the stage. As George turned to go, he found himself facing Margaret. They stood looking at each other for a moment, and George said, "How are you, Margaret? I'm sorry about your pa, and I should have said so sooner."

"It's all right, George. Thank you. I could be better. The excitement of the children allows me to escape my thoughts."

"Well…again, I'm sorry. I-I'd better be going."

The children spent most of the afternoon decorating the tree and the schoolhouse for the coming program, now only two days away. They made paper chains out of colored construction paper and long ropes of popcorn strung on sewing thread. There were a few precious shiny glass balls and ropes of tinsel, and shiny star for the top. They made drawings of Santa Claus, stars, reindeer, angels, and snowmen, colored them and hung them on the tree. The school had a collection of paper bells that folded up, and ropes of red and green paper that they used to decorate the room. At the close of the day, they viewed their work and were pleased with it.

Margaret let them go home a little early and bustled about the room, picking up debris from the day's activity, then got a push broom and started sweeping. She was halfway through, when there was a knock at the front entrance. She had already latched the door. One of the children must have forgotten something. She went to the door and peeked through a tiny hole Professor Phillips had drilled there for her safety when she was alone. George. What was he doing back here?

She unlatched the door and opened it. "George. Did you forget something?"

"You could say that. May I come in?"

"Of course." She stepped back into the entryway.

George stepped inside and stood facing her, gathering himself. He was holding something behind his back. "I'd best just come out with it. Margaret, I've been a fool."

Margaret waited for him to continue.

"I don't know if you'll forgive me, but I hope you will. I've missed you terribly, and it's all my fault. Is there a chance?"

Margaret couldn't decide how to answer. Wasn't this what she wanted? And yet, there were all those long days and night when she felt the pain of separation and uncertainty.

"George, thank you for coming over and saying what you've said. You said you've been a fool." She smiled ruefully. "Will it hurt your feelings if I agree with you?"

George smiled. "I reckon not. The only question now is, can I undo it?"

"I'm not a vindictive person, but I'd like to have some time to think about where we go from here. Can we sit a few minutes? And what are you hiding behind your back?"

"Sure. And I brought you something." He brought out a burlap bag."

"What's *that*? It's moving!"

"It's a live chicken. It might not have worked for ole Lester Coggins, but I thought it might for me."

Margaret laughed in spite of herself. "You're crazy!"

"I'm desperate!"

They went forward to the stage area where Margaret sat at her desk and George took a side chair.

Margaret said, "What do you expect to happen?"

"I don't know. It takes a while for any wound to heal, and I did wound you."

"Although I didn't agree with your reasons, I suppose I could understand what *you* were thinking. I told you then that you shouldn't worry about what others think, as long as it's none of their business."

"I guess you're right, but I just couldn't help it."

"You seem to be doing very well...congratulations, by the way...so do you have it out of your system?"

"I do. If you don't mind my quoting you, 'to *hell* with the rest!'"

Margaret pressed her fingertips to her chest. "I said *that*?"

"You did."

Margaret shrugged. "Well? Now let me change the subject. A couple of months ago, you did something that drove me crazy...which might mean admitting I still care for you. Early one morning, you drove out of here in a buggy with a stylish-looking young woman and it was not until the next night that you came home. Care to explain?"

"You were keeping track of me?"

"Yes."

"Well, I've got to swear you to secrecy, but I'll tell you all about it."

"I swear. Tell me!"

"It was Rose Harvey."

"*Rose?* That was *Rose*? How did she —?"

"Do you remember the big storm back in September, the cold rain and wind?" Margaret nodded. "The next morning, I found her wet and about to freeze under that tarp over by the shop. She'd been beaten by her pa and had run away—"

"I remember everybody looking for her!"

"Well, my ma took her in and brought her out of it.... You should have seen her—"

"Where is Rose now?"

"I'll get to that. We lost my sister, Nola, when she was eighteen. Ma just never got over it. Oh, she carried on...but she always looked a little sad. Didn't smile as much. Caring for Rose was good for her...really brightened her up. Ma's good at sewing, making things. Well, she jumped in and made Rose a whole collection, including a nice red wool coat."

"Please, George, don't keep me in suspense! I saw her in that red coat."

"As things got better for Rose, and all, I didn't know what to do. She couldn't stay hid out forever. Then something happened. The Professor dropped by the shop, like he does once in a while. It hit me all of a sudden. I swore him to secrecy and asked him if any of his friends in Springfield might have use for a maid, or somethin'."

"And he came through?"

"He did! She's working for a professor whose wife also does some teaching, and they have a couple of kids. Rose keeps house, looks after the kids."

"An *au pair*."

"I reckon that's the fancy words for it. She gets to go to school some, too."

"George, that's *wonderful*! In the old days, I would have jumped up and given you a big hug!"

George smiled. "I'll put it on your bill, collect later, I hope."

The schoolhouse was packed to standing room for the Christmas program. The school desks on runners were stacked outside, replaced by long benches. Coal oil lanterns hung from hooks in the ceiling to shed a soft gold light over the gathering and there was a prominent smell of cedar. Margaret started the proceedings by introducing Josephine Archer and Luke Johnson, who would read the traditional Christmas story from the book of Luke. His much later namesake Luke began the reading and a hush fell over the room:

> "And it came to pass in those days, that there went out a
> decree
> From Ceasar Agustus that all the world should be taxed.
> And all went to be taxed, and every one into his own city.
> And Joseph went up from Galilee, out of the city of Nazareth,
> into Judea, into the city of David, which is called Bethlehem,
> because he was of the house and lineage of David...."

The adults listened attentively to the familiar words with some of the women wiping tears from their cheeks. Small children squirmed in their seats, eager for the best part, when Santa Claus would arrive. Josephine picked up the narrative:

> "...To be taxed with Mary, his espoused wife, being great
> with child.
> And so it was, that while they were there, the days were
> accomplished
> that she should be delivered.
> And she brought forth her first-born son, and wrapped him
> in swaddling
> clothes, and laid him in a manger because there was no
> room for them
> in the inn..."

As the reading concluded with the verse about shepherds, John Johnson, Warren Harvey, and Jimmy Archer came in the side door, dressed in old bedsheets with towels draped about their heads. Warren was carrying a live lamb. A curtain made with sheets strung on a wire was drawn to show Opal Bowman and Herman Ott, similarly dressed, kneeling beside a wooden box of straw.

After a quick draw of the curtain and some bustling about, it was drawn back again to show Jimmy, Luke, and Warren wearing cardboard crowns. Jewel Bowman hustled up to the piano and accompanied their singing of "We Three Kings."

The rest of the students all gathered at the front and sang "Joy to the World," and Margaret called that portion of the program to a halt, to the applause of the gathering. By secret signal, a bell similar in sound to the teacher's bell was heard outside. "Santa Claus" himself burst into the room, to the amusement of the adults and older children, and wonderment on the faces of the small. Oley Jensen had only to powder his beard, add a white wig and glasses, and don a somewhat threadbare red suit, to pass muster.

Two of the older girls, Opal and Josephine, helped Santa Clause hand out presents to the children, all from names drawn for an exchange. Finally, the jolly man opened a large burlap bag he'd brought in and handed out paper bags to each, with an apple, hard candy, and peanuts. Edna Johnson had gathered the mothers to put the treats together.

Santa Claus "Ho-ho-ho-ed" a farewell and the evening ended with a strong singing of "Silent Night."

Ben and Anna drove the team home in the starry night, with Eva wrapped in a quilt in Anna's arms. After a brief tantrum when Anna took control of the sack of candy, Eva had gone fast asleep.

ROGER MEADOWS

-31-

THE TRIAL

The trial was scheduled for the first Monday in January and Forsyth's population had more than doubled. Sheriff Horton's predicted "God-damned circus" had come to pass. All rooms to rent were full to capacity at outrageous prices. Tent encampments sprang up on the outskirts of town using surplus pyramidal tents from The War, giving the appearance of that period when Union and Confederate armies alternated possession of Forsyth...until Union forces tired of it and burned the town to the ground. There was an invasion of pickpockets, sellers of souvenirs, beggars, evangelists, and women of suspect profession. Horton added three more temporary deputies.

This time, the invading forces were curious citizens and a collection of journalists from as far away as Washington D.C., New York, and Chicago. The new-built courthouse would house only a small percentage in the courtroom, but that did not seem to matter. The lucky number who could secure a precious seat could depend on a rapt audience to hear what they had to say when they exited. Journalists were given first priority so bailiffs would have to examine credentials carefully.

Ozark weather contributed a mix of freezing rain and sleet during the night before that carried into the morning, making unpleasant conditions for those, all men, standing in line for a seat. One of the first was a man named Nathan Roach. Roach was a righteous man. It made him angry when accused got off easy or with no penalty at all. God didn't provide the Ten Commandments to be taken lightly.

Roach was approaching middle years and lived with his aged mother, his father having passed to his reward. He wore his rust-colored hair long and his beard full, attempting his version of a Biblical look. When he was growing up, the family rarely went to Meeting, but reverence for the scriptures was pounded into him. He liked the Old Testament best. It was filled with men who went out, by God, and did the Lord's work. As he stood in the freezing darkness of the morning, he thought about some of those men—Gideon, Joshua, Samson—even David who killed that giant with a slingshot. When he was a kid, Roach had practiced until he thought he could do the same.

We'll see about this-here trial, he thought. I bet that fancy man and his lawyers get him off. We'll see…. At last, at nine o'clock, the doors were opened for the trial to begin. Roach shuffled forward on frozen feet and was at last rewarded with a seat in the gallery. He would give anything for some coffee, but at least he had brought along some corn pone and cold ham.

The courtroom was packed to capacity with the expected scent of unbathed country people, damp with the rain, still shivering from the cold. A large coal stove in the corner glowed red around its bulbous firebox, but it did little to cast any warmth into the far reaches of the room. A hush fell as Deputy Bobby Joe Duke, in his high-pitched tenor shouted, "All rise!" Then there was a noisy commotion of movement as the spectators took to their feet. Judge William Blackburn strode in, taking his place behind the high bench. He was a tall, heavy-set man with a tanned square face and a mane of white hair. His face was lined with a stern expression from carrying the weight of justice as he traveled from county to county for major cases. For this case he was dressed in proper judicial robes, a rare departure from his usual black frock coat.

Blackburn stood for a moment, scanning the crowd. All stared back in anticipation for him to speak. "Take seats! In case you-all don't know it, I'm in charge here. And I have a hair-trigger, in case you don't know *that*. When court's in session, unless you're trying the case or you're on the witness stand, you'll keep your mouths shut. Otherwise, you'll give up your seat to someone outside who will appreciate gettin' it."

He stepped forward, flopped a worn leather case on the bench, and sat down. He whacked a wood block in front of him with a gavel and said, "Court's in session! Let's get on with it. Bailiff, bring in the accused."

Bobby Joe Duke rapped on a door to the left of the bench, the judge's right, and Madison entered, flanked by deputies Jeffrey and Sloan. He was dressed in a new black suit with white shirt and black cravat. He carried himself erect with an expression of disdain, as though he were willing to tolerate a useless exercise. He was now clean-shaven and his silver hair restored to its true color. His hands were manacled in front of him, a minor flaw in the image he sought to portray.

He was delivered to the defendant's table, facing the bench to the judge's left. His lawyers, Frederick Kilgore and son, Charles, had been standing, and all seated themselves. There was a stirring in the audience, but not quite reaching the noise level for Blackburn's gavel.

Jacob Fortner from Washington, and the local prosecutor, Moses Shelby, and two clerks, were already seated at the prosecutor's table to the judge's right as Madison was led past them.

Blackburn surveyed the scene in front of him and said, "Mister Duff, read into the record what we're about."

Nathaniel Duff was a slender blond man in a dark suit who traveled with the judge on the circuit and served as court clerk. He was reading the law, but had some time to go before he could pass the bar. He stood, cleared his throat and read. "This is Taney County case number eighteen-eighty-three dash one; the State versus Mister Perry Madison, on trial for murder in the first degree." He sat back down.

"Will the defendant please rise," Blackburn said. All three at the table did so. "Mister Madison, how do you plead?"

"Not guilty, Your Honor."

"Now, in arraignment, you stated that you wished to have a bench trial—no jury. Is that still your desire? If so, the court needs to hear it again in your own words."

"Absolutely yes, Your Honor—a bench trial."

"For the benefit of those present, it means that I alone will decide the outcome of the case. I decide what I will and will not hear, and then decide on the evidence I do hear, whether the case is proven." He turned to the prosecution and said, "Now, who speaks for the prosecution?"

Shelby shot to his feet. "I do, Your Honor."

"You may make a brief opening statement, outlining the charges and your case. And I hope you've been able to locate the meaning of the word 'brief" since we were last together."

"Yes, Your Honor, by all means." He cleared his throat and glanced briefly at the other table. "On or about December first, eighteen eighty-one, Mister Perry Madison willfully, and with malice aforethought, did take the life of U. S. Marshal Elbert Strong, in the jurisdiction of Taney County, Missouri. Mister Madison did then flee the county and was later apprehended in San Francisco. The state will show beyond reasonable doubt that Mister Madison was the only one with motive and opportunity to commit said dastardly crime.

"Marshal Strong had presented a subpoena to compel Mister Madison to accompany him to Washington where Mister Madison was to be presented with charges of embezzlement and treason."

"Objection!" shouted Frederick Kilgore, rising to his feet.

"Overruled," said Blackburn. "I think you know you can't object during an opening statement and I know why you're trying. Please do not interrupt again."

"Your Honor, I believe it is within my rights to object if prosecution attempts to inject unrelated evidence in opening statements."

"Duly noted. I'll not be influenced by it. Proceed, Mister Shelby."

"As I was saying," Shelby continued, "Mister Madison did not want to go, because he knew what was what. Instead, he talked Marshal Strong into waiting until the next morning to leave, placing him in a bunkhouse alone with food and a bottle of whisky.

"The next morning the whisky, the marshal, and the defendant, and both their horses and tack were gone. It was a dark night with heavy rain to wash away any tracks. It became evident that both the marshal and the defendant were missing. Several days later the marshal's body was found hidden in a brushy ravine, his head stove-in. Nigh a year later Mister Madison was located in San Francisco living under an assumed name, his appearance changed, and in a bigamous relationship with a second wife. That's all, Your Honor."

There was a loud rush of whispers in the courtroom with a rapping of the judge's gavel and his shout of "Order!" Then, "That was pretty brief, Mister Shelby. Much better. Now may I hear from the defense."

Frederick Kilgore rose to his feet and adjusted his coat. He faced toward the judge and began, "Your Honor, and gentlemen..." turning his head toward the audience, "we have heard quite a tale of wild speculation about Colonel Madison's activities, none of which prosecution will be able to prove, except for certain facts to which we will now stipulate. Colonel Madison did leave on the night in question and he did travel to California to begin a new phase of his life. As to any activities involving Marshal Strong, he has no knowledge of those events. When we present our case, logical explanations will be provided for Colonel Madison's activities and motivations. We will not be outlining our entire case in this opening statement, but we look forward to having all facts, and I emphasize *facts*, to be brought forth. Thank you, Your Honor."

Kilgore went to his table and sat down. Madison reached over and shook his hand.

"Prosecution, are you ready to present your case?" Blackburn said.

Shelby jumped up. "Yes, Your Honor."

"Then call your first witness."

"Prosecution calls Miss Margaret Madison."

Bobby Duke was ready, and opened a door at the back of the courtroom. Margaret entered and walked up the center aisle, glancing neither left nor right. She was wearing a long black dress with white lace collar, and her chestnut hair was swept up to a swirl of curls on top of her head. All eyes followed her, the only woman in the room, as she proceeded to the witness chair indicated by Shelby. Duff was waiting with a Bible in hand, and administered the oath.

"Now, Miss Madison," Shelby began, "I'm sorry you have to be here for this situation, but I must ask you a few questions."

He seemed to enjoy his role in the proceedings, and began with the usual "get-acquainted" questions—about her family, where she went to school, what she was now doing, and so forth, until he asked how many students she had in her school.

Frederick Kilgore shot to his feet. "Objection. Is there a chance we will eventually get to the point?"

"Sustained. I believe we were all thinking the same thing," Blackburn said. "Have you forgotten why we're here, Mister Shelby?"

Shelby flushed red, and said, "Sorry, Your Honor. Now, Miss Madison, were you present and aware that the marshal had arrived and requested your father accompany him to Washington?"

"Yes."

"Were you aware that both were gone the following morning?"

"Yes."

"When did you learn that something was not right with plans of the two men?"

"What do you mean?"

"Did the sheriff come to your house?"

"Oh, that. Yes, he and another sheriff and a man from the livery in Ozark came."

"What was the nature of their visit?"

Margaret paused. "As I recall, it was because the marshal's hired horse had not been returned. I believe they had also had a telegram from Washington asking about my father."

"What about him?"

"That he wasn't there yet."

"And when did you hear further that the marshal's body had been found?"

"Mmm...about two weeks later."

"Did you believe your father had something to do with his demise?"

"Objection!" shouted Fredrick Kilgore, rising to his feet.

"Withdrawn," said Shelby, looking pleased with himself. "No further questions."

"Cross, Mister Kilgore?" Blackburn said.

"Yes, Your Honor." Kilgore walked over to face Margaret. "Good morning, Miss Madison. Thank you for being here."

Margaret nodded.

"Was it unusual for your father to be summoned to Washington?"

"No, I wouldn't say so. He'd had a similar request two or three times before in the preceding months...and he was quite involved there during the War."

"And what was the nature of his business in Washington?"

"He didn't discuss his business with the rest of the family."

"I see. Was there anything unusual about this visit? Was there anything, looking back, that you could connect to the disappearance of Marshal Strong."

"No."

"Thank you, Miss Madison."

The judge looked over at Shelby, who shook his head. "You may step down, Miss Madison," he said. Then to Shelby, "Call your next witness."

A chair had been reserved for her behind the rail in back of the defendant's table. She remained the only woman in the room.

"Prosecution calls Madison's groom, Ike."

This time, Duke ushered in a slender black man with white hair. There was a stir among the spectators, drawing a rapping gavel. It was the first time any of those present had seen a person of color in a courtroom except as a defendant. Ike made his way down the aisle behind the deputy, looking uncomfortable, and took the witness chair as directed. When Duff asked for his last name, he said, "I don't rightly know I has one. I don' remember my first owner's name and then I was owned by mista Mad'son. Well...not owned, I reckon, but 'most the same thing. Now I work for Miss Mad'son."

Nathan Roach had listened intently to the testimony of Margaret Madison and now the colored man. Why did they allow him in here? Roach heard the prosecutor lead Ike through his recollection of that rainy December night; how Madison had first ordered the surrey for the following morning, then later changed his mind and said they would use the horses. Then there was a description of the missing horses and tack, and the judge let him go.

Roach was growing impatient to hear something important. It was a little more interesting when that hired hand was brought in to describe how he had seen buzzards circling and found the dead man. That prosecutor, named Shelby, drew out a lengthy description of the corpse and its surroundings. The judge don't look too happy about that, either, Roach thought. But that lawyer on the other side didn't do a damn thing.

At last, it seemed, the judge called a halt for a noon break. "We'll break for an hour and a half," he said. "For you out there in the court room, if you want to leave and keep your seat, we will issue a return ticket. It won't be good for tomorrow."

-32-
THE PLOT

Roach was among the many who left to find a toilet and some coffee or something stronger. Food was brought in for the prisoner and his lawyers, the deputies, the clerk, and the judge. While he was outside, he huddled away from the crowd with Clyde Harvey and Orville Perkins.

"How's it goin' in there?" Perkins said.

"Real slow. They ain't touched him yet. Just a bunch of yammerin'."

"Well, we'll be here when you come out," Harvey said.

"Yeah. Let the rest know."

Judge Blackburn rapped his gavel and said, "Court is back in session. Mister Shelby, call your next witness."

Sheriff Horton was admitted and sworn in. Shelby faced him and began. "Sheriff, I'd like to take you back to early December in Eighty-one. What was your first knowledge of the circumstances of this case? Please tell us what happened."

Horton smoothed his mustache with his right hand and began, "Well, it was like this...." He proceeded to outline the visit by the sheriff of Christian County and the Ozark stable owner, and the telegram from Washington. "Seemed the colonel didn't show.

"And when was this?"

"'Bout third or fourth of December, as I recollect."

"What did you do?"

"Well, we investigated, didn't find nuthin' right then, but later, as you know, that fella found the body."

"Thank you, Sheriff. No further questions," Shelby said.

"Cross, Mister Kilgore?"

"Yes, Your Honor." He strode over to face Horton. "Thank you, Sheriff. Now, according to testimony, Marshal Strong's whereabouts were unknown for about two weeks. Do you have any knowledge about what he was doing for that period of time?"

"Well, I reckon he was bein' dead for a good part of it." There was laughter in the courtroom, gaveled to silence by the judge.

"I fail to find it amusing," said Kilgore. "But can you say for certain when he died?"

"No, Sir."

"Then he could have spent up to several days attempting to track Colonel Madison when he discovered him missing the next morning. Correct?"

"Well, I...I...."

"Thank you, Sheriff. No further questions." Kilgore walked back to his seat.

Shelby had no redirect. Instead, he called his next witness, Doctor Stevenson.

Shelby approached. "Doctor, I'll get right to it. You examined the body of Marshal Strong. What was the cause of death?"

Stevenson described the cause of death as most likely a blow to the head with a hammer. Shelby attempted to elicit more specific details, but there was nothing of importance.

"Thank you. No further questions."

Doctor Stevenson started to rise, but the judge said, "Just a moment, Doctor. Defense?"

Fredrick Kilgore had already risen and walked over to the witness. "Doctor Stevenson," he said. "Was there anything distinctive about the wound that could be matched to a specific weapon?"

"Not that I could determine."

"Was there a search, to your knowledge, to find a specific weapon?"

"There was. The sheriff let me know that they would bring anything to me that they suspected was used."

"Did they?"

"No, Sir."

"Is it *possible* that a fall on a sharp object could cause such a wound?"

"Possible, but not likely."

"Was there anything about the wound that would tell you who might have done it?"

Doctor Stevenson looked nonplussed. "No, of course not."

"Doctor, how long before he was discovered did Marshal Strong die?"

"There's no way to know precisely, with all the changes in the weather and all. I'd guess one to two weeks."

"I see. Could have been one week, could have been two. Thank you, Doctor. No further questions."

"Redirect, Mister Shelby?" Blackburn said.

"Yes, Your Honor." He walked back over in front of the witness. "Now, Doctor Stevenson, we heard testimony by the man who found the body and he said the saddle was also found near the body. Is there any way a man suffering an accidental injury such as the one described could have unsaddled his horse and driven it away?"

"I would think not."

"No further questions."

"You may now step down, Doctor," Blackburn said. "Mister Shelby, you may now call your next witness."

Shelby, who had remained standing, said, "Prosecution calls Marshal Joshua Lambert."

Joshua Lambert was an imposing figure as he walked down the center aisle. He was tall, dressed in black with a new white shirt and black string tie. He now had a neatly trimmed black beard and the thin scar on the left side of his face added to his stern appearance. His badge winked out from behind his left coat lapel and he was armed, as marshals always tried to be. He glanced at Margaret as he walked by and she smiled at him.

Lambert was sworn in and gave his full name for the record, pointing out that he had no permanent address. He was approached by the man from Washington, Jacob Fortner, rather than Shelby.

"Marshal Lambert, rather than asking you a series of questions, I'd like for you to tell us in your own words, what your assignment was and how you went about fulfilling it."

Lambert looked over at the judge on his right, then out over the crowded courtroom. "Well, I'll try to keep this short. I got a telegram to come from the Territories to Springfield and get a new assignment to track down Mister Madison...." He proceeded to describe his travels to talk to anyone who knew the fugitive, and his speculation about where the man might have gone. He talked of telegrams, and wanted posters mailed, and finally a hit from New Orleans. When he talked of finding a man who, "said he'd seen horses and a man like—"

"Objection," said Kilgore, rising.

"Sustained," Blackburn said. "You can't quote what someone said to you, but I believe you will figure out another way to continue."

"Yes, Your Honor. Well, we were able to satisfy ourselves that it was a pretty sure bet that Madison had been there, based on the handbill and the horses."

"The horses?" Fortner asked.

"Yes. There was a black stallion and a sorrel mare involved. We found out this man was using the name Jefferson, and he'd booked passage on a steamer bound for Panama. That meant only one thing to me, that he was probably headed for San Francisco. It was a pretty big gamble, I guess, but it paid off. Rode a train all the way out there, and me and Marshal Bean dug our way through all the businesses we could find until we spotted him. He'd changed his name again and his appearance, but we arrested him and I brought him here."

Fortner was back in front of his witness. "Remarkable!" He said. "Quite some detective work."

Lambert shrugged.

"Have you found that fleeing a scene is a good indication of guilt?"

"Objection!" Kilgore said, rising. "If that's all we needed, courts would be unnecessary."

"Sustained."

"Let me rephrase. In all of your professional experience, when you captured fugitives, were more found guilty than those found innocent?"

Lambert thought. "Well, it's like this. I never really kept score, and I was often off on another assignment before they came to trial. I say probably more guilty than not."

"On your long train ride back from California, did he give any indication of his involvement with the death of Marshal Strong?"

"I believe I already told you we didn't discuss it."

Fortner colored slightly. "Uh...yes. No further questions."

Judge Blackburn said, "Before cross, we'll take a short recess. Fifteen minutes." He rapped his gavel, stood up, and left the room.

Madison turned to Frederick Kilgore. "What do you think? Are we all right?"

"I believe so. They've spent their entire case on proving that you left, which we have agreed to stipulate."

"One thing," said Charles Kilgore. "The sorrel mare bothers me. If they are able to convince the judge that it's the livery mare from Ozark; that would be a bad thing."

"No way they can do that." Madison said. "There are lots of sorrel mares. That was one I picked up down in Arkansas some place."

Blackburn returned, brought the court back to order and directed the defense to proceed with cross examination.

Frederick Kilgore faced Lambert and began. "I have just a couple of questions for you. So far, you have verified to what we have agreed to...that Colonel Madison left Taney County. I'm sure, with your experience, you know that to prove guilt beyond reasonable doubt, you must have some solid evidence connecting the accused to the crime. Did you discover such evidence?"

"Objection!" from Shelby.

"Overruled. Mister Fortner urged the witness to tell his story in his own words."

Lambert shifted in his chair. "Well...."

"Well, what?"

"Well, there was the horses."

"What about them?"

"The horses he left behind in New Orleans matched the description of the ones from here."

"In what way?"

"A black stallion and a sorrel mare."

"I see. Marshal Lambert, how many sorrel mares do you suppose there are in this vast country?"

There was a titter of laughter in the courtroom. The judge rapped his gavel and Shelby shouted, "Objection!"

"Never mind," Kilgore said. "I withdraw the question. And I have no further questions." He waked back to the defense table.

"Redirect, Mister Shelby?" Blackburn said.

"Yes, Your Honor." He walked over to face Lambert. "You are tracking down the horse in question, right?"

"Yes, Sir."

"Do you expect results soon?"

"We're making every effort."

Shelby turned toward the bench. "Your Honor, we request that a continuance be granted until the evidence can be produced."

Blackburn said, "I'm sorry, Mister Shelby, but unless you can give me a specific date and it isn't far away, I can't do that. Request denied. Are you finished with the witness?"

Shelby said he was, Lambert stepped down, and the judge asked, "Any more witnesses, since the horse isn't here?" There was another slight commotion, but the judge let it go.

"Co-counsel, Mister Jacob Fortner, has a document to present that addresses the character of the witness and a strong motive for the murder of Marshal Strong."

"We discussed this at arraignment and I deferred seeing any document until I was on the bench. Now, I wish for counsel on both sides to see me in chambers, while we decide on this."

Judge Blackburn, the four lawyers, and the clerk, Nathaniel Duff, were all crowded into the small room off the courtroom where the judge had a desk. "Now, we're off the record here, so I'll explain what I have to do. Since it's a bench trial, I will be acting as judge while I examine the document. I'll rule on whether the 'jury', which is also me, should see the contents of it. If I rule it inadmissible I will not consider it in reaching a verdict."

"Your Honor, how is that possible? It's like un-ringing a bell!" said the senior Kilgore.

Blackburn stared at him for a moment. "It's possible because I am a man of integrity with a long history and understanding of the law."

Jacob Fortner spoke. "Your Honor, I believe that this document provides a strong motive for murder."

"We'll see. Now give me a few moments to read it."

Blackburn took the paper, perched a pince-nez on his nose, and began to read. The rest remained silent.

Finally, he looked up and stared at the wall over their heads. "This is an affidavit signed and sealed by an inspector general accusing Mister Madison of embezzling money during the War. Tell me, Mister Fortner, what it has to do with a murder in Taney County?"

"It seems obvious that Mister Madison did not wish to go back and face charges."

"Mister Kilgore?"

"I don't believe it is obvious at all. Colonel Madison had willingly gone back twice before. Was he told that he was being accused? We don't know. Did he have other reasons for leaving? He did. Would he have resorted to murder, or would he simply have left with the heavy rains covering his tracks? With a head start, that marshal would have had just as much trouble finding him as Marshal Lambert did some time later. I believe this is prejudicial against his character and should be excluded."

"Here's the thing," Blackburn began. "If they intended to press charges against Mister Madison, why did they bring a subpoena instead of placing him under arrest? I suppose we'll not be able to determine the answer to that question. And this accusation is merely that at this point. If we were to adjudicate the validity of this accusation here in this court, it would be necessary for the signatories of this document be produced for cross examination by the defense. And I assume they are not here, Mister Fortner?"

Fortner looked down at his hands, and replied, "No, Your Honor."

"Well, gentlemen, I will not have this document read into the record. Let's get back into the courtroom."

Judge Blackburn gaveled the court to order. "We have before us a request by the prosecution to admit a document from Washington concerning the accused. I have examined the document and decided it is not admissible. Now, Mister Shelby, do you have further witnesses?"

"I do not, Your Honor. Prosecution rests."

Blackburn said, "It's been a long day. We'll adjourn until tomorrow morning at nine o'clock. At that time we will hear from the defense. Court is adjourned."

-33-

THE DEFENSE

There was a big rush for the exits as reporters dashed to telegraph their stories, and all the rest rushed to tell their stories to those outside. Roach ran down the board sidewalk to a saloon down the street where Harvey, Perkins, and two others were waiting.

"Well, how'd it go?" Clyde Harvey said.

"Not good," Nathan Roach said. "I ain't no lawyer, but they just don't seem to have anything to really get him."

"What happens next?" said Preston Stewart.

"Well, I reckon the dee-fence has their turn," Roach said.

"You gonna' be there?" Orville Perkins said.

"Look, I'm about dead," said Roach. "Can anybody else cover it? I've gotta go check on the livestock. My maw is gettin' old, and she can't do it."

"I will," Perkins said.

"You better get there early, Perk, like 3:00 in the mornin', and wear everything you own. At least it ain't rainin' no more."

"I'll do it. I been up all night coon huntin' before. It'll be easy."

Judge Blackburn called the court into session the next morning promptly at nine o'clock, by the gold pocket watch he pulled from beneath his robe. The courtroom was full to capacity again, including Orville Perkins in a front row, and the only woman again, Margaret Madison.

"Is defense ready?"

Frederick Kilgore rose. "Yes, Your Honor." He walked over in front of the bench, half facing the judge. "So far, we've been listening to the prosecution attempt to make a case against my client. As we have all seen, they have presented nothing that ties my client to the unfortunate demise of Marshal Strong. They have merely provided testimony to confirm what we have agreed to: that Colonel Madison chose an opportune time to depart Taney County. In light of this lack of evidence, I petition the court to dismiss."

Judge Blackburn rubbed his chin and looked over the heads of those seated in the courtroom. "I hear you, but we've come this far, and quite rapidly, I must say. I believe we should hear more about your side of the case. Are you ready to call your first witness?"

"Thank you, Your Honor. I have listed only two possible witnesses, and I think it's only proper that I ask Miss Madison to leave the courtroom until, and if, she is called to testify."

"So be it," Blackburn said. "Miss Madison, if you please?"

Margaret looked surprised, but rose and walked up the aisle and out the rear door.

"Defense calls Colonel Madison." There was a stir in the courtroom. Accused were often held back to keep them away from the prosecution's cross examination.

Madison rose and walked forward, stepping around the rail and standing beside the witness chair to be sworn in. Then he took his seat.

"Please state your full name and address for the record," Duff said.

"Colonel Reginald Perry Madison. I currently have no address."

Kilgore approached. "Colonel Madison, did you kill Marshal Strong?"

"I did not."

"Did you leave Taney County on the night in question, travel to New Orleans, and thence to San Francisco?"

"I did."

"What were your reasons for leaving?"

"I'd been thinking of it for some time. I'd sunk a lot of money into the farm, but it wasn't paying off. I'm better at conducting commerce. My wife had developed confusion of the mind, and we were estranged and incompatible. My daughter had defied my orders to go back east and continue her education. And finally, I was being summoned to Washington for the third time to sit in endless congressional hearings about the past. It just seemed like the perfect time to head out."

"Colonel Madison, did you realize it is breaking the law to ignore a subpoena?"

"Yes, I did. I acknowledge it was less than honorable but I didn't think it was a big crime—missing a meeting in Washington."

"Did you have any inkling that it might be more serious than attending a meeting?"

"No. It was just a simple summons to travel all the way there, just like the other two times."

Kilgore glanced up at the judge. "I have no further questions."

Blackburn looked over toward the prosecution table. "Mister Shelby?"

This time it was Jacob Fortner who rose and walked across the room to face Madison. "Mister Madison, my name is Jacob Fortner. I have a few questions."

Madison stared back at him.

"If you did not kill Marshal Strong that night, who did?"

"Objection!" Kilgore said. "I assume procedures in Washington are similar to those we primitive people out here abide by."

"Sustained."

"Let me re-phrase. Do you agree that it is a remarkable coincidence that he shows up dead the same night you left?"

"I have no opinion on that. And I'm told he was not found dead until sometime later."

"Do you have any explanation for how that might have happened?"

"How what might have happened? Finding him?

'No, his being dead."

"No, I do not."

"Did you commit bigamy by marrying a second wife in San Francisco?"

"No, I did not. I met a widow who had a child, but we did not marry."

"How did you finance the large property you purchased here?"

"Some inheritance; savings from my military salary; and wise investments."

"Mister Madison, how about the business in San Francisco?

"I'd saved some back from the property here, and I was able to assume loans on a distressed business."

"Did you embezzle money, take kick-backs, and so forth, when you were involved in military procurement?"

"Objection!" shouted Kilgore, on his feet. "Relevance. May we stick to the case at hand?"

"Are you going someplace with this, Mister Fortner?" Blackburn said.

"It goes to motive," said Fortner. "Facing charges for past misdeeds would be a powerful motive for murder."

"I'll over-rule. Mister Madison, you may answer."

"No," said Madison, calmly.

Fortner, looking frustrated, said, "No further questions."

"Re-direct, Mister Kilgore?" Blackburn said.

"Just one item," said Kilgore, walking over to face Madison. "Prosecution seems fixated on the request for you to come to Washington again. Did you have any reason to believe you were about to face indictment?"

"No, I did not. It was just like prior subpoenas."

"Thank you, Colonel Madison. No further questions."

Blackburn told Madison he could step down, then asked, "Any more defense witnesses, Mister Kilgore?"

"Defense calls Miss Margaret Madison."

There was a delay while Margaret was located and brought back into the courtroom. After she was reminded of her swearing-in and seated, Kilgore approached her. "Miss Madison, I'm sorry for the circumstances that bring us here, and I apologize for the subject of my questions."

"It's all right," Margaret replied. "What must be, must be."

"Your father testified that one of the reasons for his leaving was the breakup of your family relationships. Will you address that subject?"

Margaret looked down for a moment, then raised her eyes to look directly at Kilgore. "It's true that things weren't going smoothly. I'd made my father unhappy with me by staying here instead of resuming my studies to be a high society lady back East."

She paused, then continued. "My mother, God bless her, was very unhappy living here, and had begun to lose touch with reality. She's now being cared for by her sister in New York, and is diagnosed as being not of sound mind. It pains me to talk of such things in public."

"Again, I apologize," said Kilgore. "No further questions."

"Cross, Mister Shelby?"

Remember his prior direct questioning of her, he said, "No, Your Honor."

Kilgore rose. "Defense rests, Your Honor."

"We will take closing arguments tomorrow morning at nine o'clock," Blackburn said. "Court is adjourned."

Again there was a dash for the exits, men pushing and struggling to crowd through the doors. Madison turned to his daughter behind him. "Margaret, I'm sorry for putting you through this, and I regret our past differences. As time had passed, I've come to realize that you have the right to be your own person. So, whatever you do, I hope you have a happy life."

The deputies led him away before he could say more, but Margaret was puzzled by the tone of his comments, so uncharacteristic. It almost sounds as though he's saying farewell.

As soon as Madison was led away, Marshal Lambert appeared beside her. "May I escort you out?" he said. "Perhaps you'll take supper with me?"

Margaret hesitated, then said, "Thank you, Joshua, but I don't think I should. In spite of your kindness to me, I don't think it would look right. I get the feeling that sentiment of the whole community, except for his lawyers, is against my father. I believe I should avoid seeming to be against him also."

"Well, I'm disappointed," Lambert said, "but I reckon I understand. I'll still see you out; make sure you're safe from the mob."

Margaret smiled, "I thank you for that."

Margaret went back to her room in the rooming house. True to his word, Lambert had protected her through the mob of reporters outside, and down the street to the rooming house where they were both staying. They made a point of separating in the lobby so that no one could get the wrong idea. Margaret regretted she had to make the decision not to accompany him in the evening. She felt very much alone, away from her home and away from her students. She missed them and she missed Etta. Professor Phillips had substituted for her in the school. And there was George to think about. She appreciated his apologies, but she was having trouble leaving behind her disappointment over their separation these past months. Then there was also Joshua Lambert. Was he looking after her in his professional capacity, or was he interested on a personal level? She yearned for the trial to be over, but was fearful of a guilty verdict, which would surely mean a hanging. Even if her father was acquitted, Lambert had orders to take him to Washington...but those were not capital charges...at least she thought not. Life has become so complicated! She ordered a meal to be brought to her room.

The sun had been out the last two days, and most of the ice had melted in temperatures above freezing during the afternoons. However, the melt would re-freeze during nighttime lows, making early mornings treacherous in places.

Back on Bull Creek, Benjamin Archer had ventured out on the afternoon of the second day of the trial, and was able to pick up a copy of the *Forsyth Beacon* at Guthrie's store where he had gone for supplies.

At the supper table that evening, Ben, Anna, and Jürgen talked of the trial, sensationalized by the reporters. Anna and Ben were able to add details of talk in the community when the body of the marshal had been discovered. Jürgen had known Madison only through his encounter when he placed Anna in service with him.

"Again, I am sorry for placing you in his household," he said. "I did not know how he was."

"It's all right," said Anna. "He was not a nice man, but according to the paper, they don't seem to think they have proved he did the murder."

Anna heaved herself up from the table to clear the dishes, thinking to herself how wonderful it would be to have her normal body back, and also the thrill of a new baby in the household. As she maneuvered her unwieldy self about, she thought of that apt phrase from the Bible that she heard recently at the Christmas program, "...*Mary, his espoused wife, being great with child....*" Such a good description of her own state of being!

ROGER MEADOWS

-34-

THE CLOSING

Court was called to order on schedule. Weather had warmed enough that the ice was gone except for a few spots in deep shade. Roach was back on duty, one of the first to claim a seat. This would be it. One or the other of them lawyers would get the judge to take his side.

At Bobby Joe Duke's command, the adversaries and everyone else in the room rose. Judge Blackburn strode in, his black robe rustling, and said, "Take your seats!" He did also, pounding his gavel and announcing, "Court is in session. Now, let's get down to business. Mister Shelby, are you prepared to give your closing statement?"

Shelby jumped to attention. "Yes, Your Honor." He had an easel set up between the prosecution table and the judge's bench, where the judge, the defense, and half the courtroom could see the large chart he placed on it.

"This is not a complicated case," he began, using a pointer. "I have here a timeline of the sequence that led to the death of Marshal Strong. All of you have heard the testimony, so I will not repeat what was said. But this chart will remind you of that testimony and show that the only reasonable explanation of the marshal's death is that it was at the hands of Mister Madison...." He stepped slowly through the arrival of the marshal, the ordering of the surrey, the countermanding of that order, the whiskey, the disappearance of both men, the visit by the sheriffs to the residence, and the discovery of the body.

"This is a compelling sequence that illustrates the mindset of premeditated murder. He cancelled the surrey when his mind was made up to eliminate his problem with the marshal. The whiskey was part of the diabolical plan; making it easier to dispatch him in the darkness of that rainy night.

"And so, Your Honor, and fellow citizens, knowing this sequence and the mindset of the accused at that time, this would have been the greatest coincidence of all time if his departure and the marshal's death would have occurred at the same time. Therefore, Your Honor, I ask for a finding of guilty of premeditated murder beyond reasonable doubt."

There was a buzz of whispers and a stirring and rustling in the courtroom. Blackburn rapped his gavel and called for order. "Thank you, Mister Shelby." He turned to the defense table. "Are you ready to go, Mister Kilgore?"

Frederick Kilgore rose and began to walk to the center of the courtroom. "Yes, Your Honor." He adjusted his blue serge coat and shot the cuffs of his starched white shirt. He paused and looked out over the spectators, then half-turned to the judge. He spread his hands for emphasis. "I have no notes or charts, because this is a very simple case. As you listened to testimony, you did not hear one thing—not one single witness or piece of evidence—connecting Colonel Madison to the unfortunate death of Marshal Strong. We do not know what happened in those days after Colonel Madison left. As Colonel Madison testified, he had been thinking of leaving for some time for the reasons we have shown you. His reasons were supported by the testimony of his daughter.

"The marshal's subpoena, the third summons to attend a meeting, was a motivating factor to go ahead and do it. You have all had something you needed to do and kept putting it off until something triggered the decision to go ahead and do it—like fixing that fence that you kept putting off until your cattle got out.

"In this case, you may *suspect*, you may *think* you know, but in our system of jurisprudence, you must have *proof beyond reasonable* doubt. In this case, that proof is missing. Therefore, the only reasonable finding is *Not Guilty!* Thank you, citizens, and thank you, Your Honor."

Kilgore was gratified to see some almost imperceptible nodding of heads at his last example, but he had no idea what the judge was thinking as he sat behind the bench with a face of granite. He took his seat beside Madison, who shook his hand.

Blackburn turned to the prosecution table. "Mister Shelby, rebuttal?"

Shelby stood, "No, Your Honor, except to state again that I do not believe such a coincidence as they claim, could have taken place."

"Very well. That ends presentation of the case by both sides. I will retire to chambers and review all of the testimony and reach a decision. It will take a little while for me to do that, and this morning's session will be transcribed by Mister Duff from his shorthand while I do that review. So we will adjourn until sometime this afternoon. You may remain here or secure a pass from the guards for your return. Court is in recess."

With his rap of the gavel, the rush for the exits began.

Nathan Roach huddled with four others down the street at the saloon. Clyde Harvey, Orville Perkins, Preston Stewart, and Jericho Ellis were all well-lubricated with cheap whiskey they had been drinking all morning. "Well," Ellis, a newcomer, said. "Which way is it a-goin'?"

"He's guilty as hell," Roach said, "but I'd bet 'most anything that that judge won't find him guilty because of all the silly rules they have."

"What are we gonna do about it?" said Perkins. "You know how they keep lettin' 'em off 'round here."

Roach said, "If it goes the way I think, plan on a late night and get the rest of the boys together. Better start on it now. We need about a dozen. We can do it like we talked about."

Some reporters stayed in their seats, consolidating their notes. Some wrote two alternative news flashes to save time when the decision came in. Margaret retired to her room to wait in anxiety, hurrying past shouting reporters. Marshal Lambert waited for a time in his seat, later going for a meal at Mabel's. The expanded population of Forsyth waited.

At precisely three o'clock in the afternoon, church bells in the center of town began ringing. Since it was not on Sunday morning, it was known by all the population that something big was happening, such as a fire, some calamity, or a need to assemble. In this case, they knew that a verdict had been reached and all flocked toward the courthouse.

Lambert caught up with Margaret, both hurrying up the boardwalk. "Margaret, have you made plans for what happens after the verdict?"

"I know it could go either way," she replied, her face drawn. "Either way, I want to leave this place as soon as possible and go back to Bull Creek. The only difference will be in what I say to my father."

"Either way, will you allow me to escort you safely back there?"

"Won't you be needed here?"

"In one case, I'll telegraph for transportation to Springfield, and the other not, but I will have some time in either case."

By this time they were at the door of the courthouse, and Margaret said, simply, "yes."

The courtroom was soon filled, everyone in place, and they rose for Judge Blackburn to take his place and announce, "Court will come to order. You may take your seats."

-35-

THE VERDICT

I have reached a verdict," the judge announced. "There will be no outbursts or demonstrations within these walls or outside, or perpetrators will be arrested. "In keeping with the law of the land, which calls for a guilty verdict to be rendered in murder cases *beyond a reasonable doubt*, I find the defendant, Reginald Perry Madison, *not guilty*."

Despite the judge's instructions, there was an outcry among the spectators and a stampede for the exits. Deputies couldn't arrest them all, so they arrested none, as the judge banged uselessly on the block. Madison rose and raised both fists in the air. He turned to Margaret, who leaned over the rail to embrace him. "Congratulations, Father," she said.

"Thank you, Margaret," he replied. "It isn't over yet, of course." He was surrounded by three deputies, ready to take him away.

She spoke after him, "I have to go back home tonight, but I'll come back and see you before you go."

Both the prosecutors and defense counsels followed the judge out the back door behind the bench. He looked over his shoulder and said, "Come on back. I expect you have some things to say to me, and I'll listen."

When they were in his office, he proceeded to take off his robe and hand it to Duff before he sat down. "All right, let's hear it. Mister Shelby you can go first, and to all of you, nothing said here goes outside this room."

Shelby, red-faced, sputtered, "*Sir,* uh, Your Honor, you *must* know that man is guilty!"

Blackburn wagged his head from side to side. "Might well be, and it pains me to say it, but you didn't *prove* he was guilty. I agree with the defense that I did not hear a single, solitary thing I could use to hang a guilty verdict on him. You can have the whole population *think* someone is guilty but law requires more."

"But, but—", he began, but he was interrupted by Jacob Fortner.

"He's correct," Fortner said. "I was afraid it would go this way. If the marshals had been able to have that witness here from New Orleans, along with the sorrel mare, or a witness to what happened in the middle of that night, it would have been different. Don't worry, though, he will face a severe trial when we get him to Washington."

By the time Margaret made it through the shouting crowd outside, again protected by Lambert, she saw her horse and buggy coming down the street, trailing the marshal's horse. During the recess, Lambert had paid both bills and arranged for a stable hand to fetch them as soon as they heard the court had reconvened.

Margaret tried to answer some questions, but soon found that all were negative, trying to get her to admit that he should have been found guilty. As they walked up the boardwalk to get into her buggy, she said, "You're amazing. Thank you."

"I've been through this kind of thing before. We'll grab our stuff and get out of here."

Lambert skillfully navigated through the crowded street as the show was over and all the weary spectators were in a hurry to leave. There was a considerable amount of shouting, cursing, cracking of whips, and occasional bumping of wagon and buggy hubs. Eventually, they cleared the outskirts of town. They settled in for the long ride, silent at first with their thoughts about what had just happened.

After a few miles of almost silence, Lambert said, "I know you've been thinking about what just took place. I reckon you're happy about the way it came out."

Margaret said to him, and almost to herself, speaking softly. "I never wanted to see him guilty, with a public hanging. He *is* my father, after all. But just between us...I think he did it. There should be some way the books, as it were, would be balanced...maybe that trial coming up in Washington."

"I'll keep your confidence, of course. I try not to judge, just do my job and bring them in. But I think you may be right. From what I hear, he does have to face some pretty serious charges."

"My father was always the person who dictated everything in our family. He was very angry with me. And my mother was never happy here, as I said in the trial. Maybe it was one reason she lost touch with reality. I guess we don't understand those things...."

They rode on, talking of other things—the break in the weather; her desire to see her school children again; getting back to a normal life. He spoke of his upcoming journey with some dread. "This has been my longest assignment," he said. "Most of the time I'm working in a given territory I'm assigned to, and usually a few days for each case."

As the day was drawing to a close and they drew nearer to Sycamore, he shifted in his seat, cleared his throat, and turned to her, "Miss Margaret, may I be so bold as to ask a personal question?"

She looked back at him. "I suppose so, depending on how personal." She was amused to see this tough-looking man, with the battle scars, look bashful.

"Well, uh...I was wondering if there's any chance that we could...be...that I could call on you, if you know what I mean. Not because of the law or the way we've been up 'til now."

Margaret smiled at him. "I'm flattered that you would ask. You've been such a comfort to me in this bad time. I...I...just don't know what to say. You see, there was someone that I thought would—"

"The blacksmith?"

"Yes."

"He seemed a good man."

"He is. I don't know why I'm telling you this. I guess because I trust you. He wanted to start a business and make something more of himself, as he tried to explain, to be 'more worthy.'"

"I can understand that. I feel the same way. You're good lookin', you're educated, and you're nice besides."

Now Margaret was embarrassed. "You're sticking up for him?"

Lambert smiled at her. "Call me a fool, I guess, but if you really loved him...."

"Well," Margaret said, "I'm all confused about what I think right now. Give me some time until we get this behind us. You have this long journey to Washington—"

"I understand. Long term, I'd like to settle down, maybe run for sheriff someplace; be able to stay in one spot."

"Sounds like a good thing."

Darkness had begun to fall and with it a drop in temperature as they reached Sycamore. There was a light on in Olaf Jensen's house. They stopped in front and Lambert went to the door to see if they had a place for him to spend the night. Margaret saw Oley come to the door and there was nodding of heads, and Lambert headed back to the buggy. Oley waved his hand to her.

"We're all set. I'll see you home, then come back."

"You don't have to do that. I'll be all right."

"Naw, wouldn't be proper."

In a short time, they reached Margaret's home. Etta must have heard them coming, and she came running out the door and down the steps, despite her advancing age. As Lambert handed

Margaret out of the buggy, Etta rushed to embrace her. "Lord have mercy, child!" she said. "I been yearnin' to have you home!"

"Me, too, dear Etta. I missed you." Then she turned to Lambert and rose on tiptoe to kiss him on the cheek, that left cheek with the scar. "Joshua, thank you for taking care of me. God be with you on your journey."

"Thank you, Margaret. My pleasure. No matter what, I hope we can meet again."

With that, he mounted his horse and rode into the night. Ike came to put the buggy away and Margaret and Etta went into the warmth and light of the cabin.

-36-

THE BREAKOUT

Twelve men gathered in a grove of trees on the outskirts of Forsyth. Frost was beginning to form on the ground and their horses puffed clouds of condensate into the chill night air. It was after midnight of the day the verdict had been delivered in the trial of Perry Madison. The moon was still casting some light, but was beginning to set in the treetops to the west.

The men gathered in a tight circle and spoke in low voices. Nathan Roach began to review what they were about to do. "You all know what we're about. That man is guilty and we all know it. So let's go over it again. We'll wait until pitch dark, maybe about two more hours. We'll lead the horses into the clearing behind the jail. Keep 'em close and be ready to pinch off any noise they might start to make. Jericho, you and Ed will hold them and wait for us. Clyde, did you put the log back there?"

"I did."

"Now this is real important: *No talkin'!* Natcherly, no names, but people can know your voice. Wear gloves so they cain't see your hands. We don't aim to shoot anybody. The idea is, when we bust in there, we'll catch 'em by surprise and tie 'em up. They's keys to unlock the cell. Get ropes and gags ready. And make sure your mask is tight. Any questions?"

"What if they're able to pull a gun?"

"Do what you have to do, but hope that won't happen. We don't want the noise, but if you have to, try not to shoot to kill. The deputies ain't guilty."

There was a thick layer of leaves on the ground among the trees, so they posted two of their number and the rest sat with their backs against trees, dozing as they waited. At last Roach walked among them whispering that it was time to go. The moon had gone down and a thin cloud layer obscured most of the starlight. As silently as ghosts, they crept out of the trees and up the alley behind the buildings until they came to the clearing behind the jail. The town was in almost absolute darkness, with only a few dim lights showing in upper stories. A dog barked somewhere, but not at a level to sound an alarm.

When they were at last in position, the two men took the reins of the thirteen horses, in two separate groupings. The rest of the men, four equipped with sawed-off shotguns, six with holstered sidearms, walked up the side of the sheriff's office, which also housed the jail. Six of the men carried an eight-foot length of tree trunk, much as pallbearers carry a coffin. All were wearing masks fashioned from bandannas. They paused when they reached the boardwalk. The street was clear, in total darkness, totally deserted. They moved into the street and noted dim lights shining through the curtains on the window of the office.

The six men with the log lined it up with the front door with two shotgun bearers on each side. From six feet away, one of them whispered, "On the count of three. Now, one…two…three, go!"

The log hit the door at latch height and the door crashed open, the men staggering and dropping the log as they struggled to regain their footing as they charged into the room. The four others were right behind them.

Jake Sloan and one of the temporary deputies were seated at a table playing checkers. *"What the hell!"* Jake yelled as they both leaped to their feet reaching for their guns. It was too late.

They were immediately overpowered and disarmed. They were gagged just as quickly and lashed to their chairs.

Roach cast about for keys, searching desk drawers, finally finding a ring of keys on a peg behind the door to the sheriff's office.

As he opened the door to the hall leading to the jail cells, he heard a shout, *"Hey! What's going on out there?"*

He ran down the hall with two men with shotguns right behind him. There was Madison, peering through the bars of his cell. One of the men rushed to point the shotgun at his face, holding a finger to his mask where his lips would be.

"What are you doing?" Madison said.

No one spoke. Roach went through the keys until he found the right one. Two more men came down the hall and pinned Madison's arms behind him and at the same time tied a gag around his mouth. They half-carried, half-dragged him down the hall and into the front office area. The two deputies' eyes were wide as they saw what was happening.

All of the men quietly carried their captive out the front door and down between the buildings to the back lot. They tied Madison on the extra horse, all mounted, and they rode away into the darkness. They followed the back outskirts of the town and on into the wooded hills to the west. From the breaching of the front door to their departure, the operation took less than fifteen minutes.

Joshua Lambert rode along the wagon track southwest of Sycamore at a fast walk on his hired sorrel mare. He'd had a good sleep and was well-fed by Maybelle, Oley Jensen's wife. The sun was clearing the treetops behind him, and he felt good. Shapin' up to be pretty warm for January. Good to daydream about Margaret. Had to face the fact that it probably wasn't going anywhere, but pleasant to think about it. Glad to get that trial over with and get that man to Washington and be shed of him.

He heard the sound of hoof-beats ahead of him. Somebody comin' at a fast pace up ahead around the bend.

Subconsciously, he eased the tail of his coat clear of his Colt before the rider burst into view. He recognized the sheriff's deputy, the one called Bobby Joe Duke.

Duke reined his horse to a stop, almost colliding with Lambert's horse, clumps of dirt flying in the air. *"You've gotta come quick!"* he shouted. *"They've got him!"*

"Madison?"

Bobby Joe turned his horse around beside Lambert's. The horse was blowing hard and lathered with sweat.

"They broke in right in the middle of last night and took Madison!"

"They who?"

"We don't know, but they was maybe a dozen. Sheriff's gettin' a bunch together to follow 'em. Lotta tracks headed west."

"Anybody hurt?"

"No. Happened so fast, they couldn't even get a gun out. Was Jake and another guy. They tied 'em up and they didn't get loose 'til almost daylight this mornin'."

By this time, they were both headed toward Forsyth, so Lambert said, "I'm goin' on ahead. You better come at a slower pace and not kill your horse. I'll get there as fast as I can."

Later, when Lambert came charging into Forsyth from the east, he saw a group of riders coming toward him from the west. As they drew closer together, he saw Sheriff Horton at the head of the group. When they were close enough, Lambert shouted, "Did you find them?"

"We found *him*, but we didn't find *them*." They reined to a halt as they drew close. Lambert saw a man's body draped over the saddle of one of the horses, a man astraddle behind the saddle.

"Oh, *hell*," Lambert said. *"Damnation!* I should've been here. I should've thought to put more guards on him."

"Don't blame yourself," Horton said. "I've been second-guessin' myself all mornin'. Don't do no good. I just thank the Lord nobody got shot when they broke in."

"Where'd you find him?"

"'Bout a mile up in the woods, hangin' from a' oak tree."

"Any chance of catchin' them?"

"We'll try, but I doubt it. Looked like they split up and doubled back. All the roads are all tore up from the crowds that was here. Be hard to sort out the tracks, but we'll try."

"Well, we'd better get the body taken care of...and Sheriff? Somebody needs to tell the daughter before she hears it. If you don't need me, I'll do it."

"Go ahead. I'll tell that fancy lawyer from Washington what happened and he can send a telegram."

"I'll get a fresh horse and head right back."

Some hours later, Lambert was again nearing the ford below Sycamore. He was riding a chestnut gelding this time, not the sorrel mare that had brought back thoughts of the trial. The horse was long-legged and a good traveler, so it was just late afternoon, the sun still fairly high in the west. He tried to remember what day of the week it was. Thursday...or Friday? Based on what she said about her school, I'll probably find her there. How the hell am I going to do this? Wonder if I should find some woman to stand by...or the blacksmith? His mother? Margaret's bound to know her. No, she's pretty strong. I'll just go for it and let her tell me what she needs.

He rode up the dirt road, right past the mill, the general store, and the blacksmith shop with its attached buggy shop. A couple of idlers on the store's porch hollered a "good afternoon," and waved. George...that was his name...raised up from his work on a buggy wheel...and stared, then waved his hand.

The school was all closed up with the still cool weather. He dismounted and tied his horse to a rail out front. As he climbed the steps, he thought, I don't look forward to this. He knocked on the door.

Margaret had just finished organizing the last hour of the day and all of the students were busy again, or at least pretending to be. A couple of the older girls were in a corner listening to first graders working their way through their reading. One of the older boys was dusting erasers on the back steps. Margaret heard the firm rapping on the front entrance and made her way to the door. She leaned forward and peeked through the peephole. *Joshua!*

She quickly slid the bolt and there he stood, a grim look on his face.

"Joshua? What is it?"

"I'm so sorry, Margaret. I have bad news."

"It's Father, isn't it?"

He nodded. "They took him in the middle of the night. They...they—"

"You needn't go on. A lynching, right?"

"I'm afraid so." She looked so beautiful standing there, looking up at him, and he could see the faces of her students up the aisle behind her, staring in his direction. "Look, can we go someplace to talk? Would it be all right to let the kids go? Tell me what I can do."

-37-

THE HILLSIDE

George Zinn had seen the marshal ride by. Seemed in a hurry as he rode up to the schoolhouse. Then Margaret appeared and they talked. What's going on? Her pa's trial is over and he was let off. I'd have thought the marshal would be gone, taking the colonel to Washington, if the newspaper was right.

Margaret disappeared back into the school, and right away the kids were all coming out behind her. A little early for school to let out. Wait! Now him and Margaret are headin' over here.

George stood in front of his shop as they approached. When they drew closer, Margaret said, "George, may we have a word with you?"

"Of course. Come and sit." He indicated the facing benches. How'd do, Marshal." They shook hands.

Before she sat, Margaret surprised him by giving him a hug. George could see a look of worry on her face.

"George, a mob took my father out of the jail last night and lynched him."

"*What?* How could such a thing happen?" He looked at Lambert.

"Bad judgement on my part and on the sheriff's part. We just failed to expect it. We had two deputies on duty, but the mob was well organized. They busted the door and were on them before they could react. I feel terrible about it."

"There's been some of that vigilante stuff going on, but not on things that serious," George said. "What a thing to happen! What can I do, Margaret?"

"My head's been buzzing since I heard. You know he and I weren't close, but I'm the one who will have to bury him."

"Let me...and the Marshal...help. I'm sure he will."

Lambert nodded.

"Where do you want him buried?"

Margaret looked up at the hillside across the way, and pointed. "Up there, I guess. He doesn't have any family back east that I know of, beyond immediate. Mother wouldn't know anything."

"All right. If we can get the body prepared in Forsyth, I'll take the wagon and go get it. We can tell Oley and he can get things going here. Funeral?"

"I don't think so. We'll see if he can say a few words at the grave, but I can't see any community outreach, knowing what they thought of him."

"You may be surprised, Margaret. Not because of him, but for you." George said.

Margaret looked at him. "You remember how we first met?"

"Of course I do. The burying of Anna's mother."

Margaret said to Lambert, "My father forbid me to mix with the local population, but when I heard of the tragedy of this woman's death, I sneaked out when he was gone, and joined the rest of the community. Of course I didn't know anyone, including Anna. By chance, I was standing behind George and his father, and when that large gathering started to sing together, *Amazing Grace*, it was a most moving experience.

"It started to rain, and George helped me catch a ride with the Archers, and the oldest son, Ben, drove me up across the flooding creeks until I could reach home."

Margaret paused and both men were silent, sensing her emotion. She wiped away a tear with her finger. "Amazing, the circle of life," she said. "I first saw Anna grieving beside her mother's grave; I met George; and Ben, Anna's future husband, helped me home. And it's all entwined with the domineering nature of my father, who will eternally rest on that same hillside. Amazing."

"It *is* amazing," Lambert said, feeling more outside the circle than before. He continued, "I have to go back to Forsyth. I'll get there late tonight and start things moving first thing in the morning."

"Good," said George. "I'll talk to Oley...unless you want to, Margaret...then maybe I can let Tom Archer know. He can spread the word, help with the grave. I'll head to Forsyth early in the morning."

Margaret said, "Thank you George, and Joshua. I have to tell Anna myself, so I'll go right home and leave in the buggy to see her and Ben. Oh, and I'll notify Professor Phillips."

Twilight was falling as Anna looked out the window to see if Ben and her pa were through with the milking. She had a big pot of vegetable and meatball soup simmering on the stove and cornbread in the oven. Eva was by the fireplace talking with her rag doll. Anna didn't see Ben at the moment, but movement down toward the creek caught her eye, a horse and buggy approaching at a fast trot.

She was surprised to see it was Margaret, so she grabbed a shawl off a peg by the door and went out on the porch. If not for the ponderous change in her body, she would have bounded down the steps. As Margaret stepped down, she shouted, "Margaret! It's so good to see you! Come in!"

Margaret hurried to the steps and up on the porch to embrace Anna, "My goodness, Love, it's good to see you looking so motherly!"

"I am *that*," Anna said. "It won't be long. I'm so surprised to see you, but I've missed you so." She led Margaret inside. "You're just in time for supper."

"I'm sorry. I didn't even think of the time. I'll explain...."

Eva came running and Margaret scooped her up and hugged her. "Hey, sweet girl."

Eva put her arms around Margaret's neck and said, "I love you, Auntie Margaret!"

"I love you too, Sweetie. Let me put you down a minute and talk to your mother, then you and I can talk some more."

She saw the puzzled expression on Anna's face and knew she must explain. "Anna, I came to tell you what has happened. My father is no longer alive. He was taken out of the jail in the middle of the night and lynched by a mob."

Anna raised her hand to cover her mouth. "Oh, my! I'm so sorry!" She reached to embrace Margaret. "What a shock it must be!"

"It was…at first. But when I think of the life he led, as you well know, maybe I shouldn't be too surprised."

At that moment, Ben and Jürgen entered the front door. Ben crossed to Margaret and embraced her. "Margaret! A nice surprise! What brings you here?"

Margaret repeated what she had told Anna.

"They keep doin' stuff like that around here. They should let the law decide."

"They didn't do right by you, Ben." Anna said.

"True, but at least everybody knew it, and they let me go free."

Anna saw her father standing aside. "Oh, I'm sorry. Margaret, I want you to meet my pa. You saw him only that one time, I think."

Margaret held out her hand. "I heard you were back."

"Yes, yes. Out of her goodness, Anna has forgiven me." There was a small break in his voice.

"Well, that's the way she is," Margaret said.

After they ate supper together, Ben saddled a horse and escorted Margaret back down the creek to her home. It had been some time since they'd heard anything out of Ferdinand Harvey, but he didn't believe they'd heard the last of him. Nobody with the warped mind of a man like that could ever be trusted.

Two days later, on a cold, windy day, with low clouds scudding across the tops of the hills, Margaret drove her buggy down the wagon road on the east side of Bull Creek. She was dressed in black and wore a black hat with a veil. She dreaded what she had to do; stand alone, or almost so, beside a dark hole in the clay soil. She knew George would be there and possibly some of the Archers, since Tom had promised to have everything ready. And of course Oley Jensen, who would say a few words for the redemption of her father's soul. It would be better if she could summon honest grief, she thought, instead of this numb feeling of confusion.

As she rounded the last little bend in the road and Sycamore opened up to her view, she was confused by what she saw. Wagons and buggies of all types lined the road on both sides, and there were dozens of people standing among them, apparently waiting for something. What was going on?

As she continued, she began to recognize her students from past and present, along with their parents. Other families from the community were there also. They all remained silent, but the women nodded and the men lifted their hats as she drove by. The children and young people raised hands in a salute of sorts. Tears started in her eyes and coursed down her cheeks.

She kept driving until she was in front of Guthrie's store. Henry Guthrie was standing there waiting for her and led her horse up to the hitching rail. Margaret looked behind her as she drew to a stop and saw that all of those she passed had followed her in a silent procession down the dirt street. George appeared and helped her step down.

"What is all this, George?"

"I told you it might happen. I didn't organize a thing. It's all spontaneous. And it's all for you."

Margaret looked across the street and saw Tom and Rebecca Archer standing beside their buggy and still seated in it was Anna with Ben standing beside her. It had all been something of a blur, but now she could see the other Archer children standing alongside the wagon behind them with the Johnsons.

"George, I don't know what to say. I'm overcome."

"Now you know, if you didn't already, what 'community' means. Are you ready to walk up the hillside?"

She replied that she was, and they walked up toward the open grave. It was off to the side along the south margin of the graveyard. She could see the pine coffin, placed on two short logs beside the grave. The crowd fell in behind her and George, and all of them walked up to gather around behind George and Margaret when they reached the grave site. Oley Jensen was waiting there with a Bible in his hand, one stubby finger inserted to keep his place. He stepped forward to take Margaret's hand. "Bless you, Miss," he said. "Are you ready to begin?"

"Yes, I am. And thank you for all you've done for me."

Oley took his stance at the head of the coffin and faced the crowd. He was dressed in his Sunday-meeting clothes; clean overalls, white shirt, black broadcloth coat, and black felt hat. His curly brown beard was washed clean of the mill's flour dust.

He raised his booming voice. "Folks, we are gathered here on a sad occasion to commit the body of a fellow human being, Perry Madison, to the soil. God gives us one life to live here on earth, in this human vessel, and he also gives us a choice about what we do with it, how we choose to live that life. It's not for any of us here to judge another on the choices that other might make.

"Some of us may have been tempted to violate the command to *judge not*, in the case of this man, but if you do, you are failing to obey God. Seek rather to find it in your heart to pray for our sister Margaret, and give her comfort in her time of trouble.

"In our community here, the words believed to be from King Solomon have meaning to me and I hope to you also. I'll read a few selected verses from Ecclesiastes, Chapter Three:

To everything there is a season, and a time
to every purpose under the Heaven.
A time to be born, and a time to die;
a time to plant, and a time to pluck up that which is
planted.
A time to weep, and a time to laugh;
a time to mourn, and a time to dance.
A time to tear, and a time to mend;
a time to be silent and a time to speak.

"None of us can know what was in the heart of Colonel Madison throughout his life, or when he knew he was facing the end of it. We can hope he came to peace with the Lord in those final hours and now rests in the eternal home we all seek. So as he has been plucked up from this earth, let us all use this as a time to weep, a time to mourn, but also a time to mend. I commend all of you who came here to do just that; to show your love and support for Miss Margaret. So before my final words, Miss Margaret, would you like to say anything?"

"*I don't know if I can,*" she whispered.

"Take your time," he replied.

Margaret lifted the veil from her face and up over her hat. She took a deep breath and was able to summon the voice she used in the classroom, "God bless all of you for being here for me. My father and I had our differences, but the last time I saw him, I found him changed. Maybe he was taking stock of how he had lived his life. In any case, I regret that his life had to end as it did.

"This community and all of you mean the world to me, and I thank you all. I truly appreciate Oley's words of comfort and wisdom. So, as he said, for everything there is a season." She bowed her head.

There was a murmured chorus of "Amen."

Oley nodded toward four men standing by; Tom and Ben Archer, and Rafael and Matthew Johnson walked forward and grasped the plow-lines on each side of the coffin. Jimmy Archer and Mark Johnson got on each end and the six of them carried the coffin to the end of the grave, Jimmy stepped out of the way, and they carried it suspended over the grave to slowly lower it to the bottom. They pulled the plow lines out and stepped out of the way.

Oley stepped forward and spoke, "And so we commit the body of Perry Madison to the soil of this hillside; earth to earth, ashes to ashes, dust to dust; and his spirit to God, who gave it. We leave his soul in the hands of Almighty God and hope he will share in the sure and certain hope of the Resurrection unto eternal life."

Margaret was standing beside him and said in a soft voice, "Well, it's over. Thank you, Oley."

He closed his Bible and held it against his body with his elbow. He took her hand, covering it with his other hand. He said, "You're most welcome, Miss. Do you want to take part in the usual custom of the shovel? Most times only the men do it."

"Of course."

He handed it to her and she poured a shovel-full of dirt into the grave, the clods and stones clumping on the pine. George appeared beside her to do the same. Margaret saw a long line of men form behind him and they all did the same. As each came by, they would murmur a comforting word or two to her.

She turned and walked away. Behind her, she heard the sounds of the men filling the grave.

-38-

THE FAREWELL

The wind was still blowing and the sky darkening as Margaret and George descended the hillside back toward her buggy. All the rest were heading to their wagons and buggies. She was surprised to see a tall figure standing beside hers. She had thought that Lambert was gone, headed to his next assignment, but there he was.

George stopped and said, "Go ahead, Margaret. I'll wait over toward the shop."

"Thank you, George. I'll just be a minute. I believe he's closing a chapter, as I just did."

A few drops of rain began to fall as she approached Lambert. "I didn't expect to see you here."

"I had to be here; had to tell you goodbye."

"I'm glad you came. I thought you'd be gone."

A steady light rain began to fall. "Climb into the buggy," he said. "I'll drop the side curtains for you while we speak."

"You'll get wet. Get in with me."

"I can't stay. I'm headed back to catch the mail coach to Springfield."

They both climbed into the buggy.

"You should stay until the rain is gone."

"I have a slicker. Look...I'm sorry we met because of your father. But I'm glad we did. I'm going back to the Territories."

"Be safe. I hope you find what you're looking for."

"I believe I did, but what I found wasn't available to me."

She reached over and squeezed his hand. "I'm sorry…any other time or place…."

He lifted the curtain aside and the buggy rocked as he climbed out. "You take care of yourself, Margaret," he said, as he turned to walk away.

"You, too," she called after him. "And write to me sometime; let me know how you are."

She watched him go to his rented horse and pull out a rolled yellow slicker and put it on. Then he mounted and rode away, tipping his hat to her as he left.

Margaret sat for a moment as he rode down the dirt street and turned right to head toward the ford. She picked up the reins and turned her trotter toward George's shop. As she approached, she saw him standing in the open doorway, waiting for her. Tom Archer's buggy was parked in front.

Tom climbed out and both he and George approached her as she drew to a stop.

"Margaret, we'd like for you to come to the house and spend some time with us." Tom said. "Anna and Ben are coming. You too, George. The Johnsons are taking the kids home with them and will bring 'em back after supper."

"I would like to, thank you," she said. "You come, too, George. You can ride with me and I'll bring you back by here."

He looked at Margaret. "You're sure it's all right?

"Of course."

"I'll close up the shop."

As they drove along, following the Archers' buggy, Margaret said, "This day takes me back, as I was saying a few days ago…that hillside, the rain…."

"Yes. I'll never forget that day. It was the first time I saw you, Margaret. You and I have quite a few memories…."

"That we do. And they're all good, except for that time one of us went on a divergent course."

"Who would be foolish enough to do a thing like that?" George put his hand over his face and peeked between his fingers.

242

"Hard to imagine," she said.

"Is the marshal gone?"

"Yes, George, he's gone.   There was never anything between us. He's a good man and he looked after me in this strange episode. He's going back to that Oklahoma territory. I feel sorry for him. I think he's getting weary of that kind of life."

"I wish him well, then," George said. "Uh...Margaret, this may not be the time or place, but when we can, I want to be alone with you and spend some time talking about us. As I told you before, at the schoolhouse, I want us to get back to the way we were."

Margaret reached over and took his hand. "After we put this day behind us, we'll talk."

They continued behind the Archer buggy, up along Hanson Creek to ford it on the lane leading to the Archer home place. The light rain had continued, prompting George to remark, "I hope folks were able to keep dry on their way home."

"I think most did. Before the burying, I noticed several had the hoops up on their wagons, ready for canvas. And you see more buggies nowadays. Several of yours?"

"Yes. We're keeping pretty busy."

They parked the buggies in front of the house and the three women went inside. The men unhitched the horses and led them to the barn to be rubbed down and fed a measure of oats. Inside the house, Rebecca took Anna's and Margaret's wraps and hung them up. She embraced them in turn. "Edna Johnson was kind enough to take care of all the younger folks so we could visit. She said they'd play games and she'd parch some corn."

"How nice of her," Margaret said. "Although it would have been fine to have them here."

Rebecca smiled. "Of course. However, Edna and I think Mark and Josephine may have encouraged her to do it. You know...young people...."

"Right," Margaret said.   "Not many chances to get together."

The three men came in, and Rebecca said, "Why don't we sit at the table? I've made a couple of gooseberry pies and fresh coffee."

When they were all seated, Tom said, "Let me say again, Margaret, I'm sorry for your loss."

"Thank you, Tom. It's been hard for me to sort out my own feelings. Sad, of course, the way he had to die. I'd begun to quit thinking much about him after he'd been gone for a while. Then he's found, he's tried, not convicted, and now gone permanently...." She shook her head.

Anna, seated next to her, put her arm around Margaret. "Don't forget you have a sister here, who'll do anything for you."

Margaret hugged her. "I know, my sister. I heard very little from my other family, and expect they won't bother to ever come back here. So, if it's all right...." She looked around the table, "I'll consider this to be my family. And I was overcome by the response of the community."

"I told her it might happen," George said. "I know how we all feel about her."

Ben and Anna exchanged a look.

Rebecca said, "We will always be your family."

Tom said, "I hate to bring it up, but there remains a worry to me." He looked at Ben and Anna. "We haven't seen much out of Ferd Harvey lately, but he's still there and I can bet he's still brooding over Clint...and also Rose is still missing."

George looked at Margaret. "Shall I tell them? Yes, I will. It goes without saying that this must remain our secret."

"I'm eager to hear it, but let me pour more coffee," said Rebecca.

All waited until she was seated, then George began, "First of all, Rose is alive and safe...." He proceeded to tell them the whole story of her discovery and rescue. They all listened with rapt attention until he finished. Then Rebecca jumped up and ran around the table to embrace George from behind. Tears were streaming down her cheeks.

"George, what a wonderful gift to me! I've thought of her every day! My dear niece! What a relief!"

"I'm sorry I had to keep it a secret. But I'm afraid if word ever gets out, he'll try to track her down."

"You did the right thing," Tom said. "Of course it won't leave this house. I doubt she'll be safe until he's gone. And I doubt we can relax our vigilance, either. Who knows what he'll think of next."

ROGER MEADOWS

-39-

DEVIOUS PLANS

Ferdinand Harvey sat at the plank table in his long underwear. It was once red, now faded to pink with sweat stains under the arms. His graying hair was in disarray, reaching almost to his shoulders and was entangled with the fringes of his beard. His only visible features were weathered cheeks, close-set pale eyes, and a bulbous nose. "Bring me more coffee," he said, banging his cup on the table.

Estelle shuffled over to the table on bare feet, coffeepot in hand, and filled his cup. She was skeletal and bent, her threadbare dress hanging from bony shoulders. She had gathered her hair into a knot on top of her head, but strands had come free and hung about her face. She said nothing and turned to go back to the stove, where she was boiling cornmeal for mush.

Ferd took a drink of the coffee and said, "This tastes like piss!"

"It's all old grounds," she said meekly. "We ain't got any new."

Their two remaining sons sat quietly, knowing it was dangerous to speak at the table unless told to do so.

Ferd chose a new tack. "What are we havin' for breakfast?"

Estelle said quietly, "Cornmeal mush, like yesterday."

"Again?"

"Yes. We ain't got no pig. We done et it all."

"Well," Ferd said. He looked at his two sons across the table. "Looks like tonight we'd better see if we can find another one."

The eldest, Bob, said, "Hope we don't get caught."

"You're a scaredy-cat," said his younger brother, Buford.

"He's right," said Ferd. "When Clint was alive, he never backed down from anything."

"Yes, and where is he now?" Bob said.

Ferd half rose from his chair, "You watch your mouth! You just might join him!'

"Sorry, Pa. I didn't mean nuthin'."

Ferd settled back in his chair. He stared at the wall behind them. "I wonder what happened to our Rose?" he said.

Estelle, still with her back to them, thought to herself, You beat her up and ran her off, that's what happened to her. Tears started in her eyes, tears she thought had long since been depleted. My Rose, my only joy, my only hope in life, now gone from me. But I cain't say nuthin'.

Ferd continued, "You'd a'thought somebody'd a'found her bones in a ditch someplace by now, or out in the woods. Maybe somebody's hidin' her, but for this long? Don't think so, but if they did, I bet those damned Archers had something to do with it.

"That gives me a' idee. I think we have a granddaughter we ought'a see about. Remember from the trial? Stelle, you was there. Bob, you was there. Remember what Clint told you, Bob? They didn't use it in the trial, but I believe what Clint told you. That Archer kid is prob'ly Clint's little girl. What is she, three or so? 'Bout time she met her real grandpa. I bet if I can look her in the eye, I can see some of our Clint in her. That 'ud be somethin'…make up for losin' Rose."

Oh my, Estelle thought. Will it ever be over?

Ferd poured sorghum over his mush and attacked it with a spoon. Between bites, he began to plan. "What if you boys was to take turns watchin' that place? We could pick a time when that Benjamin was gone. We could wear hoods and swoop in and take the girl. The female is big as a sow right now and her old man is there I think. But if he gets in the way, he can be taken care of. Should be easy."

"Pa, wouldn't they know it's us?" Bob said.

"Not if we do it right. Like I said, we wear hoods. And we don't talk. We'll put the horses in that little patch of woods by the pond and go in afoot. Buford will watch 'em."

"But what'll we do with the kid?"

"Don't you worry about that, Bob. We'll prob'ly keep her if she's Clint's. We got as much right...."

Bob just looked down at his empty bowl and quit talking. He believed his pa had gone nuts, but there wasn't much to be done about it.

"All right," Ferd said. "You can go first, Buford, startin' today. Just don't let 'em see you. They's a dog, so watch out for him. Then tonight or tomorrer, we'll see if we can get a shoat somewheres. We're needin' some pig."

Anna hummed a hymn to herself as she prepared breakfast. They'd had coffee earlier, but the men would be back in soon. It had been a week since the burying of Margaret's pa. Yesterday, they'd gone to Meeting in Sycamore, and she felt that she might not make the trip anymore until after the baby came. Should be a few more weeks, but jolting along in a wagon might not be the thing to do. Eva tugged at her skirt and held up her slate. "Look, Mama, I drawed a horse."

"You say, I *drew* a horse, but that's real good, Eva. You can show it to Papa and Gramps when they come in."

Benjamin and Jürgen came in and washed up after finishing the milking. Ben went over to the stove and put his arm around Anna. "How ya feelin', Babe?"

Anna smiled, "Tired and a little too heavy, but I'm all right."

As they ate breakfast, they discussed plans for the day. Ben said, "Since the rain stopped last week, it's dry enough to work the woods again, I reckon. Will you be all right, Anna? Would you like for your pa to stay around?"

"Yes, I'll be all right. I feel fine, and I know you two will get more done."

"You're sure? Another thing I've got to do is get another mate for Silver before spring plowin'. I tracked down where he and King came from, over the other side of Ozark. Need to get one soon and let them get used to each other."

Anna said, "Remember, we still have that gold piece we saved that Missus Madison gave me."

"We should have enough without it, but we'll see. I'll go in the next few days."

When the men had left, Anna swept the floor and cleaned the kitchen area. She added sticks of wood to the fire in the fireplace and managed to get Eva occupied looking at a picture book Rebecca had given her. It would keep her busy while Anna went to the outhouse...*again*, then to gather eggs at the henhouse, and make a trip to the springhouse for a bucket of fresh water. The weather was still chilly but the sky was clear. She did not know that she was being watched from the small copse of trees near the pond.

With her chores done, she settled in her rocker near the fire to work on her knitting. Getting ready for this baby was easier than the first time. She smiled to herself when she thought of those days. We were both so young and so ignorant. We were living in secret and had no idea what it would be like when it was time for the baby to come. And during the trauma of that birthing it was just Ben and me! Thank goodness Ben had had some experience with livestock. I hope the midwife is available this time. Of course we know now what to expect...and they claim the next one is easier. But now I know what God meant when He said us women would have a hard time of it when we gave birth, thanks to that first Eve and that serpent doing what they did.

Baby had taken some time to settle down after she started knitting. At first the needles wanted to bounce as her forearms rested on her considerable stomach. Now it seemed to be nap time in there. She looked down at Eva sprawled on the hearthstones in the firelight, and smiled again. It was surely worth it. The fire lit the shining red curls on her daughter's head and Anna's heart was filled with love. *For you, my child, you came to me through pain twice; once when you were conceived and again when you were born. At your beginning, I could not have imagined anything worse; now that you're here, I can't imagine not having you.*

Anna started another row on the baby blanket she was knitting. It was blue, a little tribute to Ben's hopes. If it was another girl, well, blue was a good color anyway. Eva interrupted her musings by closing her book and coming to stand by her chair.

"Whatcha makin', Mama?"

"It's a blanket, sweet girl."

"A *blanket*? It's awful little."

Maybe it was time. "Yes, it's little, because it's for a baby."

Eva's eyes grew wide. "A *baby*? Whose baby?"

"*Our* baby. You're going to have a little brother or sister pretty soon."

Eva opened her mouth wide in surprise. "We *are*? How do you know?"

"Your papa found a stork feather, and that's a sure sign."

"Why?"

"Well, the stork delivers babies, and he drops one feather off to let you know he's coming."

"Can I see it?"

"See what?"

"The feather."

"I'm sorry. A big gust of wind came up and blew it right out of his hand."

Eva was not to be disappointed. She started jumping up and down chanting over and over, "A baby, a baby, we're gonna have a baby!"

Buford rode home that evening all excited to report what he had seen. He found his father and brother in the barn, finishing milking the two scrawny cows. "Pa, it's gonna be easy! They don't seem to watch out much. The men went off to the woods south of the place and spent all mornin'. Then they come in for dinner and went right back. The woman was outside quite a bit. She waddled around to the chicken house and the outhouse, and such. It should be easy."

"Well, ya done good, son. Ya hear that, Bob?" Ferd said.

"Yessir." Bob frowned.

Ferd ignored him. "'Course, they'll not do the same thang ever day. We'll think on it. Tommerrer is your turn, Bob. Tonight, we'll get us a pig."

-40-

THE RENEWAL

When the first day of February dawned, the hills and coves were covered with new snow, clean and glistening white. In the stillness, all of the trees and bushes were laden and drooping. Most citizens did not pause to appreciate the beauty of it. It was cold, well below freezing, and the snow made morning chores more difficult. Ferd Harvey congratulated himself on stealing a pig before the snow arrived to show footprints. On the other hand, now he'd have to wait for a melt before activating other plans.

For Tom Archer, Ben Archer, and other citizens, the snow meant an extra ration of feed for the livestock, and allowing the horses to seek the warmth of their stalls.

Anna felt that her time was approaching. The baby had been shifting about more than usual, and seemed be positioned lower down. She hoped that the weather did not hamper efforts to get the midwife if the baby came early. She expected the baby to wait another week at least, maybe two weeks. It was a little hard to calculate. Let it be soon, she thought. I'm so eager to see what we have and to release this burden. She bustled about the kitchen stove, preparing breakfast. She smiled at Eva's excitement over the coming sibling. Ben had planned to go to the horse farm today, but postponed his trip until the snow melted.

Margaret walked the pristine path down the west side of Bull Creek, the first to leave tracks in the ankle-deep snow. She loved the crisp, clean air, and the near silence except for the burbling of the crystal Creek as it flowed over its bed of stones. Some of the children might not make it to school, but she'd get the fire going and be there for them.

When Margaret climbed the ladder to cross the swinging bridge, she noticed a plume of smoke rising from the chimney of the schoolhouse. George, she thought. She crossed, holding to the icy cables with her mittened hands. Sure enough, when she had descended on the other side and walked the short distance to the front steps, she saw his tracks coming from his shop.

Snow had been cleared from the front landing. He'd left a broom by the door, so she swept the snow from her boots before entering.

"Good morning, George!" she said. "Thank you so much!"

He turned from dropping an armload of wood into the wood box. He smiled. "It was nothing. I wanted you to be warm."

She approached and dropped her book bag on the floor. She put her arms around him and said, "I've always felt warm and protected when I'm with you. I missed that."

He embraced her, folding her in his arms as they used to do. "Me, too. In spite of my foolishness, it was always you I wanted. I always worried that having you was far beyond what I deserved."

She smiled at him, their faces inches apart. "You foolish man. I wanted you from the first day I saw you. I was prepared to be 'the old maid schoolteacher' because I couldn't imagine being with anyone else."

They came together in a hungry kiss, teeth clashing, and lips searching. The front door opened, and they jumped apart as Opal Bowman called out, "Good m-o-r-n-ing, Teacher!" in a singsong voice. She was smiling as she came in, followed by her sisters and brother.

Margaret flushed, with knees trembling, recovered and answered her as calmly as possible, "Good morning, children. I'm glad you made it safely through the snow."

George grinned at her. "Well, Miss Margaret, if there's anything else I can do, just let me know." He hurried out the side door.

Two days later, Ben said at the supper table, "Since the snow's all melted, I think I'd better go see if I can find a horse to make a team. Do you think you'll be all right?"

"I think so," Anna said. "Papa will be here, and it's not our time for another week or two."

"Yes, I be here," Jürgen said. "I watch over her."

"And you know where Ma Bright lives," Ben said.

"Yes, yes. I know from when we lost Anna's mama."

"Good. Then I'll plan to leave right after chores in the morning. Probably be gone 'til late."

"Is all right. I do the chores if you are late," Jürgen said.

Buford Harvey watched from the copse of trees. He'd been there since before dawn. Weren't too much fun gettin' out that early in the cold, but at least it got me out of milkin'. Everything looked pretty normal at the Archer place. The two men got out before daylight and did the chores at the barn like always. Now they were in the house with smoke coming out of the chimney. Must be havin' breakfast, he thought. I could use some hot coffee. Wait...somethin's goin' on. He's goin' out to the barn by hisself.

Buford watched as Ben rode out of the barn lot and started down the lane toward the crossing of Bull Creek. The dog trotted along behind him. This might be it, Buford thought, and he was excited. He observed as Ben crossed the creek and turned north along the wagon road, heading away from the direction of Sycamore.

Buford mounted and rode toward home, careful to stay screened from sight. When he rode into the Harvey place he went straight to the front porch, throwing the reins over the hitching rail and bursting into the house. "This is it, Pa!" he said. "I think he's gone and left the place, and the dog went with him."

Ferd and Bob were at the table and Ferd turned to him. "Good work, Buford. You think he's gone?"

"Shore is. He's bound to be goin' someplace away from here."

Ferd jumped up from the table. "Come on, Bob. Let's get goin'."

As he headed up the wagon road toward Ozark, Ben looked forward to getting this task taken care of. Ever since King had been shot, Silver seemed to be in mourning. He wanted nothing to do with the mules, which left him alone as he grazed the hillside pasture. Silver came often to hang around the barn whenever Ben was there, to get his big velvet nose stroked or receive a pan of oats. Now if I can just find him a good buddy, Ben thought, everything will get back to normal. Thankfully, Rebecca was able to find the name of the farm where her late husband, Charlie, had bought the pair. Ben had asked around and found directions to the horse farm, a man named Chester Williams, who specialized in draft horses.

He hurried his chestnut gelding, Charger, along at a fast walk, and thought of another big event to come, that new baby. I hope it's a boy, he thought. And I hope it's better for Anna this time. We got through it, but it was kinda scary. She's so brave after all she's been through. What a lucky man I am! Almighty God had surely blessed us both, but 'specially me.

Ferd and his two sons had made it back across Bull Creek and stealthily made their way to the copse of trees by the pond overlooking the Archer houseplace. Although no one was near, Ferd spoke in a soft voice, "We'll just wait and watch for a little while. No hurry. Then Buford, you'll keep the horses quiet, while Bob and me go get her. This is how we used to do it during the War, when me and Clyde was young fellers, ridin' with Alf Bolden. Them was the days!"

"Pa," said Bob. "I don't want to do this."

"*What?* Whatta ya mean, you don't want to do this?"

"Just that. Somebody's bound to get hurt, and we'll get caught for sure. I don't want to hang."

Ferd's cheeks reddened. "*What did I do to get a chicken-shit coward for a son?*" He exploded in a harsh whisper.

"I'll do it, Pa," Buford said. "I ain't afraid. Bob can watch the horses."

"Good for you, Son." He whirled about and cuffed Bob on the side of his head.

After Ben left, Anna cleaned up after breakfast, then went to sit by the fire and add a few rows of knitting to the baby blanket. Eva sat beside her on the hearth and drew with chalk on her slate. After a short time, Anna said, "I guess I'll gather the eggs, Sweetie. You just keep on with what you're doing and I'll be back in a few minutes. All right?"

"I will, Mama."

Anna went to the front door and donned her coat and scarf, putting the Colt revolver in her coat pocket as Ben had urged her to do. She picked up her basket and went outside and down the steps, thence around the house to the hen house out back. She went to all the nesting boxes and got the usual dozen eggs. She put cracked corn in the chicken feeder from the covered barrel in the corner, then went back outside to head back to the house. The weather is pretty nice for Ben's ride, she thought. Sunny and not quite so cold.

As she came back around the house, she froze at what she saw. Two men with sacks over their heads, holes cut for their eyes, charged toward her. One of them carried a shotgun. She dropped the basket of eggs and managed to get the Colt out and fire a shot at the one with the shotgun before they were upon her. That one dropped the shotgun, so she must have hit him, but it was too late. The other man grabbed her and slammed her against the house. Her head hit the squared log wall, and everything went black.

ROGER MEADOWS

-41-

THE ATTACK

"Pa, I'm hit!" Buford cried. He was lying on the ground, holding his right side under his armpit. "It really hurts! Shoot that bitch!"

"Let me have a look." Ferd knelt beside Buford and unbuttoned his coat. "You're sure 'nuff bleedin'." Ferd tore open his shirt and looked. "Hit ain't too bad," he said. "It just cut a groove in your side. We'll wrap her up so's she don't bleed too bad. Set up and let's get yer coat off." He jerked the bag off Buford's head and folded it several times. "Here, hold this over it while I fix a bandage."

Just as Ferd completed this action, he saw Jürgen running toward him from the barn, with a shotgun in his hands. Ferd grabbed his shotgun. Jürgen stopped and hurried a shot at Ferd, but missed with the center of the load, only a few bird shot ripping through one side of the bag over Ferd's head. Ferd answered with a more accurate shot. A full load of double-aught buckshot, enough to bring down a deer, hit Jürgen squarely in the chest and he fell backward, his gun flying.

"Now get *her* while you're at it," Buford said, nodding it the direction of Anna, lying unconscious nearby.

"I ain't gonna do that, son, her bein' the little girl's mama. It wouldn't be right."

"*What?* She tried to kill me!"

"She was just pertectin' herself, just like I was just now. Let's get you fixed up, then we can get the girl."

"Give it to me! I'll do it!"

"No. I wouldn't be right. Now hold still while I fix you up." He pulled the bag off his own head and proceeded to rip it in strips and bind Buford's chest.

"It *hurts*, Pa. Let me do her."

"I said no. Now shut yore face. Let's get what we come for."

They both hurried to the front of the house and clumped across the porch, pulling the latch string and entering the house. There was the little red-headed girl, sitting on the floor looking at a book.

Eva jumped to her feet and yelled, *"Mama! Mama!"* Then she turned and ran to her parents' bedroom and crawled under the bed, Ferd in pursuit.

Buford stood looking about him, then walked to the table and picked up a piece of left-over ham and started eating it.

Ferd hit the floor and reached under the bed and grabbed one of Eva's feet and dragged her out. Eva screamed.

"Be quiet!" Ferd said, and he put his hand over her mouth. Eva bit him.

"Ow!" Ferd said. Then he laughed. "Yore a feisty rascal."

Ferd pinned her arms to her sides and carried her out into the main room. "Buford, find her coat and hat. Quit what yore doin'. Let's get out'ta here."

Anna awoke to find herself on the ground, not knowing what had happened to her. She struggled to sit up, and it came back to her. Two scary men... a gunshot...a struggle.... Then she looked to her right and saw someone lying on the ground several feet away and was horrified. Was it...Oh, no! She managed to get to her feet and went to him, then sagged to her knees. "Oh, Papa, Papa!" She reached to stroke his face. It had lost its color and his eyes were staring, sightless. His chest was a mass of blood. In her confusion and anguish, she found it difficult to focus her mind.

Then it hit her…Eva! "Oh, my baby," she cried out, and rose to her feet and hurried as best she could toward the house.

The door was standing open, confirming her worst fears. She entered, calling her daughter's name, *"Eva! Eva!"* She went into her bedroom and looked in every corner of the house, her despair growing. They had taken her. She sank to the floor, sobbing. Oh, Ben, I need you! sprang into her mind. Then she prayed aloud, "Lord Jesus, please help me! Please keep my baby safe!"

Finally she was able to collect her thoughts. There is no one here now but me. Poor Papa gave his life trying to help. I've been in trouble before. What can I do? Must I wait for help to arrive? Should I try to hitch a team and go for help? In my condition? What to do…what to do?

She was still sitting on the floor before the fireplace, having these thoughts, when a spasm of pain gripped her body. Starting at her back, a cramping pain moved around her lower abdomen, causing her to gasp. She knew what it was, of course. Well, that does it, she said to herself. I can give up in grief over Eva and Papa, or I can, with God's help, get busy. As the pain went away, she set her jaw and rose to prepare for what was to come. First things first….

Ben was able to find the horse farm and arrived around noon. Chester Williams was a big man, in keeping with his love for big horses. He was well over six feet tall and Ben guessed he'd go over three hundred pounds, or in horse terminology, nineteen hands and twenty-two stone. He was on the front porch of the spacious frame house and called out as Ben rode up. "Hey there, young fella; climb down and come in!"

Williams descended the porch steps and greeted Ben with a handshake. "Pearline is settin' dinner on as we speak. Come on in and join us."

Ben grasped the big meaty hand and replied. "Thanks. I reckon I'd like that. I'm Ben Archer from down on Bull Creek."

"Right pleased to meet ya. I bet you're lookin' for horses."

"That's right. I need one." Ben found Williams to be as welcoming as was possible. He had twinkling blue eyes and a ruddy face above a long white beard. Ben thought of renditions of Santa Claus in a childhood book.

Pearline proved to be just as friendly, almost as tall as her husband, but much less like a draft horse in build. Over a meal of beef stew and cornbread, Ben told of the provenance of his horses and the tragic loss of one of them.

"I remember them grays and I remember that fella Charlie Tate. You say he's gone?"

"Yes. It was bad thing. Slipped and hit his head they say, fell in the creek in the winter time. Anyway, as time went by, his widow married my pa. We'd lost my mother years before. That's how I come to own the team. Now I need to replace the one. Somebody shot and killed one of them, either an accident or on purpose. I'm pretty sure it was on purpose."

"Who'd do such a thing as kill a horse!"

"Well, it's a long story, but he's a really bad one, the one who I think did it. Hard to prove."

Williams shook his head, looking down at the table. "After we eat, we'll have a look. I've got about twenty comin' on, most broke to harness to some extent. They'll be gone by spring plowin'. That's not countin' all the brood mares and colts. I still have the mare that birthed that team of your'n, a year apart, but she's too old for any more. Good thing is, I still have a couple of her geldings you might be interested in. They don't match in color, but would be half-brothers."

After the noon meal, Williams showed Ben around with some pride, well justified. There were four corrals, well-built barns, and spacious pastureland. He asked Ben to wait and mounted up on a sturdy saddle horse. With the help of a shepherd dog he rounded up a half-dozen horses and brought them into a corral for Ben to look at. Ben walked among them. One was a dappled gray like Silver, but he settled on a black half-brother. Seemed right, somehow. They soon arrived at a price, low enough that Ben could hang on to the original gold piece of

Anna's. After they agreed, Williams surprised him with a proposition. "What if I throw in his mama? I can't rightly sell her, but she's sound. You have to feed her, o'course, but she'll work some...plow the garden, snake logs outta the woods, that kinda thing."

Ben thought a moment. "I'll do it. Thank you. I got plenty a' pasture. I don't know if horses remember each other, but it won't hurt to find out."

"I call her 'Queen'."

Ben left at mid-afternoon, two horses on long leads. Probably won't make it home 'til after dark.

42-

THE HIDEOUT

Anna knew that she was to face alone what was to come. The chance that anyone else would come by was remote. Years before, Colonel Madison had cast her out of the house in early winter with only what she was wearing and with no place to turn. And she overcame it. This time she knew Ben would be coming to her; she just had to make it through the next several hours. Eva, my love, she thought, may God protect you until we can find you. Be brave.

After that first spasm subsided, Anna got to her feet and put a kettle on the stove to heat. Next, she made her way out to the tack room where her father slept, avoiding looking at his body as she walked by. She removed a quilt and the corn-shuck mattress from his bed and took two pennies from the drawer in his bedside table. As she did so, another pain gripped her body and she gasped, standing still until it began to subside.

She went to where he lay and knelt beside him. Her tears began to flow again, as she tenderly closed each eye, placing a penny on it. "Oh, Papa," she whispered. "I'm so sorry. Rest in peace with the Lord." She rose and carefully draped the quilt full length over his body.

When she was halfway to the house, carrying the mattress, her water broke, a sudden warm gush that wet her underclothes, her skirt and shoes, puddling on the ground. Better here than in the house, she muttered. As soon as it was finished, she went into the house and back to the bedroom to change into a nightgown.

Another spasm struck. Was it the same delay? Is it coming sooner?

In anguish over her daughter, she found it difficult to focus. Now think, she told herself. There will soon be another child. The cradle is ready and in the main room. Get out baby clothes, diaper, belly band, wash cloths, and blankets. Get out scissors and some cord. Get towels and rip up an old, clean sheet to fold cloths for my bleeding. Bedsheet and pillow for the mattress. Bucket for the afterbirth. As she checked off her list in her head, she went from place to place until all was gathered in front of the fireplace. *Eva, my sweet girl, we'll get you as soon as we can!*

Should I pull the latch string? It will be hours before Ben gets here. I'd hope that some way I'll be able to let him in and keep those crazy men out. I'll pull it.

She stoked the fire and sat in her rocker while she still could, and waited out the next labor pain. Well, little boy or girl, it's just the two of us now, so let's get this over with.

Ferd Harvey and his two sons rode on the trail through the woods to their cabin. Ferd made Bob carry the girl on his horse. Eva struggled in his grasp and cried out for her mother, seeming more angry than afraid, yelling in defiance, "Let me go! I want my mama! You're mean!"

Bob managed to control her by pinning both of her arms, after dodging tiny flying fists. He talked softly to her, "I'm sorry. Just settle down. You'll be all right;" pleas that did no good.

He was relieved when they arrived and he was able to dismount and carry her into the house following after his pa. Buford came in last, whining about the pain in his wound.

Estelle Harvey turned from the stove, where she was attempting to prepare something for them to eat. She saw the struggling little girl in Bob's arms, and in a rare event, spoke up. "Now what have you done, Ferd?"

"Went and got my granddaughter, that's what. Come and take a look at 'er."

Estelle came closer and looked at Eva, her face set in a worried frown. She said, "I'm sorry little girl. What's your name?"

Eva stopped struggling, stared at her with curiosity, but did not answer.

"Don't she look like Clint?" Ferd said.

"Not to me," Estelle said. "She has red hair and green eyes. Clint had brown hair and gray eyes, if you ever bothered to look."

"That don't mean anything. Look at her ears and the shape of her nose."

"I don't see it. I'll say this once and then no more. Take her back, or they'll be comin' for you."

"I'm keepin' her."

Buford had been ignored too long. "Ma, I need help. I been shot."

Estelle whirled to look at him. "Where? How bad?"

Estelle had Buford sit in a chair and take off his shirt. She unwrapped the crude bandage and looked at the angry wound. "I'll get some stuff to wash it out and wrap it up again."

While she tended to him, Buford in loud protest, Ferd took Eva from Bob and sat her in a chair. "Now, you stay right there, or I'll tie you up. You got it?"

Eva stared at him.

As soon as he started to turn away, she jumped down and ran toward the door. Bob caught her in time.

Ferd came after her, his face red, "Now you mind what I say. Don't ever do that again or you'll get a whippin' you won't forget."

This time Eva stayed in the chair, her arms folded, and her chin jutting out.

Ferd had been thinking about the next step. Maybe Stelle was right for once. They might come 'round looking for him. Better come up with a plan. After a few moments, he said. "Here's what we're gonna do. We're gonna use one of the hideouts we used during the war. We'll take some quilts and stuff and one of them hams and some cornmeal. Where I'm thnkin' there's plenty of good water. One of you boys will be here all the time and switch off. Anybody comes around, me and the other-un is out huntin'. Trying to get a deer. How's that sound?"

No one said anything.

"Well?"

"Shore, Pa," Buford said.

-43-

THE ARRIVAL

A nna could no longer sit in the rocker and had moved it out of the way. For the most part, she felt better to lie on her back with her knees elevated, waiting for the next round of pain. Sometimes she would lie on her side for a few minutes, or even get up on hands and knees. She'd lost any sense of the passage of time, but it seemed that hours had passed. It was difficult to think about what was happening, for thinking of Eva. Is she all right? Where is she? Is she afraid?

She hadn't kept time on the mantel clock, but she realized it was after mid-day. The pains were closer together, she knew, and had started counting to keep track. At first she could stand them with just a gasp, then later a groan. Ben had told her to yell out loud if that would help, and she'd now reached that stage.

She'd forgotten just how bad the pain was when all the muscles of her body contracted to try to rid itself of that foreign object living within her. Ben had coached her that first time to try to relax and not strain herself, but as the contractions drew closer together and the pain greater she couldn't help herself. It was push! push!, face red and crying out to the empty house. She'd gotten a pan of hot water to be in her reach and hoped it hadn't cooled too much. She could feel a heaviness in her lower body and the pains were coming closer together. Less than a minute apart.

The next waves of pain merged into one. She arched her body and looked down over her cramping stomach and pushed with all her might. At last, movement! She felt the release of tension and felt the moment had come at last. She raised herself on her elbows and saw something emerge between her legs. A baby at last! Exhausted and in pain, she managed to sit up, legs spread wide, and picked up the bloody, slimy, creature and brought it into her lap. She quickly grabbed a warm wet cloth and wiped its little face and heard a first cry! She quickly placed a folded clean piece of bedsheet between her legs to staunch the bleeding. She broke into uncontrolled sobs and brought the baby to her breast, wrapping it in a towel. She rocked back and forth and said aloud. "Thank you, Lord, for this great gift of life. Please bring Ben safely home to me to see his *son*!"

The little pink baby continued his plaintive crying, as she continued to wash him and dry him with the towels she'd arranged nearby. As soon as he was clean, she retrieved the scissors and yarn and tied off the cord twice, cutting it between the ties. She hurriedly dressed him in a little knit jacket Rebecca had made, wrapped a band around his middle, and expertly diapered him.

Now I am not alone, she thought. "Sweet baby boy, let's see if you know how to have dinner."

Her breasts were swollen and full, a miracle of preparation for the next step. She untied the top of her gown and brought her new son to her breast, helping him find the erect nipple. A thrill went through her as he began to suck. Although she had seen it before, she was still struck by the miracle of it all. *How does he know how to do that?* She stroked his head with her finger, smoothing the light brown hair. He hasn't opened an eye yet to see this new world he had entered after the months of darkness. *Evie, wherever you are, you have a little brother!*

The fire had died down and she could see by the fading brightness in the east window that it was late afternoon. Her son had finished sucking and was sleeping, so she painfully arose and swathed him in blankets and laid him in the cradle. Only then was she fully able to feel her weariness, remember the sorrow of the morning, and renew her concern for her precious daughter.

She added split oak firewood to the fireplace and the flames crackled to life. Those are the last sticks of wood from the hand of papa, she thought.

Her stomach started cramping again so she lay back down on the spoiled mattress and was able to expel the placenta, wrapping it in the old towel and putting it in the bucket. She replaced another of the folded cloths between her legs and pulled on some drawers to hold it in place. She walked stiffly over to the water bucket and took a long drink, then tried to decide what to do next. I need to eat something to keep up my strength and Ben will be hungry when he comes home. She decided on cream of tomato soup from her summer canned tomatoes, and a johnny cake to go with it. What I really want to do is lie down and sleep. I feel sorry for what Ben will encounter when he returns...except for the joy of his son.

There was no moon as Ben rode down the wagon road, illuminated only by the great canopy of stars and the Milky Way. It was just enough light for him to find his way. The temperature had fallen and he was growing cold and hungry. He could feel Charger beneath him growing tired also. Luckily, he had only about a half-mile to go before the lane that crossed Bull Creek and led home. Anna would be waiting for him and he couldn't wait to tell her of his success. Being a mother herself, she'd appreciate his bringing the mother of his horses home with him. He smiled to himself when he thought of how Eva would be excited. And Anna's gonna' be a mother again! I hope it's a boy, but more than that, I hope she'll be all right.

When they reached the ford, he stopped in the middle of the creek to let the three horses drink. He'd wait himself until home. Wouldn't be long now. He could see faint light in the distance shining through the window, and behind it, she'd be waiting for him.

He rode directly to the barn lot and dismounted. Silver was on the other side of the lot and whinnied. One of his new acquisitions answered. He tied up Charger and led Queen and the other horse into the corral and removed their halters. There was water in the tank and hay in a rack that Jürgen had put there that morning. He went back and unsaddled Charger, put the tack away, and led Charger into the corral with the others. He was surprised that Jürgen had not come out to see what was happening. Must be inside with Anna.

He ran up the porch steps and started across the porch. The door opened and there was Anna, silhouetted by the light of the fireplace behind her. It looked like she was wearing her robe and it looked like she was holding something in front of her. She rushed into his arms, careful of the bundle she was holding. At last she could let go of her composure, and she broke into sobs, "Oh, Ben, Ben! I need you so...Oh, Ben!"

"Anna, what *is* it? What...*what's happened?*"

Through her sobs, *"Oh, everything's happened...first, you have a son, but Eva's been taken and Papa is dead—"*

"What? Wait, wait, I don't understand!"

"Take your son and help me to a chair by the fireplace and I'll tell you."

As they walked toward the fireplace, Anna spilled out the events in a torrent of words, "To make it fast, I was out gathering eggs. When I came around the house, two men charged at me with bags over their heads. I dropped my basket and was able to get off a shot at the one carrying a shotgun. I think I hit him, because he dropped it, but the other one threw me against the house and knocked me out. When I woke up, I found Papa dead. When I went in the house, I found Eva was gone. Then my labor started."

Ben rubbed his face. "Oh, my, oh my! It's a nightmare! Was it the Harveys?"

"I don't know."

He knelt beside her chair and held her hand, cradling the baby in his other arm. "I can guess. Who else could possibly do such an evil thing? Let me think. I haven't even looked at my son!" He lifted aside the blanket and gazed at the sleeping child, his expression relaxing for a moment.

"How did you do it, Anna? Who helped—"

"*You* helped, when you were with me that first time. Otherwise, it was just that little one and me."

"Oh, my, Anna. You're so strong, you're the world to me. I'm sorry I wasn't here for you."

'It's all right, Ben. You were here in spirit. Knowing you were coming kept me strong."

Anna said, "It's been a horrible day except for our son you hold. I yearned for you to come, but dreaded telling you about our precious girl, and Papa, course."

He bowed his head for a moment. Then he looked up. "I'll ride down to Pa's. He can send Jimmy for the sheriff, and I bet Rebecca and him both will come back with me and help out. Where is your pa?"

"In the side yard. I covered him with a quilt."

"All right. I brought us a couple of horses. Charger's gonna be weary, but maybe he can take me that far."

"I'll get you something to eat. You must be about to starve."

"Always thinking of me. If you have a chunk of cornbread or something, I'll eat it on the way."

ROGER MEADOWS

-44-

THE CONFESSION

It was nearing midnight when Ben knocked on the door of his parents' home. They were astonished when he told them of the events of the day. They immediately began to activate Ben's plan: Jimmy was dispatched for a fast ride to Forsyth to get the sheriff. Josie took charge of the younger children, and Tom and Rebecca were soon headed out in their buggy. Ben rode with them on Beauty, Tom's horse, while Charger took a much-deserved rest.

Anna had been nursing the baby when she heard them arrive. She arose and went to the door and unlatched it when Ben identified himself. Rebecca entered first and enveloped her and her bundle. Tears flowed all around. Rebecca promptly took charge of the house, allowing Anna to finally go to bed and try to rest. Tom and Ben went out to take care of the horses, stopping first by the body of Jürgen Friedrich.

Tom said, "Of course we won't move anything, but I see a shotgun layin' over there in the grass. I bet Anna's pistol is here somewhere. We'll let the sheriff do his thing."

Tom insisted Ben get some sleep and he proceeded to milk the cows and feed the other livestock, taking a look at the horses Ben had brought home. Finally, he and Rebecca sat by the fire to await the arrival of the sheriff.

Tom did not realize he had been dozing, but he snapped awake at the baying of Bone. He rose and looked out the front window and heard the sound of approaching horses. He stepped out on the porch in the morning darkness, faint light just beginning to detail the trees in the distance and the outbuildings. There was a tinge of pink in the east. Sunrise was not too far away. Then he saw the two riders begin to emerge from the faint light and recognized Sheriff Horton in the lead.

As they drew closer, he saw that it was Deputy Henry Jeffrey who accompanied him. Jeffrey had been the one who had come out to examine the dead horse, King. As they drew up and dismounted, Tom went to shake hands.

"Thanks for coming, Sheriff. And you, too, Henry. Come inside and have some coffee."

"Glad to do it," the sheriff said. They both wrapped the horses' reins around the hitching rail. "That boy of your'n did a good job. He headed back home like you tole him."

Rebecca came forward. "Come in and sit, gentlemen," she said. "I'll pour coffee. Anna and Ben are sleeping, but I'll wake them up. Yesterday was a hard day."

The sheriff removed his hat. "Thank ya, Ma'am. Much ablidged."

Anna had been sleeping only a couple of hours since the last feeding, and struggled to awaken. She did what she must, however, and soon came into the room where they were drinking coffee, dressed in her long, quilted robe, her long hair hastily gathered in a queue down her back. The men all leaped to their feet, and spoke good mornings. Tom placed a chair across from the sheriff for her and Anna seated herself.

"Thank you, Sheriff," she said. "I have a horrible story to tell and we need your help."

"I'm sorry, Ma'am. I'll do all I kin. If you will, just take your time and start at the beginning. I'll wait 'til you're ready, then I'll ask my questions."

Anna gratefully took a drink of coffee Rebecca set before her and began, "We got around early yesterday morning and Ben left for Christian County to buy a workhorse to replace the one that was killed. That left me and Papa and Eva here. Midmorning, I went out to gather eggs, and when I was coming back around the house...." Anna continued her narrative through the discovery of her father and the subsequent birth of her son, leaving out any description of the latter in the presence of men not her husband. That would not be proper. Ben had joined them, and all listened in silence. When she had finished, the sheriff spoke.

"Any idee who they were?"

"They had bags over their heads with eyeholes and they didn't speak. If I had to guess, it would be the Harveys—the old man and one of the boys. They've been nothing but trouble, as you know."

"Yes, Ma'am, I know. And now they have your little girl. It's startin' to get light out. Do you feel up to goin' outside to show us where you was, and so forth?"

Anna was stiff and sore and felt a bit dizzy from yesterday, but she said, "Yes, Sir. I'll slip on some shoes and a coat. It may be improper to say, but I think I could summon the strength to get my shotgun and go with you to get my girl back."

Out in the side yard, Anna pointed out about where she was at the time she was attacked. They found the pistol where she had dropped it and the basket with broken eggs. Deputy Jeffrey picked up the pistol and smelled the barrel, then checked the load. "One round gone," he said.

"When I came to, I was about here, next to the house. As I said, I looked over there and saw Papa." She led them to where Friedrich lay. Horton went to lift the quilt and Anna turned away. "Sorry, Sheriff, I don't want to look again."

"It's all right, Ma'am. My, my! I'm so sorry."

Again, Jeffrey checked the shotgun and reported one barrel fired, the other loaded.

The sheriff said, "After you shot at the one, your pa must 'a come at 'em and was able to get off one shot before they shot him."

"Looks that way," Tom said. "Too bad about poor Jürgen. He tried."

"My God, Anna!" Ben said. "They could have killed you, too!"

"I don't know why not, but thanks be to God, they didn't. And it would have been two of us, you know."

The sheriff turned to Anna and Ben. "Folks, I'm thinkin' you might be right. What we're gonna do is, we're goin' to check out the Harveys, see what they have to say for theirselves. I assume one of you men will want to come along."

Tom looked at Ben. "Son, let me do it. Somebody needs to stay here and guard the house. And you had a hard day yesterday."

"Pa, I've had some rest. And I'd like to be there for Eva when we find her, and you can guard the house as well as I can." To himself he thought, I want to be there in case they resist arrest.

Reading his thoughts, Horton said, "Let me get something straight; if it is them, we take 'em alive to stand trial."

Tom said, "I told Jimmy to let some others know after he got some rest and took care of the livestock. We should have more people here pretty soon. But I'm sure you won't want to wait."

"You got that right!" Ben said.

"Sheriff," Anna said, "Whatever you have to do, *bring back my girl!*"

Ben was familiar with the back trails and led the sheriff and deputy across the creek and up the ridge trail to the Harvey place. There was a light showing in the front window as they dismounted and tied their horses to the rail. Ben carried his Winchester, Deputy Jeffrey was armed with a short shotgun, and Horton pulled his Colt Peacemaker as they mounted the steps to the front door.

Horton held the Colt by his thigh, rapped on the door, and called out, "Sheriff Horton here. Open the door."

Ben and Henry stood to either side as they waited. Then there was the sound of the bolt being lifted and the door opened a crack to reveal the pinched face of Estelle Harvey. "What do you want?" she said.

"Like to have a word with your menfolk, Ma'am," Horton said.

"They ain't here." Estelle was still peering through the cracked-open door.

"Where are they?"

"Bob's at the barn. The others is huntin'. Don't know where they're at."

"Well, Ma'am, Deputy Jeffrey is goin' to come in and have a chat with you, so open the door. Me and him will go out to the barn." He nodded first at Jeffrey, then at Ben. "Henry, you know what to do."

They found Bob Harvey milking a scrawny cow. He stopped and stood to face them. His face above a grizzled dark beard was set in a worried frown. "Sheriff?" he said.

"That's right, Bob. Set your bucket somewhere. We'd like to talk a bit. You know Ben Archer here, I think."

Bob nodded, and set the milk bucket on a high shelf.

"Now, Bob, I think you might know why we're here." Horton stared at him, face to face. They were about the same height.

Bob dropped his gaze, staring at his feet. Horton waited. Then Bob said, almost in a whisper, "He's gone crazy. I tried to tell him. Now I don't know what to do."

Horton said, gently, "Do the right thing, Bob. It'll be best for everybody."

"But he'll hang, won't he?" Bob looked back at the sheriff. He was about to cry.

"That'll be up to a judge or jury, Bob. Ain't nuthin' gonna get any better to let this go on."

Bob nodded and looked down again.

Ben spoke for the first time. "My daughter better be all right."

"Last I saw, she was jest fine."

Horton said, "I reckon you know where they are."

"Yessir."

"Take us to them."

Bob fidgeted, wiped his nose on his sleeve. "I don't think it would work, just comin' at 'em. Buford's trigger-happy and it could cause trouble for the little girl."

Horton looked at Ben. "He's got a point." Then to Bob, "What do you suggest?"

"Tomorra's my day to be there and Buford will be here. If I'm there, I could be holdin' the girl and run out with her. That 'ud work. You could get Buford as soon as he gets here tonight, after milkin'. That's when I ride down to replace him. It'll be dark when I get there, but you could take up on both sides—"

"Both sides of what?"

"Oh. They're at Pigeon Roost Cave."

Horton turned to Ben. "You know it?"

"Yes. It was used as a hide-out by the raiders, Pa told me. I've been there."

"What do you think of his plan?"

"I think it would work, if we can trust him."

"You can trust me. I didn't want any part of this and Pa's crazy as a loon. Kept talkin' about a granddaughter. I knowed you'd come. Best get it over with."

"What we're gonna do, Bob, is we're gonna set on you and your Ma until it's time for Buford to get here. We'll hide, and we'll take him first. Then you'll go down jest like you been told."

Bob nodded. "I'm to take him some supper and I ride down carryin' a lantern."

"That's good, Bob." Horton clapped him on the shoulder. "Now let's get to the house and wait there. Ben, if you will, go on back to your place. Bobby Joe's supposed to be comin'. You or your pa can fetch him over here. We'll set tight and wait for this evenin'."

When Ben arrived at his home, he found the yard between the house and barn filled with numerous wagons and buggies, with several neighbors from the coves and hills going to and fro.

Oley Jensen, Homer and George Zinn, Rafe and Matthew Johnson, and others came to meet him. Bobby Joe Duke was there, also.

Oley spoke first. "Any luck finding her?"

Ben dismounted. "Yes, we know where she is. Ferd Harvey has her and she's all right, we think. We have a plan, and it's really important that we don't do anything to tip him off. We'll have to wait for evenin' to make our move. So we sit tight until then."

There was a murmur of voices, and George spoke up, "What can we do to help?"

"The sheriff and Henry are guardin' Miz Harvey and Bob at their place. He'll tell us if he needs anybody. Bobby Joe, I'm to take you to him soon's we're ready."

Rafe Johnson said, "Let me do that. You need to be here."

"All right," Ben agreed.

After he had checked with Anna and found her surrounded by friends, including Margaret, George took him out to the tack room so see Jürgen's body. The men had already bound up the terrible wound, washed his body, and dressed it in clean clothes. Ben thought they'd done a good job. His beard and hair had been trimmed, and he looked to be sleeping in the pine box George had brought. He was wrapped in a quilt, which would be folded over him after viewing. Others were already digging a grave in Sycamore beside his wife.

"You've done good, George," Ben said.

"It's little enough. So sorry about this."

The neighbors had brought abundant food, and Ben was urged to eat and lie down for a rest before the evening rendezvous with Sheriff Horton. Tom prepared to go with him for the evening to come, for whatever was needed for the rescue of Eva. George asked to go with them, on a borrowed saddle horse.

ROGER MEADOWS

-45-

INTO DARKNESS

As the winter sundown approached, Sheriff Horton held a last-minute briefing on the front porch. Bobby Joe was inside, keeping watch over Estelle and Bob Harvey. "Here's the way we'll do it," he began. "Bob said Buford would prob'ly come straight to the house 'cause he'd be done milkin'. However, supposin' it might be different, two of us will hide in the barn, just in case. Two more will wait in the house. I'm gonna send Bobby Joe, and you, George, if you will, back down the trail with all the extry horses, so's his horse don't tip him off there's somethin' goin' on. After we get him, I'll fire one shot, so's you can come in. Come to think of it, if there's a buncha shots, come in anyway.

"How about me and Ben in the house and Tom and Henry in the barn?" They all nodded and he continued, "That's it, then. Bob'll come out to milk, just like reg'lar. Try to take Buford easy if he comes in there first. Shouldn't be a problem."

Ben and Horton went into the house and sent Bobby Joe outside. All went to their stations to wait. Bob sat in a rocking chair in front of the fireplace. He stared at the wall, saying nothing, waiting. His mother stood at the work table along the wall, peeling potatoes and turnips. She turned to face the sheriff, her face wrinkled in pain. "Please don't hurt ma'boy, Sheriff."

"We'll do our best, Ma'am. I'm sorry we have to do this. He won't know we're here, so there shouldn't be a ruckus."

The sun went down and twilight settled over the hills. Bob went to the barn to milk the two cows by lantern light. He ignored the two men waiting in the shadows. No one spoke. Estelle Harvey finished her work in the kitchen corner and sat in a rocker, staring into the fire. Ben and the sheriff sat in straight chairs beside the front door, on the hinge side when it would be opened. All was silent except for the crackling of the fire. They waited...and they waited.

Estelle got up and went to the work table. She stirred up a bowl of cornbread, poured it into a cast iron skillet, and put it in the oven. The sheriff and Ben tensed and rose as they heard footsteps on the plank porch. "Bob," the sheriff whispered, but he eased the Peacemaker out of his holster. Sure enough, the latch was lifted and Bob walked in.

"He should be comin'," he said. "He'll ride up here and I'll take the same horse back down there."

"All right," Horton said. "You get on over there at the table, if that's what you'd be doin', and we'll all wait. You'll not interfere, or you'll be in big trouble." Bob did as he was told. They continued to wait.

Finally, one of the hounds under the porch started baying and they heard the sound of a rider. Horton moved to the other side of the door and flattened himself against the wall. They heard footsteps on the planks outside, the latch went up, and Buford burst through the opening door. Horton was upon him immediately and Ben joined him from the other side.

Buford yelped in pain as they bore him to the floor, face down. "What the hell!" he yelled.

"You're under arrest, young fella," Horton said. And to Ben, "Bring that arm over here."

The sheriff shackled his wrists, and together they dragged him to his feet. Buford cried out in pain again, "You're hurtin' my arm! What the hell's goin' on? Me and Pa was just out huntin'."

Bob said from across the room, "They know everythin', Buford. Just as well give in."

"You sonofabitch!" Buford yelled back. "You told 'em."

"We knew everything," Horton said, "So ya just as well shut yore mouth."

As they set him in a chair, Estelle came forward. "He's been hurt, Sheriff. Kin I take a look at his wound and see if I kin fix it?"

"Yes, Ma'am, soon as we can."

The sheriff put leg irons on Buford and freed his arms so Estelle could tend to him. Horton went out on the porch and fired his pistol in the air. Soon Tom and Henry came from the barn, and a short time later Bobby Joe and George arrived with the horses.

Buford's wound was rebound and Horton gave instructions to all of them. "Bobby Joe, I'd like for you to watch this young man and his ma. Mister Zinn, would you be willing to keep him company?"

"Yes, be glad to." George was eager to have a talk with Estelle Harvey, tell her about her daughter, but he decided to wait until it was all over. Maybe it would ease the pain.

Bob went to his mother and hugged her, whispering, *"Sorry for all this, Ma, but it had to happen sometime."*

Estelle nodded. *"Yes. You be careful. No tellin' what he'll do."*

In a short time, all five men were mounted and headed east along the ridge, Bob leading with a lit lantern, the rest in single file on the narrow trail through the scrub oaks.

Margaret sat in a rocker beside Anna's bed while she slept. She was holding Anna's infant son, even though he was asleep and the cradle was nearby. She smiled down at the little boy, the warmth against her bosom a pleasant feeling. There can't be much better duty than this, she thought. She and Rebecca were taking turns. The rest of the neighbors had gone home to tend to their own, except for Rafael Johnson and his son, Matthew. They had taken care of the evening chores, milking the cows and putting out feed. Now they stayed to provide security. The other Johnson sons would take care of their place.

As Margaret was about to fall asleep in her contentment, the little one awakened and started to squirm. His whimpering sounds turned to full cries of indignation. Time to feed me or change my diaper or both! Anna's mother instinct brought her instantly awake.

"Somebody wants something," Margaret said. "I'll check his diaper."

Anna, yawning, scooted herself up in bed. "I'll get ready for my part."

"When does the little fellow get a name?" Margaret said.

"As soon as Ben and I can talk. We've hardly seen each other. I'll be so glad when this is over and I have Eva...and Ben...safe."

"Oh, me, too." Margaret finished the changing, and brought the baby to Anna. "Here he is. He did his duty."

The riders traveled down the steep north slope of the ridge in total darkness except for the circle of wavering light from the lantern Bob carried. Apparent overcast had moved in, obscuring even the faint light of the stars. Bob knew the trail, but the ruggedness of their path increased, making the horses stumble from time to time. After some time and several twists and turns, Bob reined in and turned his horse around. The others drew close, their faces dimly lit by the lantern light.

Bob spoke softly, "We're about a quarter-mile away. Best let me draw ahead. The trail starts to bend to the left and slope down. Might want to tie the horses up right away and follow on foot, so's they don't make a racket. I'll go slow enough for you to keep up. The cave's at the base of a ridge up ahead and faces south, so you'll see me get there. He'll have a fire goin' so it'll be lit up some."

"What kinda cover we got around the mouth?"

"There's buck brush and scrub cedars on both sides. Pretty much hides the cave unless you're straight-on...and there's a little creek comin' out of it that trickles off to your left, lookin' in at it."

"All right. Soon's we get close enough, Henry, you and Tom slip around to the left, across the little stream. Me and Ben will take the right side. After Bob goes in, if all goes well, try to get in close enough to cover him when he comes out with the girl. Now, Bob, don't let us down. Take your time until all is settled. Then you're gonna grab her and run out, right?"

"Yessir."

"Again, keep it relaxed. Take your time. We'll wait. Keep safe."

"Yessir, I will."

"Christ, it's dark! I've got a little vision, though, and it'll get better once we quit lookin' at that lantern. Let your horse make plenty a'noise to cover for us." Horton said.

Their plan in effect, Bob rode his horse down the rocky trail, making the noise a horse makes. Four shadowy figures trailed behind, dividing when they came within sight of the cave mouth. Sure enough, they saw the silhouette of Ferdinand Harvey as he emerged, a shotgun in the crook of his arm. Carefully watching their footing, at the same time the four saw Bob ride up to him. As they took up their stations, they silently observed as Bob dismounted and unsaddled his horse, handing to Ferd a sack of food he'd brought. Bob hobbled the horse and turned him loose. Must be some grazing available, but it was too dark to tell.

The two men entered the cave. The cave mouth was in the shape of a half-moon on its flat side. A wall of rocks had been built long ago, closing half of the opening, leaving the steam and a walkway open to the left. The four watchers settled in to wait. Henry Jeffrey, to the left, was equipped appropriately with a .44 caliber lever-action Henry he'd pulled out of his scabbard, leaving behind the stubby shotgun. With him, Tom Archer carried a shotgun loaded with buckshot. To the right, Ben had his '73 Winchester, while the sheriff stayed with his long-barreled Colt. Their orders were to take Ferd alive, but do whatever it took to protect Bob and Eva. It could be a matter of minutes or hours before Bob would emerge with Eva—if he emerged at all. It would take courage to defy his father after the years of living in that family.

Tension mounted as the four men waited, their eyes focused on the cave opening, their weapons ready. Suddenly, Bob burst into their view, carrying a burden in his arms. He ran to the right, toward where Horton and Ben waited. In seconds, Ferd emerged in the cave mouth. He raised a shotgun and fired at his son. Bob stumbled and fell, twisting his body to keep from falling on top of Eva.

Sheriff Horton yelled, "Drop it, Ferd! Drop it!"

Ferd yelled back, "Like Hell!" and raised the shotgun to fire at the prone figures.

A hail of gunfire brought him down.

-46-

CONCLUSIONS

Sheriff Horton and Ben both charged forward, the sheriff to determine the status of Ferd Harvey and Ben to check on his daughter. Ben saw movement in the darkness and was thrilled to hear a little voice cry, *"Mama! Mama!"* In seconds, he was beside her and took her in his arms. "Papa's here!" he said. She put her arms around his neck so tightly he could scarcely breathe.

"Oh, Papa," she said. "I want to go home!"

"We're gonna do that right away. Are you all right? Are you hurt?"

"No, I don't hurt, but I'm hungry and I want Mama."

"We'll take care of that."

Bob was struggling to sit up, gasping in pain.

By this time, Tom Archer had arrived and asked, "Is Eva all right?"

"Yes," said Ben. "How bad off are you, Bob?"

"I'm hurtin' bad," Bob said. "It's mostly in my left shoulder, but the shot scattered."

Tom said, "Let's get all of us to the cave where we've got some light and we'll see what we got. Henry went to see if the sheriff needed anything."

As they approached the cave, Horton said, "He's done for. Sorry, Bob, jest couldn't help it. How are you?'

"I'm hurtin', but I think he'd of killed me for sure if you hadn't stopped him." He passed by the sprawled body of his father, and shook his head sadly.

Tom threw more branches on the fire and it flared up. "Sit down over here, Bob, with your back to it, and we'll see what we can do." Bob did so, and they removed his jacket and carefully peeled away his shirt to reveal the damage. The pattern was centered on his shoulder blade, but scattered enough that his ear was nicked and other shot had hit his back, his neck, and upper arm. He was bleeding badly.

"We'd best just tie a patch over the worst part and get you to Forsyth, let the doctor take care of it. Lucky it wasn't double-aught." He proceeded to do so, pulling out his shirttail and ripping it off, doing the same to Ben's to make a proper bandage.

Meanwhile, Henry Jeffrey had gone out into the darkness and come back leading two horses. The sheriff had rolled Ferd's body in a quilt, and they made ready to depart, Ferd's body draped over his saddled horse. Bob was helped onto his horse, his left arm in a sling made from his belt. They doused the fire with water and using the light now of a second lantern, began walking back to retrieve the other horses. "We'll have somebody come back and clean out the place in a day or two," Horton said.

Ben judged that it was somewhere halfway between midnight and dawn as the cavalcade of riders reached the barn of the Harvey place. It had been a long, weary ride for all, and his arms were tired from holding his sleeping daughter. He switched arms from time to time and could rest part of her weight against the pommel of the saddle; still, he looked forward to dismounting.

Horton, in the lead, held up his hand for a halt. He said, "Henry, you need to stay here for a little while 'til we break the news about Ferd. We'll come and get ya soon's we can."

Jeffrey nodded and dismounted, holding the reins of his horse and the lead rope of the horse holding the body. The rest rode on to the front of the house and wearily dismounted. Tom helped Bob climb down. Those inside heard the commotion and George came out on the porch.

"I see you got her, Ben. Good news. Uh, where's the rest?"

"We'll come inside and explain," Horton said.

Those inside were weary also, having kept anxiously awake, waiting. Deputy Bobby Joe and Estelle arose, but Buford was shackled to his chair. Estelle rushed to Bob, but saw his condition and didn't embrace him. "What's wrong, Son," she said. "Where's your pa?"

Bob put his right arm around her and said, "It ain't good, Ma. I brought the little girl out of the cave and Pa shot me in the back. He was gettin' ready to finish me off, but the rest...well, they kept him from doin' it...."

"He's...?"

"Yeah, Ma. He didn't make it."

She put her hands to her face, "Lord, Lord. What's to become of us?"

"We'll figger it out, Ma. Now let's all set down."

Horton stepped forward, "I'm terrible sorry, Ma'am. It couldn't be helped."

Estelle nodded without speaking. Then she saw Eva, now awake, standing by Ben. Estelle went to her and knelt down. Eva stared and moved closer to Ben's leg. Estelle said, "Are you all right, Honey? Are you hungry?"

Eva nodded.

"You and your pa sit down, and I'll find you somethin', then I'll tend to you, Bob."

While the rest sat, Estelle got a pan of warm water, a washrag, and soap, and brought it to Ben, having noticed how grubby the little girl was. Next she brought Eva a piece of johnnycake with butter on it.

Bob said, "Ma, I think I'll make it 'til a doctor looks at it. What's next, Sheriff?"

"Well, here's the thing. We've gotta make it all the way to Forsyth. Kin you do it, Bob?"

"I reckon so. It hurts like the devil, but it'll hurt anyways."

George spoke. "Miz Harvey, is there anybody who can come and stay with you?"

"No. I ain't got nobody. They's all been chased off. Usta be Rebecca was a friend to me, but...."

George said, "How about I stay here until it's all sorted out. Mister Archer can get things goin', and Ben has to get his little girl home to her mama. I've got something to talk to her about anyway."

All went into action, first laying out Ferd's body in the smokehouse, then the sheriff and his deputy and the two Harvey boys left for Forsyth. Before they left, the sheriff took Bob aside and spoke quietly to him, "You understand, Son, your brother has to go to jail to wait on a trial. You're goin' to the doctor, but you can come home after that. The solicitor will prob'ly want to talk to you, but I doubt he'll charge you. I'll speak in your behalf."

Bob nodded, "Thank you, Sir."

Tom and Ben left with Eva, and George was alone with Estelle. She'd made coffee and they sat in rockers in front of the fire, the house now quiet.

"I'm George Zinn, Miz Harvey and I have something you'll want to hear."

"You're the blacksmith's son."

"Yes. Now you've had a big dose of bad news, but I have some good. Rose is alive and well—"

Estelle jumped up, *"What? What did you say?"*

"She's alive and doing well. She's working in Springfield—"

"Oh, praise the Lord; praise the Lord! Tell me how it happened." Tears were streaming down her face.

George was able to calm her down and get her to sit. Then he told her the whole story, leaving nothing out. "She's written some. She misses you, but was afraid to make contact. Now I'll write to her so she may be able to come and see you."

She clasped her hands together and said, "Oh, God bless you and your family!" And for the first time since Rose disappeared, she smiled.

The overcast had cleared and the stars began to fade as the faint light of dawn lit the eastern sky. Eva had gone to sleep again and Ben's arms ached as they rode into the yard in front of the house. Tom had offered to spell him, but Ben could not stand the thought of giving her up. Rafe Johnson stepped out onto the porch at their approach.

He called out softly, "You did it, I see!"

"Yep," said Tom as they dismounted. "You're still here? We'll come inside and tell you all about it."

Rafe and his son, Matthew, had waited with Rebecca throughout the night, keeping the fire going and alternately dozing in chairs. Rebecca and Margaret had stayed by Anna's side. Rebecca now rushed forward to take the waking Eva from Ben.

"Come to grandma, sweet girl," she said.

"Gramma," Eva said in a tired voice.

Anna had heard them arrive and she and Margaret came out of the bedroom. Anna held her infant son in her arms. She handed the baby to Margaret and went to Rebecca.

Eva reached for her, crying, *"Mama, Mama!"* Then she saw the bundle Margaret was holding and pointed, "What's *that?"*

Margaret came to them and Anna moved the knit blanket aside to reveal his face. "It's your new baby brother!"

"Oh, oh, oh!" Eva said, "We have a baby!" Then, "What's his name?"

Anna glanced at Ben, "He doesn't have one yet, but your papa and I will give him one, now that big sister is home again."

Tom said, "Margaret, George is just fine, he's staying with Miz Harvey right now. I'll explain it all."

Ben embraced his wife and daughter.

As the new day brightened outside they all gathered around the fireplace and Tom told them of the events of the night. They were horrified that Ferd would shoot his own son and that he would have killed Bob if the sheriff and others had not intervened. Ben said that he felt a great weight lifted from his shoulders, at the same time regretting that it had come to this. Anna was filled with gratitude that Eva was back unharmed, but mourned the sacrifice her father had made in trying to defend them.

"I doubt any charges will come Bob's way. Don't know what we would have done without him," Tom continued. "Buford will have to spend some time in jail, I reckon. Don't know what will happen to Estelle and Bob in the long run. As I said, George stayed behind with her until anyone else can come. I'm sure by now he's given her the good news about Rose."

"Maybe I can go over there in the buggy after breakfast," Rebecca said.

"I'm sure she'd like that," Tom said.

"Me and Matt will milk your cows and head on home." Rafe said.

"No, no. You've done enough," Tom said.

"I insist. You get some rest. You've had a hard night."

Tom sighed. "You're right, of course. I owe you a lot."

"No ya don't. We've all got a lot to do, with two graves to finish, and all. And we'll all have to pitch in and help Bob and Miz Harvey until he gets on his feet."

Tom rested for about an hour, then he drove to drop Rebecca off at the Harvey place, and on to Sycamore. He'd need to help organize the community to accomplish all that had to be done. George came by to get his horse and buggy. He had another pine box to deliver.

When all were gone, Ben and Anna were alone with their family, now numbering four, the two little ones sleeping. Ben embraced Anna as they watched George disappear in the trees down at the crossing. "Anna, you're just amazing! I love you more than life," he said. "I'm the luckiest man alive—or maybe I should say 'most blessed by God.'"

Anna looked up at him, "I'm the one that's blessed. Since that day you found me standing in your hayloft, trembling with fear, threatening you with a pitchfork, you've been my world."

She stood on tiptoe to kiss him, then smiled and said, "Maybe now we can name our son and begin to live in peace."

EPILOGUE

S pring had come to Bull Creek. The Creek was running full from the spring rains, the sparkling flow making nature's music as it tumbled over the limestone ledges. Coves were white with blooming dogwood, complemented with the dark pink of occasional redbud trees. There was a fresh scent in the air from the budding trees, the greening grass, and the rich smell of freshly turned earth.

On this Saturday morning there was a large gathering of the community on the grounds of the Sycamore schoolhouse. A pig was roasting on an iron frame over a fire pit since the midnight hours, and tables were set out to receive the potluck noon meal to come.

The celebration taking place was because of a wedding ceremony in the schoolhouse, today a church. The groom was the owner of a local business and the son of the Sycamore blacksmith. The bride was the community's much loved teacher, who spent many working hours in this same building. This time, however, she was radiant in a long white dress of satin and lace. Their attendants were a handsome young married couple; she with flaming red curls; he tall and handsome with blond hair.

After the ceremony they emerged, smiling and happy, to the applause of the gathering; the standing room crowd inside and all those outside. After a joyous meal under the trees, the new-married couple drove away in a new buggy adorned with flowers, a buggy of the groom's own manufacture, for a honeymoon in Springfield.

The marriage of Margaret and George was the culmination of a healing process that took place over several weeks following the kidnapping of Eva Archer and her subsequent rescue.

Ben and Anna Archer named their new son Thomas Frederick Archer. They wanted to honor both grandfathers, but compromised on a near-spelling of Anna's father's last name. Anna's father was buried next to her mother in the hillside cemetery in Sycamore two days after his death. George drove the family there in a new two-seat buggy with spring chassis, comfortable for Anna so soon after her confinement. In a tribute to Jürgen Friedrich's sacrifice, there was a large turnout for the funeral and graveside service.

On the following day another burial took place at the Harvey farm, this one sparsely attended. Oley Jensen did his duty and conducted a simple graveside service for the handful of attendees. None of Ferdinand Harvey's children were there; Rose too far away, Bob recovering from his wounds, Buford in jail, and Clint's remains in the grave beside him. His brother, Clyde, and family attended, as did his sister, Rebecca Archer. Tom went with her.

It would take some time for Bob Harvey to recover full use of his left arm, so the men of the community, including his Uncle Clyde, worked out a schedule to keep the farm going. Despite the troubles in her family, Estelle Harvey began to feel some hope for the future—no more physical and verbal abuse; and the anticipation of seeing her daughter, once lost, now found. That event took place a week after Ferd's death. She was preparing a noon meal for herself and Bob, when there was the sound of a buggy driving up outside. Soon, the door swung open and a tall, elegant young woman walked into the room. Estelle was puzzled for a moment, then she knew. She was overcome with emotion and sank to her knees, sobbing.

Weeks went by before Buford Harvey's trial. He was charged with murder and kidnapping and convicted after only two days in court. His lawyer pled for leniency in his case, due to his youth and the fact that he did not actually fire the shot that killed Jürgen Friedrich. He avoided hanging for his client, but Buford was sent away for a long prison term.

In the months following the death of Anna's father, a healing had gradually taken place with Anna and Ben, and they felt a freedom from worry that had plagued them while Ferd Harvey was alive. Anna was pleased to receive a letter one day from her brother Evan. He was still working on a ranch in Texas and had met a girl he planned to marry. Anna now had an address for him and wrote back a long letter, telling him of all that had taken place since he had left. She urged him to return if he could. In any event, she was glad to be reconnected.

A few days after the wedding, Ben came in for the noon meal Anna had prepared. As soon as she saw him, she knew there was something wrong.

"Is something the matter, Ben?" she said.

"Well, it's just…while I was plowin', I kept thinking over and over about this whole thing with Ferd Harvey. Was there anything along the way we could've done different to cool it down? It seemed to start over not much and it just got worse and worse."

"I certainly don't know. I think you have to just put it behind you, because nothing can be done now."

"But," he replied, "It just doesn't feel right to be glad he's gone, but if I'm honest, I do feel a great relief."

"You're human. All you can do is pray for forgiveness. Sit down and I'll pour you some coffee while I get things taken up."

Ben continued, "It seemed to start when Pa bought your folks' place, then there was the fence dispute and Clint was killed. He even started that by shootin' first. Clint kept tryin' to bait me even before that. Bob was always different, as he showed lately.

Buford was more like his pa. I keep thinkin' about what Ferd did to Rose, his own *daughter*." He glanced over at Eva playing by the fireplace. "How *could* he? And poor Estelle. What her life must have been."

Anna walked over and put her hand on his shoulder, "You're a good man, Ben. I love you with all my heart. Try to leave it behind you. Maybe time will help. In any case, I thank God every day that we found each other. Now we can live in peace."

* * * * *

Although Anna and Ben were not directly affected, lawlessness and disorder worsened in Taney County over the next few years, with thievery and unsolved murders increasing. Outlaws and renegade holdovers from guerilla bands during the Civil War began to thrive and exercise control over law enforcement and jury selection.

Frustrated community leaders gathered in secret and established a vigilante group which became known as Bald Knobbers. Eventually, that group grew out of control and was forcefully disbanded before peace and lawfulness were regained.

About the author:

Roger Meadows was born in the hills of Missouri, not far from the setting of *Devil's Lane* and *Return to Bull Creek*. He grew up on a remote farm without electricity in his early years and attended a one-room school all eight grades, conditions not too different from the generations before him.

After college and a tour as an Army aviator, he began a career in industry, completing graduate school along the way. He conducted business throughout the world, dealing with many cultures.

He has written dozens of essays and short stories, and edited the works of other writers. He has participated in writers' groups in Spartanburg, Greenville, and Hilton Head, South Carolina; and Knoxville, Tennessee. He and his wife, Wanda, are members of the local chapter of Sisters in Crime.

Mr. Meadows enjoys reading, sailing, kayaking, travel, and working with wood. He and his wife live in the Upstate of South Carolina. They have three adult children and two grandchildren. He welcomes your comments to him at RDM730@aol.com. See his web page at
https://www.amazon.com/author/rogermeadows

Made in the USA
Coppell, TX
17 December 2021